BLACKTHORN COTTAGE

BLACKTHORN COTTAGE

Rowena Summers

Severn House

This first world edition published in Great Britain 2006 by
SEVERN HOUSE PUBLISHERS LTD of
9–15 High Street, Sutton, Surrey SM1 1DF.
This first world edition published in the USA 2006 by
SEVERN HOUSE PUBLISHERS INC of
595 Madison Avenue, New York, N.Y. 10022.

British Library Cataloguing in Publication Data

Saunders, Jean, 1932-
   Blackthorn Cottage
   1.   Inheritance and succession - Fiction
   2.   Villages - Somerset - Fiction
   3.   Young women - England - Bristol -
        Family relationships - Fiction
   4.   Domestic fiction
   I.   Title
   823.9'14 [F]

ISBN-13: 978-0-7278-6411-6
ISBN-10: 0-7278-6411-4

Except where actual historical events and characters are being
described for the storyline of this novel, all situations in this
publication are fictitious and any resemblance to living persons
is purely coincidental.

All Severn House titles are printed on acid-free paper.

Typeset by Palimpsest Book Production Ltd.,
Grangemouth, Stirlingshire, Scotland.
Printed and bound in Great Britain by
MPG Books Ltd., Bodmin, Cornwall.

One

As the country bus jolted through the lanes alongside the sweet-scented fields of waving wild flowers, Jasmine fingered the letter in her bag for the tenth time. It still seemed totally unreal that the old gentleman she worked for had bequeathed the cottage to her. It was even more unreal that after another almighty row with her father she had slipped out of the house while everyone else was busy that morning and had waited, shivering, at the bus-stop until the only country bus that passed through to her destination, Horton, on the way to some larger town, came trundling along.

She wasn't shivering with cold, just anticipation and more than a little apprehension. The only person who knew what she was doing today was her sister Grace. She had been sworn to secrecy, even though Grace's ability to keep a secret was as likely as flying to the moon, and everyone knew that would never happen. Her smile faded a little. Everyone said there was never going to be another war, either, but if her father's dire portents about Chancellor Adolf Hitler were anything to go by, it was quite likely to happen.

Jasmine brushed aside such gloomy thoughts. Only last year the Olympic Games had been held in Munich in Germany, and had been a huge triumph, despite Herr Hitler's astounding and insulting refusal to shake the hand of the great American athlete, Jesse Owens. According to Jasmine's father, wars had been started on lesser grounds – but then, her father always had something to say about anything that was topical. He seemed to thrive on starting a discussion that other people would call an argument that soon developed into a shouting match, and it was one of the reasons why Jasmine had finally known she had to get away before they killed one another. Not literally, of course. Deep down,

1

however scratchy they were, she knew love existed between them, but they simply couldn't get on together, and when the solicitors had sent her the letter, she had known that this was her golden opportunity.

It was a daring thing for a young woman to do, and some would say she was taking the women's rights that Emmeline Pankhurst had finally won a decade ago, too far. In fact, seeing her own determined reflection in the window of the bus now, she recalled the moment when she had confided in Grace. Her older sister had been aghast, not that she was leaving to look at this cottage her employer had left her, but in the way she was apparently prepared to sneak off to take a look at it. And by herself too. Even though Grace was the elder by seven years, she had none of Jasmine's eagerness to go out and meet the world, as she called it, and was content enough to work with her father in their haberdashery shop.

'You can't just leave without telling Dad, Jassy!'

'Why not?' Jasmine had tossed her head, her fine brown hair tumbling about her face before she twisted it up into a workaday knot on top of her head, and stabbed it into place with a large tortoiseshell comb. 'I don't have to work in his shop for ever, Grace, and neither do you. You could come with me!'

She hadn't even considered it before, but seeing Grace's flushed face, she knew it would never happen. Grace might be the older sister, but as far as their father was concerned she was far more docile than Jasmine had ever been. But then Jasmine had had to assert herself very early in life. Their father had turned away from his second daughter completely when his wife had died in childbirth, as if blaming the tiny mite for his grief. It was as if he couldn't bear to look at the baby who had caused his beloved wife's death, and twenty years later, Jasmine was sure he still resented her for it.

'I can't leave him,' Grace had stated. 'It's all right for you. You've already had a different sort of life, working as a private secretary for Mr Devenish at the big house. But Dad needs me here.'

'He needs you, but he never needed me. He probably didn't even notice I've been working elsewhere these past few years, so why would he need me now?'

2

'That's not true. He's proud of you, Jassy. He admires your skills in shorthand and typing, and that you were so determined to learn it, which is something I've never mastered properly.'

'It's a pity he never showed his admiration then.'

She couldn't help her anger. In any case, Grace could do anything as far as their father was concerned, and he easily overlooked any of her business shortcomings. Owen Wyatt was a self-made man with rigid ideas, and the fact that his elder daughter was perfectly happy to go along with them, only made his attitude to his more self-willed younger daughter seem more extreme.

'It's hard for someone like Dad to show his feelings, and you know it,' Grace continued. 'Ever since Mother died, it's been difficult for him.'

Jasmine bit her lips hard. It was tempting to lash out at Grace whenever she mentioned their mother, showing a jealousy she knew was pointless and unworthy, just because Grace had known her mother for seven years, and Jasmine had never had that chance. Even her own name . . . her flamboyant, unusual name, had come about because Owen was too full of despair even to name his new child, and it had been Grace, with the help of their Aunt Lucy, who had named her after the delicate jasmine flowers in the Wyatt garden.

Jasmine sighed, her reflection in the bus window showing how her shoulders had drooped as she recalled that conversation, and she straightened them at once. She had made her decision, leaving a note for her father, explaining what she had done, and that she would return as soon as she had seen the cottage. He knew all about the solicitor's letter, of course, and the fact that she had been floundering at home ever since her old employer had died and left her out of a proper job. In one of their flare-ups Owen had told his daughter she must do as she thought best. She was no longer a child, but right now, despite her bravado, she felt as indecisive as if she was. If only things could have been different between herself and her father. If only she had a mother to turn to for advice . . .

To give herself something to do, she took the letter out of her bag once more, her hands inside her cotton gloves

3

shaking a little. She didn't need to read it again, since she knew it by heart, but it prevented the few other passengers on the early morning bus wondering why such an attractive young woman should have a sudden shine of tears in her velvety blue eyes.

'Dear Miss Wyatt,' the letter on the impressive headed stationery stated:

> Further to our recent communication regarding the Horton property that Mr Giles Devenish has bequeathed to you, we will be pleased to arrange for local Estate Agent, Mr William Hedges, to meet you at the cottage at your convenience. Please contact Mr Hedges for details of the property.'
>
> J. J. Jones, pp Jones, Barker and Stone, Solicitors.

To Jasmine it sounded more like a musical act. Jones, Barker and Stone, tripping across the stage of some auditorium and doing a sand dance . . .

When the bus began slowing down, Jasmine realized with a start that they had finally reached the small village of Horton, deep in the Somerset countryside, and that, as expected, it was about as different from Bristol as anyone could imagine. There was no great river winding past buildings and into the heart of the city, bringing commerce and prosperity; no magnificent suspension bridge built by Isambard Kingdom Brunel spanning the River Avon; no busy shopping centres and dirty, crowded streets alive with every kind of humanity.

Compared with Bristol this was just a backwater – and no place for a lively young woman of twenty years. Why had Giles Devenish ever thought she would take up residence here? Jasmine's bravado began ebbing away again. What on earth was she doing here, and why hadn't she instructed the solicitors to sell the place and send her the profit . . . knowing all the while that she couldn't do that to the kindly man who had left the cottage to her. Not without seeing it first, at least.

She owed him that much – and a lot more, she thought with a rush of affection for her elderly benefactor, mixed with a sense of sadness at his passing. Abandoning her inheritance before she had even seen it was a defeatist attitude, and Jasmine had never been one to shy away from what had to be done. She was here now, and she had made her decision.

She alighted from the bus on the outskirts of the village and she watched as it moved away on its journey in a cloud of dust, and for a moment she felt totally isolated and disorientated. The village ahead of her revealed a cluster of cottages, the spire of a church, and a meandering stream alongside the main street where a family of ducks was noisily splashing about in its morning ablutions.

Jasmine knew it would have made more sense to let this Mr William Hedges, Estate Agent (upper case initials to show his importance, she had noted in the solicitor's letter), know she was coming. Even without knowing anything more about him, she had disliked him. Some pompous old goat, she guessed. But how foolish was it not to have contacted him through Messrs J. J. Jones, Barker and Stone, to ask for details of the cottage? She didn't have a key to it, and she had no idea where it was.

Acting on impulse was never a good thing, as her father was constantly telling her. But she hadn't come all this way for nothing, and she walked purposefully towards the buildings ahead of her. The difference between here and the noisy, bustling city of Bristol was marked. The silence was broken only by the family of ducks, the chirping of birds, and the drone of a tractor somewhere in the distance. It was somewhat eerie to someone who had been brought up in the heart of that city, and then cycled to work at an elegant estate on its fringes, but that wasn't going to deter her, either.

In any case, she didn't have to stay. She certainly didn't have to live in the cottage. She could still sell it and do what she wanted with the money. And then she thought of how kind Giles Devenish had been to her and, without even giving it a chance, she knew it would have been like throwing his generous gift back in his face. It was a frustrating fact that had to be faced.

As she walked on, she realized that Horton wasn't quite as silent as she had first thought. There was a hum in the air of people going about their daily business, and the village wasn't as devoid of life as it had seemed. The few thatched cottages on the outskirts gave way to more and more of them, opening out into a large village green with a huge old oak tree in its centre, under which were rustic benches where people could sit and dream. There were already several old men sitting on the benches, as gnarled as the branches of the old tree as they took the morning air. She could feel their stares following her as she walked.

Around the village green there were small shops selling basic commodities, and a pub, the Rose and Crown. Jasmine couldn't see anything that looked like an estate agent's, but there was a tiny post office wedged in between the green-grocer's and the bakery, and it was to there that she made her way, perfectly aware that the old men on the benches were probably discussing her now. Strangers would obvi-ously attract curiosity here, and when none of them answered her tentative smile, she stuck her head in the air and tried to ignore them.

The post office shop had a bell that tinkled prettily, announcing a customer's arrival. Jasmine felt as though she had stepped back in time as she realized it didn't merely sell stamps and postal orders, but that half the shop was taken over by counters and shelves full of sweets and newspapers and magazines, and clearly did double duty as a newsagent's as well. The plainly clad postmistress, peering over wire-rimmed glasses, and whose only sense of fashion were the heavy beads clanking around her neck, also seemed like a relic of an earlier age, and Jasmine wondered for a moment just what kind of community this was. Creepy was the word for it, she decided.

'Can I help you, Miss?' the woman behind the post office counter said, with the same appraising look the old men on the green had given the newcomer.

'I'm looking for Blackthorn Cottage,' she said, deciding to forget all about Mr William Hedges (Estate Agent) for the moment, and take a look at her property by herself.

The woman nodded. 'Oh yes. You'll be the young lady from the city. I guessed it must be you. William said you'd be here before long. We were taking wagers on how long it would be.'

Seeing Jasmine's astonished look, she spoke archly. 'Don't look so worried, my dear. You haven't come to a den of debauchery.'

It was a weird thing to say, and the last thing Jasmine had thought, but she managed not to let her expression betray the thought that nothing here could remotely be described as a den of debauchery!

'I'm Mrs Lester, and William's my nephew,' the post-mistress went on. 'There's not much that goes on in the village that one or other of us don't get to hear about. So you'll be wanting to take a look at Blackthorn Cottage, and a bit of a shock you've got coming to you, I daresay, a smart city girl like you.'

Jasmine couldn't mistake the slight inference in her voice that smart city girls had no place here in the wilds. Well, amen to that, she thought.

'I didn't say I was going to live in it. But naturally I want to see what the cottage is like,' Jasmine found herself saying, as if it was any of this woman's business! But she tried to keep her voice civil. She had been brought up to be polite to her elders at all times, even if it was sometimes difficult to do.

'I'll let William know you're here.'

'There's no need! If you just direct me to the cottage, I'll find it by myself.'

She found herself talking to thin air. Mrs Lester had disappeared behind the swishing bead curtains at the back of the post office. The nerve of the woman, Jasmine fumed. If she'd wanted an escort she'd have contacted William Hedges herself. And why would she have a bit of a shock coming to her when she saw the cottage, Jasmine wondered suddenly? What was wrong with it?

She felt a tiny stab of unease. Giles Devenish had a lot of small properties scattered about a wide area of the county, and rarely visited them himself. Jasmine only knew about them because of her work. Of course she had heard the name of Blackthorn Cottage in the village of Horton, but that was all she had known about it – apart from commenting that it sounded very pretty and olde worlde.

Was that the reason Mr Devenish had remembered her in his will, which was something she had never expected?

Certainly not with such a gift! If she had ever expected anything at all, it would have been no more than a trinket or a small sum of money, never for a young woman like herself to become a property owner! She still couldn't forget her father's scathing remark when she had received the solicitor's first letter, six months after her employer had died, when the complicated details of the will had finally been sorted out.

'Why would the old boy leave anything to you, a glorified clerk? You weren't toadying up to him in some way, were you, my girl? We've never had any of that kind of scandal in this family, and we don't want any hint of it now.'

Jasmine hadn't understood what he meant for a moment, and when she did, her face had become beetroot red with rage.

'That's a beastly thing to say! Mr Devenish was never less than kind to me, and everyone said he'd been devoted to his late wife. I'd been privileged to know what he planned to leave for several members of his staff, but he never mentioned anything about this cottage to me. In fact, he treated me more like a daughter than an employee, but that's something you wouldn't know about, isn't it!'

It wasn't done for young girls to speak to their father in such a way, and she had never done so before. For a minute she thought he was going to hit her. She trembled at the furious look on his face, and then he seemed to slump as he turned away and blundered out of the room. Moments later Grace came in, clearly having heard everything, and her face was pained and shocked.

'You shouldn't have said that, Jassy.'

'He shouldn't have said what he did to me! If you heard it, then you'll know what he was implying. That I was some sort of – of – *trollop*.' Her lips trembled as she said the word.

Grace had taken her in her arms. 'He didn't mean it. He does care for you, Jassy, and he only wants what's best for you.' She hesitated. 'Unfortunately, whenever he looks at you, he sees Mother, and it broke his heart that he couldn't do anything to save her when you were born. But you're so like her, Jassy, and she could always turn men's heads.'

8

'You're not telling me that she—'

'Oh, good Lord no! But Aunt Lucy used to tell me how he'd ramble to her in his grief after Mother died, and how he'd never really believed that someone as beautiful as Mother could be content with a stick-in-the-mud like him. He was always afraid she'd go off and leave him and cause a scandal.'

As Jasmine raised her eyebrows Grace gave a rueful smile. 'I know what you're thinking. Which would have been worse? Heartache at Mother leaving him, or the scandal to his good name? Take it from me, Jassy, he was *truly* heartbroken when she died, and if you'd seen him then you wouldn't need to ask that question. I was only a child but I still remember how he'd gaze at her photo for hours on end.'

'You have the advantage of me then, don't you?' Jasmine had retorted, shaking her off. 'Knowing Mother, and knowing how much he loved her.'

There was nothing Grace could say to that, and nor could the past be changed. Jasmine couldn't forgive the things her father had just said, but grudgingly, she felt as though she understood him a little better at that moment. And if she was hotheaded and impulsive, so was he in lashing out at her in the way he had! They were more alike in that respect than she had ever credited before.

She jumped suddenly at the sound of voices seemingly coming from somewhere out of the ether. She had been so wrapped up in her own memories and emotions at that moment, she had completely lost touch with where she was until she realized the voices weren't disembodied at all, but were coming from the other side of a bead curtain in a village post office.

'It's all very irregular. I've already got far too much to do today, and an appointment should have been made through the proper channels,' said an impatient male voice.

'Oh William, don't be so stuffy. In any case I'm sure she won't be staying once she sees the state of the place, and she'll be happy enough to go back to the city where she belongs and let the old ghosts lie.'

Jasmine's heart jolted now. What was this? Old ghosts? She was as level-headed as the next person, but she wasn't too keen on the thought of the cottage being haunted, if that was being implied. She recognized the woman's voice as that of the postmistress, and she had no doubt that the other one belonged to William Hedges. He sounded just as pompous as she had imagined, and she mentally played down his importance to 'estate agent', lower case initials.

And what could be so all-fired important in this backwater that he couldn't spare half an hour to show a client around her own property! She was on the point of leaving, sure that she could find someone else to direct her to Blackthorn Cottage, when the bead curtain was pushed aside. The postmistress appeared, followed by a large, dark-haired man who seemed to take up all the space around him.

'This is my nephew, William Hedges,' the woman announced, as if Jasmine hadn't already guessed.

Instinct had told her he would be an aggressive type of man – didn't estate agents need to be? But other than that, her instinct had been totally wrong. Here was no pompous old goat in the same age bracket as her old employer, but a young man some years older than herself who was glaring at her now with piercing dark eyes, and who was clearly annoyed at the interruption to his day.

Well, pardon me, thought Jasmine, her hackles rising, but I'm the client here, and you're the dogsbody whose job it is to tell me that the property I own is every city dweller's country dream. She wished she could think of some smart sarcastic remark to put him in his place, but the words never materialized.

'You must forgive me for appearing so ungracious, Miss Wyatt,' he said, although the impatience he couldn't hide rather belied the contrite words. He came around to the front of the shop and put out his hand, and Jasmine automatically put her hand in his and felt his firm handshake. 'You'll be here to see the cottage, of course, but it would have been far more convenient if you had made an appointment through your solicitors. Never mind. Now that you're here, it can't be helped.'

Well, if that was supposed to be an apology, then politeness was certainly not one of his assets, Jasmine thought, fuming.

'My time is limited too,' she said as sweetly as she could. 'There's only one afternoon bus back to Bristol out of this – place – and I need to be on it.' She couldn't have put it any clearer what she thought of Horton. Godforsaken wouldn't have been too strong a word for it, although she wouldn't have gone that far.

'Then we'd better make a start,' William Hedges said briskly. She didn't miss the smell of paint about him, and noticed that there were splodges of brown paint on his shirt-sleeves and his hands. For a businessman, he looked extremely casual without wearing a jacket and tie. Presumably this was what country living did for you. It made you sloppy in the way you dressed. At least there weren't hayseeds sticking out of the corner of his mouth, she thought uncharitably, knowing she was putting him into a mould, and not caring.

He caught her glance and gave a half smile. 'I'm sorry if my attire offends you, Miss Wyatt. I've been painting a neighbour's fence. We turn our hands to all sorts in the country. Even my aunt here has done a bit of laying out for the undertaker in her spare time when his helper has been unwell.'

Was he trying to shock her now? Putting her in her place as a city girl who knew nothing about the rudiments of real life? Jasmine found herself bristling until she realized his smile had become more mocking.

'Oh, I think I can cope with an ungentlemanly appearance without having an attack of the vapours, Mr Hedges,' she replied lightly.

'Then let's go,' he said after a moment. 'The cottage is less than a mile from here. I presume you can walk that far?'

'Do I look as if I'll fade away?' she snapped back, finding it extremely hard to be polite to him after all, and knowing it was because she was nervous. Her hands felt clammy inside her gloves. She wanted to get this over and done with, and to get back to civilization. It hadn't taken very long for her to decide that she didn't want anything to do with country life. But she had come all this way – and besides, there was no bus back until late afternoon.

'Come back here afterwards and take a cup of tea with me, if you've a mind to it,' his aunt called out to her as they went out of the door together.

'Thank you. If there's time,' Jasmine said.

She would rather sit and take tea with a – a scorpion – than anyone in this place, guessing that the woman would want to find out all about her in order to spread the gossip. Jasmine had a job to keep up with William Hedges' long strides as he walked past the green and out towards the far end of the village, passing the church where they could hear the faint sound of the organ playing. She had no intention of asking him to slow down. He couldn't make it plainer that she was being a nuisance and ruining his day. A neighbour's fence was obviously of far more importance than she was! But her shoes began to rub her toes, and she decided that this couldn't go on. She stopped abruptly, folding her arms across her chest, obliging him to turn around and wait.

'It's not much farther.'

'You said less than a mile,' she accused him.

'That's walking distance. I live just around the corner in Holly Lane, and with those shoes I thought you'd prefer to ride.'

There hadn't been much evidence of motor cars here, Jasmine realized, and what she had seen looked like decrepit vehicles. She looked at him suspiciously.

'On what? A donkey?'

William Hedges hesitated a moment. Then he laughed, and his face changed completely. He was quite a handsome man when he didn't have that brooding frown on his face, but it wasn't going to influence her one bit.

'Not quite. We don't live at the seaside here, but a horse and cart would be unique to a city girl, I imagine, and quite an experience.'

'A horse and cart,' she repeated. 'You're not serious, I hope.'

Visions of a rustic farmyard affair with its attendant aromas flashed into her mind, not endearing her to the prospect at all.

'My dear Miss Wyatt, you shouldn't believe all you read about country life,' William said with amusement in his voice now. 'We're not all born with corn in our mouths, and some of us are quite civilized.'

She ignored his words and glared at him. She wasn't his

12

dear, either. 'Where is this Blackthorn Cottage then? Is it out in the wilds?'

'Something like that. Or, in estate agent's jargon, it's in a secluded, picturesque rural setting. If you had contacted me through the proper channels, I would have sent you a photograph and details, of course. As it is, it will be a delightful surprise.'

Somehow Jasmine doubted that. From the small smile on the man's face now, she doubted it very much.

Two

William's cottage in Holly Lane was larger than some of those in the centre of the village. It had an outhouse alongside, where Jasmine could see the cart. It wasn't old and rickety as she had half expected. It was smartly painted in bright colours, but even so, William didn't miss the horrified expression on Jasmine's face as she wondered just where he stabled the horse. He hadn't intended to tease her . . . but neither had he expected such a vision to turn up to view old Giles Devenish's cottage.

'Your carriage, my lady,' he said in a slightly barbed voice.

'You're not really expecting me to go anywhere in that, are you?'

'I'm not offering you a ride in a farm cart, Miss Wyatt. The local villages hold competitions every year for the best dressed horse and cart during the annual fair on Midsummer Day. I told you – it's not all hayseeds and cow dung in the country.'

'Are you laughing at me?' She felt her face grow hot, because it was exactly what she had been thinking. It was exactly what Grace had warned her about in trying to dissuade her from doing anything rash.

'I'm sorry, but you do rather ask for it, coming here in your smart city shoes.'

'If I'd thought it was going to be all hayseeds and cow dung, I'd have worn wellington boots, wouldn't I?' she flashed at him. 'If I had any, of course.'

After a moment, William said, 'I think perhaps we should begin again. I'm pleased to meet you, Miss Wyatt, and it will be my pleasure to show you around Blackthorn Cottage and explain its merits to you.'

'And its drawbacks, I daresay!'

14

'And those too,' he agreed, making no attempt to suggest that there weren't any. 'Then, when we return to my office, you may take away the paperwork I would have sent to you beforehand, and decide what you want to do about the cottage. If you so wish, I will be happy to arrange its sale for you once we have agreed on a suitable price, and I will organize advertisements to be put in various newspapers, since I am assuming you won't want to live there.'

'Why not? Is it haunted?' Jasmine said directly.

'Good Lord, what gave you that idea?'

'Your aunt. She said something about letting old ghosts lie.'

'That's nonsense, and no more than old wives' tales,' William said briskly. 'But since you seem like a young woman of spirit, no pun intended, why don't you see it for yourself and make up your own mind?'

Jasmine half expected him to whistle for a horse to come trotting up before he helped her into the cart, but to her surprise he led her instead to the other side of the cottage where a small black motor car stood on the gravel outside a garage.

'I'm afraid I couldn't resist teasing you,' William said with a grin now, 'but I'm sure this mode of transport will suit you far better.'

'Thank you, but I assure you I'm not made of cotton wool,' Jasmine replied, although with a certain amount of relief. 'So where do you keep the horse?'

'Oh, he's safely stabled at Cooper's Farm,' he said easily. 'If you're still around on Midsummer Day, you'll get to meet him.'

She very much doubted that she would be, she thought stonily. As he held open the passenger door of the car, she stepped inside thankfully and waited while he turned the starting handle. It occurred to her that if city girls were reputedly patronizing of so-called simple country-folk, it was more than reciprocated. Ever since she had arrived in Horton, she had felt a sense of suspicion from people here. She had only spoken to two of them, she realized, but the glances and mutterings on the village green had been plain enough. They didn't welcome strangers.

15

She ignored the thought and turned to William as the car ground its way along the lanes. Speed was clearly not desirable nor possible here.

'So are you going to tell me more of the supposed old wives' tales about Blackthorn Cottage. If anybody has a right to know, I do!'

'It does have a bit of a history,' William commented, 'but not a bad one, unless you're overly superstitious, and you don't strike me as anything other than a level-headed young woman.'

'So tell me,' Jasmine insisted. Was he being patronizing now? Or was she just being oversensitive and reading things that weren't there?

'The cottage has been empty for over a year. During the four years before that, it was rented on a short-term basis. Giles Devenish never bothered to sell it after the incident. Of course, it was thoroughly cleaned and all soft furnishings removed, but the basic furniture is still there.'

'What incident?' Jasmine said as he paused. If he was deliberately trying to make a drama out of some minor village affair, it wasn't scaring her.

'The last long-term tenants were a young city couple, not much older than yourself, who were excited by the thought of living in the country. All they saw was the charm of the cottage and none of the dangers round about.'

'What dangers?' Jasmine said, refusing to show any alarm, and annoyed with herself at beginning to sound like a parrot.

'Oh, they wanted to immerse themselves in country living, growing their own food and making their own wine, and proving that they could cope just as easily as country-bred folk. It's a pity they kept to themselves and didn't ask for any local advice, because they didn't heed that some of nature's bounty can be deadly. Instead of the mushrooms they thought they had gathered for their breakfast, they had picked the Death Cap variety, and they were both found by the young boy delivering the weekly newspaper to them a few days later. When they didn't answer his knock to ask for the money as usual, he pushed open the door – and there they were. I won't describe the state they were in.'

There was no doubting his meaning, but shocked as she

16

was, she had to hear him say it. 'You mean they were both dead?'

'As dodos.' He glanced at her, aware that he sounded insensitive, and then shrugged. 'It was terrible, of course, and just as terrible for the young teenager who found them. The physical effects of deadly fungi on a body can be horrific after a few days, especially since they had called no one to help them. It could have scarred the boy for life.'

She stared at him. 'It was you, wasn't it?'

At once, she realized it couldn't have been him, not if it had been a young boy who found the bodies. She shuddered at the thought.

William spoke grimly. 'No, it was not. It was my cousin – my adopted cousin, strictly speaking. His mother isn't my real aunt, but I'm sure you're not interested in our family history. But it was quite a day for us when he came rushing back to the village, terrorized at seeing death for the first time, and in such circumstances. From then on, the cottage has had rather an unhappy reputation.'

'I don't want to hear any more.'

She shivered, even though common sense told her that what had happened was no fault of the cottage – nor did he have to be quite so graphic about it, even though it had obviously struck a nerve for him to have to retell it, considering it was his adopted young cousin who had found the couple. All the same, it was hardly part of an estate agent's job to put off a prospective client. She wasn't just that, she reminded herself. She was the owner. She tried to ignore the thought of a petrified child finding two dead people, and to concentrate on where they were going.

Once out of the village and away from the main road, the narrow lanes with their high hedges seemed to twist and turn all ways. It might be a relatively short ride in a car, but if you didn't know exactly where you were going, you could probably get lost quite easily. At least it was accessible by car . . . she squashed the thought. Ever since she had heard that Giles Devenish had left the cottage to her, she hadn't really thought seriously about living here. She wasn't thinking about it now. She just wanted to see it for herself.

She had no plans at all. Since Giles Devenish's death, a

17

company had taken over the running of the estate, and everything personal about it had gone. Jasmine had felt neither needed nor comfortable there and so she had left. But she freely admitted she had been in a kind of limbo ever since, not really knowing what to do. She had enjoyed her work, and filling in time at her father's shop, as he expected her to do now, was no substitute. She was no more than an extra shop assistant alongside Grace, and they didn't really need her either. She bit her lips, wondering if her father had ever needed her.

'I'm sorry if I've upset you, Miss Wyatt,' William said, mistaking her silence. 'I assure you there's nothing to fear about Blackthorn Cottage, but it's as well to know the history. If I hadn't told you, someone else would be sure to have done so.'

'Oh, yes, I'm sure they would. Country-folk seem to delight in scaring outsiders and keeping them out, don't they?'

Now why had she said that? She didn't mean to sound so cynical, so sarcastic or superior . . . but somehow she felt she had managed to convey all those things to William Hedges, and she could see by the tightening of his mouth that he hadn't missed the inflexion in her voice, whether real or imagined.

'I'm sorry. That was insensitive of me after what you've just told me,' she said, apologizing.

'Well, perhaps we had better both stop apologizing to one another and get on with the business of the day,' he said briskly. He brought the car to a halt, and she realized they had arrived at Blackthorn Cottage, and Jasmine gasped.

Hansel and Gretel immediately came to mind . . . or *Little Red Riding Hood* . . . and all the deliciously scary fairy stories of her childhood that Grace had read to her. Not that the sight of it scared her. Bathed in April sunshine it was just beautiful, even with its slightly neglected air and the tangle of weeds and blackthorn bushes in the small garden. At night, or on misty, murky mornings, she could imagine that it would have a sinister appearance. But today it was an enchanted, whitewashed cottage and she fell in love with it instantly.

'Is it what you expected?' William asked when they had

got out of the car, and she was standing motionless without saying a word.

'It's *beautiful*.'

'I don't need to sell it to you then, do I?' he said, somewhat taken aback by such an enthusiastic reaction.

'You don't. It's already mine.'

'Of course. It was merely a figure of speech. So shall we go inside? I must warn you, it's in need of some love and attention, and the thatch has certainly seen better days.'

'Whatever's wrong with it, I'm sure it can be fixed. It's a shame to let such a picturesque place fall into disrepair because of some superstition from an unhappy episode.' She had a sudden thought as they walked up the short garden path. 'By the way, how well did you know Mr Devenish?'

Her question took him by surprise. 'Not at all. I merely acted for him through his solicitors. Why do you ask?'

Jasmine smiled. 'He was a wily old fox, that's why. He knew very well that the instant I saw the cottage I would fall in love with it and want to live in it.'

'And is that what you want?'

She could hear her Aunt Lucy's voice in her head at that moment, telling her she was always too impulsive, to think before she spoke, and not to let her sudden excitement run away with her. Aunt Lucy was long gone, but her words had always been intended to tell Jasmine to slow down and not rush into things. Sometimes it was unavoidable to let those words of wisdom enter her thoughts. It was also just as easy to ignore them ...

'I won't know what I want until I see it properly,' she said in answer to William Hedges's question, 'so why are we waiting?'

Back home in Bristol a long while later, when Jasmine had more or less placated her father at going off without a word the way she had, she and Grace were at last alone in Jasmine's bedroom and she could spill out everything about her extraordinary day. It *had* been extraordinary, she admitted. She had thought it would be just another cottage, just another village, just another estate agent giving her the same old spiel they usually did about some tumbledown place that was a probably like a millstone on his books. He didn't have to do any of that, of course. The cottage was already hers.

'So tell me everything, Jassy,' Grace demanded. 'What was it like? Were you disappointed?'

'I don't need to tell you. You can see for yourself.' She fished out the paperwork William had given her from her bag and handed it to Grace without a word. Admittedly, the photograph of the cottage had been taken some time ago before the garden became quite so overgrown, but even so, it was the sort of idyllic retreat that many a city dweller would covet. There were photos of the interior as well: the twisting staircase, the small sitting-room with the inglenook fireplace that would keep it so cosy on winter evenings, the quaint kitchen and outhouse, the two small bedrooms and a box room.

'The box room's not as small as it looks,' Jasmine said. 'In fact, the whole place was bigger than I expected. They have more room for building in the country. The place hasn't been lived in for a year, though, and is badly in need of some tender, loving care.'

As yet, she wasn't going to tell Grace about the young couple who had died there. She wanted Grace to see the cottage without prejudice or bad feelings about it, and she wouldn't admit to herself why that was.

'So what about the village?' Grace said next. 'It's only a dot on the map, isn't it? You wouldn't want to live there, would you, Jassy?'

'I haven't made my mind up about that yet.'

'Well, you need to think hard about it before you commit yourself to it. What would you do there all day? I can't imagine there's much work, and it's hardly a big enough place for you to be the lady of the manor.'

'Funny, that's what he called me. My lady,' she said without thinking.

'Who? The pompous estate agent?'

Jasmine laughed. 'That's the one, except that he wasn't at all as I had imagined, and I had tea with him and his aunt when we'd finished viewing the cottage and I'd had a tour of the village.'

'You didn't fall for him, did you?' Grace asked.

'Not likely. Don't worry, I'm not smitten, nor likely to be!'

'You seem to have got in with a few locals soon enough. So what's next?'

Jasmine looked at her thoughtfully. The idea had only come to her on the way back on the bus, when the noise and pall of the city had contrasted so sharply with the cleaner air and slower pace of life in the country. It could drive some people mad, of course . . .

'I want you and Dad to come with me on Sunday to take a look at it and tell me what you think. We could take a picnic after church and have it inside the cottage. You're always saying you don't get enough driving practise in that little car of yours, so you could drive us there, and it would be good for Dad to get away from the bad air from the river here. I hear him coughing in bed every night, and his chest isn't getting any better. What do you think?'

Grace began to laugh. 'I think you let your enthusiasm run away with you far too much! I also think you'll have a hard time persuading Dad to get away even for an afternoon, Jassy. His roots are here.'

'It's time he was uprooted then, if only for a few hours, just to see how other people live,' Jasmine said smartly. 'And *I* wasn't thinking of persuading him. He wouldn't listen to me, so you're the one to do it.'

Grace looked at her sister's determined face, and knew with a pang that she was probably right. Jassy was the image of their mother, and when she got that special, eager look on her face that made her eyes so startlingly alive, it was no wonder that Owen could hardly bear to look at her for remembering his beloved wife. But Grace sometimes felt uneasy, thinking that his grief had gone on too long. It was as if it was his crutch, something to cling on to, but he had clung on to it for twenty years now, and it was time he threw it away and lived the rest of his life without such bitterness and regrets.

'I'll try,' she told Jasmine now, knowing she would get no peace from her sister until she agreed, 'but don't hold out too much hope.'

'If anyone can find a way to persuade Dad to have a day out, I know you will,' Jasmine replied without rancour. 'Besides, I'm sure he wouldn't agree to my moving out without having a lot to say about the cottage. And before you say anything to that, I haven't decided anything yet, but it wouldn't hurt to let him know I'm considering it, would it?'

Grace looked at her thoughtfully. 'You know he missed you being around when you went to work for Mr Devenish, and he was very proud of you for getting that job.'

Jasmine shrugged. 'I doubt that he missed me at all, and if he was proud of me, he never told me!'

'You shouldn't be surprised about that. You know the sort of man he is, Jassy,' Grace said. 'He finds it hard to express his emotions, and even harder to praise his children. He belongs to the old school that thinks too much praise is bad for them and will make them big-headed. You should know that – and anyway, when did he ever praise me? It's not his way.'

'Well, if I ever have children I shall praise them whenever they deserve it. Not that I can see it happening for years, if ever.'

Grace laughed out loud. 'You didn't say that when you took a fancy to that young estate gardener, if I remember.'

'I don't want to talk about him,' Jasmine said, remembering that painful episode only too well. His image swept into her mind, unbidden and unwanted . . . Freddie Patterson, tousle-haired and bohemian, and more exciting than anyone she had ever met before. He had turned her head with his smooth lies. She had believed him when he said he loved her, and he had stirred up all kinds of feelings and longings in her that she had never known before. Then she had learned to her horror that he was practically engaged to another girl. It had been the biggest let down of her life, and a bitter one to accept, since they had to go on working at the same place and she couldn't avoid seeing him every day. She had cycled home from the estate that day with her eyes blinded by tears, and shut herself in her bedroom until Grace had banged on her door, demanding to know what was wrong.

She took a deep breath. This wasn't the time to be thinking

22

about Freddie Patterson and how she had fallen for him so heavily, thinking he was the love of her life . . . until she discovered he was somebody else's. Even when she had discovered the truth from one of the women who worked on the estate, Freddie had still pursued her, saying they could still have a bit of fun and nobody would get hurt . . . the rat that he was! Jassy had vowed that the next time a man looked at her, she wouldn't be so gullible, and she meant to stick to it.

'So what was this estate agent like then?' Grace decided to change the subject quickly when she saw how Jassy's eyes had become clouded. 'Was he fat and forty, or a white-haired old goat like you expected him to be?' she said, trying to cheer her sister up.

Jasmine smiled. 'Neither. He was about your age, and I suppose he was all right once we had got the measure of one another. I'm not sure which of us thought we were more superior – the city girl or the country boy!'

Grace raised her eyebrows. 'He obviously made an impression on you, though. And you had tea with him and his auntie afterwards?' she persisted.

'Well, you needn't read anything into that! We had business to see to once I'd seen the cottage, and I couldn't wait around twiddling my thumbs until the bus came, so it seemed rude not to accept. The auntie was quite nice, once she'd found out all she wanted to know about me!'

Right now, Jasmine didn't want to tell Grace about William's young cousin who had found the dead couple in the cottage. She hadn't met him, thankfully, and she didn't want to influence her sister or father in any way before they went to see the cottage. She just wanted their honest opinion over what to do about it. The more she thought about it, the more she knew she wouldn't want to live there by herself. It was too remote, too quiet, too everything she had never known . . . she also knew that with a lot of attention to the neglected garden, a bit of paint here and there, and some new thatch, it was also the most beautiful little cottage she had ever seen.

She couldn't ask Grace to leave her father to share it with her either, and the thought of all three of them living there together – even if her father would agree – would be heading for ructions and certain disaster. Reluctantly, it seemed the only sensible option would be to sell it.

It seemed such a shame. Being a property owner had felt good and Jasmine didn't deny it. Even the flat and shop here were only rented to her father, and to her knowledge he had never owned anything outright. For a moment, no more, the idea of handing over ownership of Blackthorn Cottage to him as a loving and magnanimous gesture for his old age, flitted into her mind, and just as quickly, flitted out again. She could just imagine his outraged pride at what he would consider a condescending offer from a daughter.

'You'd better stay up here while I suggest to Dad that we all go down to Horton on Sunday, then,' Grace said, bringing Jasmine's thoughts back to the present. 'If you hear him shouting, you'll know the answer before I come back.'

'You'd like to see the cottage, wouldn't you, Grace?'

'Of course I would. It sounds lovely – and don't let Dad put you off. I'm sure he's glad for you really, Jassy, even if he finds it so hard to show it.'

She gave her sister a quick hug and clattered down the stairs to find their father, while Jasmine stared gloomily at the wall. Why *did* people find it so hard to show their emotions and feelings? Hers seemed to be always glaringly obvious, just as the old saying went – *wearing your heart on your sleeve* – as even William Hedges had discovered. He was probably in no doubt that he'd met a very determined young lady – any more than she was in much doubt that he more than matched her in temperament.

She felt her shoulders relaxing as she thought of their encounter, unable to think of it in any other way. For the first time, she wondered what he had expected of her, and if he had even bothered to speculate, anyway. She was just another client to him. Even so, would he have expected to see some smart, city slick female who would look down on country folk?

Then there were her own expectations, she thought with a grin. Already putting him into a mould before she even met him . . . fat and forty, or a white-haired old goat! And he had been neither.

Her eyes gleamed as a sudden thought surged into her head. He would be a perfect match for Grace. They were about the same age, and it was time Grace had a man of her own, despite the fact that she always said she wasn't interested in marriage. Grace had looked after her father and sister for years now, and she would make a perfect wife and mother, and William Hedges was just the one she needed.

With her usual breezy disregard of any obstacles between them such as distance and inclination, Jasmine decided that this was a project that was definitely worthwhile. She'd never thought of herself as a matchmaker before, but all it needed was being able to throw them together at every opportunity – and that was the first problem! But with her usual quick thinking, visions of spending a good few Sunday afternoons in Horton came to mind, with herself and Grace doing a bit of gardening, and whatever renovations they could manage at the cottage. Whether or not their father came with them on those occasions would be up to him.

In any case, Jasmine was quite sure she was wily enough to enlist the help of a certain person in Horton who was allegedly a dab hand with a paintbrush. If the cottage was to be renovated to a high enough standard to be put on the market again, it would be to a local estate agent's advantage to oversee a couple of helpless females muddling along.

Three

'Absolutely not,' Owen Wyatt said in answer to his elder daughter's pleas. 'By the time I've done a week's work in the shop, then listened to the vicar spouting on about rights and wrongs on Sunday morning, all I want to do is put my feet up and have a bit of shut-eye. You go with Jasmine if you must, Grace, but I've no intention of bothering my head about it. It's all a lot of nonsense, anyway. The girl should have told the estate agent fellow to put the place back on the market and be done with it. She'd have been wiser to invest the money in something sensible, and I'm sure she'll see the folly in not doing so before long.'

'When did Jassy ever stop to think of doing something sensible? She's far too headstrong to think of anything but the charm of this cottage and none of its drawbacks. I couldn't bear to think of her living there all by herself, practically out in the wilds. That's why I want you to come with us, Dad. She won't listen to me, but you'll be able to point out all the flaws in the idea, and make her see it's no more than a white elephant.'

Owen looked at her thoughtfully. 'Sometimes I think you should have been a diplomat, Grace, but if you think such flattery is going to win me over, you can think again.' Then he paused, his eyes narrowing. 'She hasn't really got any lame-brained idea of living there by herself, has she?'

'Well, I don't know how serious she was, but she certainly mentioned it,' Grace said, mentally crossing her fingers. 'I'd hate to think of her living there all by herself too. She's not exactly the world's best cook and housekeeper, is she?'

'There's something else that you've either overlooked or chosen to ignore,' Owen said sharply. 'The girl's not twenty-one until August, and until she is, she needs my permission to do anything.'

'But what if she just leaves, anyway? You wouldn't be so cruel as to drag her back, would you, Dad? It would be so shaming for her. At least if you come to Horton with us and look at the cottage you can persuade her what a bad idea it would be. Let her think it's all her idea to put the cottage up for sale.'

He gave a heavy sigh. 'I think you'd better go away and leave me to think about it. Between you, you make my head ache.'

He began a bout of coughing that had Grace feeling alarmed. It was just as Jassy had said – he coughed and wheezed far more than he used to, and the cloying air of the city couldn't be doing him a lot of good. The doctor often told him a few hours in the healthier air of the country was just what he needed, but that was one argument she wasn't going to put to him yet. One step at a time, and for now it had to be enough that he was thinking about the drive on Sunday.

She knew he wouldn't have been comfortable mentioning Jassy's birthday, either. It was a day of mixed feelings for him. He had wanted this second child as much as his wife had ... but Jassy's birth also coincided with the day his beloved Celia died, and for that he could never quite forgive her. His head told him it was no fault of the child's, but his heart had said otherwise, and still did, after all these years. Nearly twenty-one of them now, and the pain of that day was still as searing to Owen as when it happened.

And the older Jassy got, the more like Celia she became ... he couldn't expect the girl to understand, and nor could he ever try to explain, but sometimes he could hardly bear to look at her, seeing his beautiful Celia all over again. It should have been a comfort, but it never was, and never would be. Maybe if she did move away, it would lessen the heartache he couldn't overcome ... and he instantly told himself it was an unworthy thought. A father should protect his children, not turn them away because of something over which they had no control.

By the time he joined his girls for supper that evening, he had given himself a good talking-to and made up his mind. He forced himself not to sound grudging when he gave them his answer.

'You're wanting us to go on a joyride with you on Sunday to see this cottage, I understand,' he said to Jassy. 'I daresay I can spare a couple of hours. But don't read anything into it, mind. I only said I'd look at it.'

Her face lit up with the look he didn't want to see, but could hardly have expected otherwise. It was a look that took his breath away. Even more so when she came around the table to give him a spontaneous hug, and the scent of her hair was in his nostrils, so poignantly feminine, the way Celia's used to be, that it made his eyes blur for a moment.

'Oh Dad, I'm so glad you've agreed. You'll love it, I know!'

He disentangled himself with an awkward laugh, and spoke gruffly.

'I'm not so sure about that, but at least I can give you my opinion and see if I think it's worth a pinch of salt.'

Nothing he said was going to put Jassy off now. She was bubbling inside, wondering if she should send a note to William Hedges or telephone him to say that she and her family were coming to view the cottage properly on Sunday. But why should she? It was hers, and she could go there whenever she wished. She put him out of her mind, but she was barely able to contain her excitement as the week passed. They were obliged to sit through the interminably long sermon at church on Sunday morning which didn't put Owen's occasional churchgoing in the best of humours, and as soon as it was over they went home and got ready for what Grace was indulgently calling Jassy's wild adventure. Considering they rarely went anywhere in Grace's car except for errands around the city, or the occasional summer visit to the seaside at Weston-super-Mare, it *was* something of an adventure, Jassy supposed.

Earlier that morning, Grace had prepared a picnic basket with cooked sausages and pork pies, bread and cheese, and a flask of tea. At the last minute she included a bottle of beer for Owen, thinking this might soften him up if he started to make too many objections to Jassy's cottage. *Jassy's cottage* ... it gave Grace an odd little thrill just saying the words in her head. She had never coveted such a thing herself, nor had any aspirations to country living, but it sounded so grand to think of her little sister as a property owner.

Not so little now, she thought, eyeing Jassy as she put on her jacket and gloves and had a final tweak at her hair to make sure it was tidy. She was a lovely young woman, and she was certainly going to find love one of these days. Grace wasn't too sure that the back of beyond in Horton was exactly the right place to find it, but stranger things had happened, and Grace was a great believer in fate. If fate had decreed that Jassy ended up living in Horton, then no matter what a pang it would be to Grace herself, and how much she knew she would miss her, then it was the right place for Jassy to be.

'Are we all ready?' she said quickly, before she began to get gloomy. 'You sit in the front with me, Dad, and Jassy can sit in the back with the map.'

She knew her sister would much prefer to sit in the front seat, but one look from Grace told Jasmine it would be better to do as she was told. Then, once they were well away from the smoke of the city and the stink of the waterfront, her father would have the benefit of seeing the countryside unfold in front of him in all its springtime glory.

Jasmine was still asking herself exactly what she was trying to achieve today, but in her heart she knew it was a bid for her father's approval. He seemed to disapprove of her so often, especially her impulsiveness compared to Grace's steady nature – and apparently her likeness to the photographs of her mother – as if she could help that! It would have made her so much happier if it had made him warm towards her, seeing the echo of his wife in his daughter. But all her life she had known that this was a barrier between them, and one that it was impossible for her to breach.

Well, she wasn't going to think of that now, making herself downhearted when this was going to be a special outing, and a rare occasion for them all to be going out together. It occurred to Jasmine how rarely that happened, and how much less of a family they really were. She hadn't thought of it too much before, but she was thinking of it now, when the three of them sat in virtual silence in the car, seemingly unable to have a natural conversation with each other.

Whenever she and Grace had the occasional day out together, they usually ended up singing in the car. She didn't imagine that was likely to happen today, but someone had to break this silence . . .

'Have you been anywhere near the Horton area of Somerset before, Dad?' she said brightly.

He gave a grunt. 'No. If people ever went anywhere on their day off, it was to the seaside, not to the middle of nowhere. Traipsing around farming country and stepping in all kinds of unmentionable stuff is not my idea of heaven.'

'You'll like Horton then,' Jassy went on, determined not to let him get the better of her. 'I didn't see any sign of a farm, and it's a proper little village, not only with pretty thatched cottages but with a village green, and proper shops like ours, and – well, everything,' she finished lamely.

'I think I'll reserve judgment until I get there as to whether I'll like it or not,' Owen said, 'but at least we've got a nice day for it.'

Grace gave a chuckle. 'And that's about all the enthusiasm you'll get from Dad, Jassy. Never mind, I'm sure things·will improve when he sees the place, and I've put in a bottle of his favourite beer to go with the picnic, so that'll put you in a good mood, won't it, Dad?'

'I hope so,' Jassy muttered as he laughed, wondering why it was that Grace could always tease him and get away with it, when it was considered cheek if it came from her. From what she knew of other families, it was usually the youngest who could always get around the father, but not in their case.

Then Owen turned around in the car and gave her a brief smile.

'I promise I'll give you my honest opinion as I always do, girl. I can't say fairer than that, can I?'

She supposed he couldn't, and as always she forgave him for what she considered his shortcomings in the father-daughter relationship as far as she was concerned. He couldn't help it, any more than she could help rushing into things and seeing the excitement of it all before looking for any drawbacks. Being an optimist was surely preferable to being a pessimist. Even William Hedges hadn't been able to cover the enthusiasm in his own voice when he pointed out the charm of the twisting staircase in Blackthorn Cottage, and the inglenook fireplace. He was essentially an optimist too, Jasmine thought – although, of course, that could just have been the estate agent talking . . . but somehow she didn't think so. If he had been brought up to country living, as she supposed he had been, he too could hardly fail to find Blackthorn Cottage utterly enchanting.

'You're deep in thought, Jassy,' she heard Grace say. 'I hope you're keeping your eyes on the road map and not just dreaming about the cottage and what you're going to do with it.'

'I'm not!' Jassy said, annoyed that she had forgotten all about road directions, and even more annoyed that she had been thinking about William Hedges. But since he was going to figure largely in her life from now on, no matter what she intended, it was hardly surprising. It would also be better to get along with him than to be at loggerheads – especially if she thought of him as a possible suitor for her sister.

She looked at the back of Grace's elegant head, and noted the way she drove the car so competently. Her name fitted her so well, and she and William Hedges would be well matched, so efficient in their different ways, and Jassy found it completely easy to ignore the little matter of the distance between them.

'What are you thinking about now?' Grace said in exasperation, as if Jassy's gaze was boring a hole in her head.

'You'd be surprised,' Jassy said with a laugh, wondering just how often she could persuade Grace to make this journey without revealing any devious intentions.

It was probably best to let nature take its course, she reflected. The village was so small, and they would have to venture into it from time to time to buy anything necessary for the cottage. Grace and William would be obliged to meet, and once they did . . .

'I hope this isn't going to take the rest of the day,' her father interrupted her thoughts. 'You know I do need to have my rest on a Sunday.'

'Oh Dad, you can close your eyes and rest in the car,' Jassy said.

'Nobody could rest if there are too many more bumps in

the road,' he said feelingly. 'And I daresay it'll get worse when we get downcountry a bit.'

Jassy sighed. He was determined not to see any good in today's outing, and she was just as determined not to let him depress the three of them. He wasn't always such a grouch, but today seemed to be bringing out the worst in him. He was also coughing more than usual, and ignoring the doctor's advice to take his medicine. But once he saw the cottage, she knew he'd be impressed. It was so beautiful, and she could still hardly believe that it was actually hers. Today, in the spring sunshine, it would look idyllic, and she spent the rest of the journey anticipating the pleasure and surprise on her father's and sister's faces when they saw it for the first time.

'Oh, dear Lord, who could have done this!' Jassy whispered, her face stricken, and feeling as though her heart was plummeting to her boots.

She had guided Grace through the village in high spirits, noting more than a few interested stares at the sight of a strange car in Horton on a quiet Sunday afternoon, then out through the lanes towards the cottage. And there it stood, amid the tangle of overgrown garden that could so easily be put right; the thatched roof looking not too bad at all; the whitewashed walls gleaming in the sunlight . . . apart from the trails of red paint on either side of the front door, as if someone had maliciously thrown a bucket of paint at it.

'Good God, is this what you've brought us to see?' Owen roared as they all stepped out of the car and stared in horror.

Jasmine burst into tears. 'You don't think I knew about this, do you? It wasn't like it when I came here before. Someone has done this since then. Someone who doesn't want people living here, especially outsiders.'

Grace was holding on to her shaking body and glaring at their father. After a moment he had recovered himself a little.

'I'm not blaming you, girl,' he said roughly. 'I've seen the details of the place, and I'm not denying that it looked well enough in the pictures. This is the work of vandals, and they're not going to get away with it.'

'There'll be time enough to think about that later,' Grace

said quickly. 'I'm sure it'll be all right inside, and it needn't stop us having our picnic. I think we could all do with a cup of tea to calm ourselves. What do you say, Jassy?'

She nodded slowly. She was still shaking, but the first shock and distress was giving way to anger that anyone could desecrate a property like this for no reason.

'Yes, let's go inside,' she said in a choked voice. 'Will you bring the picnic basket, Dad? Whoever did this, they're not going to spoil it for me.'

She thought she saw a flicker of something like admiration in his eyes, but then he turned away to take the picnic basket from the back seat of the car and follow his daughters inside the cottage. For a few minutes nobody spoke, each of them relieved to find the interior was intact, and then Grace couldn't contain herself.

'Oh Jassy, it's just perfect,' she said at once, just as Jassy had known she would. Who could fail to be enchanted by such a place – even though, for Jassy, it no longer felt quite the same. It *would* do, she vowed, and she definitely meant what she had said. Whoever had vandalized the outside walls, they weren't going to spoil it for her.

She was still feeling unnerved, but once they had taken a quick look around downstairs and found everything in order, she felt better when they had all had a reviving mug of tea from the flask. They needed to get their breaths back before they inspected the rest of the cottage. Besides, Owen's stomach was rumbling and telling him it was long overdue for food.

'Pass around the plates, Grace,' he said. 'There's no point in starving ourselves just because of a bit of red paint.'

Jassy gave a weak smile. Whatever else happened – famine, war or pestilence – her father believed in feeding the inner man, as he called it. She didn't argue, knowing it would put him in the best mood of all for dealing with today. In an odd way, the sense of outrage he had obviously felt at the attack on the cottage, might even be to her advantage. She desperately wanted her father to approve of her, even if this might be the strangest way to achieve it.

'We'll all eat,' she said shakily, 'and then I'll show you over the rest of the cottage. There's more to it than this one room.'

'It's a very nice room, Jassy,' Grace said, as if to reassure her that their visit here wasn't all bad news. 'I bet it would be cosy and warm in the winter.'

Owen was comfortable in one of the soft armchairs now, and he took a long drink of tea before he commented.

'That's because the walls are thick, with none of your cheap and shoddy building materials. Folk knew how to put a sturdy home together when cottages like these were built, I'll say that for them. From first glance, the thatch needs some repair work, but a good thatcher should be able to put that right.'

Jassy flashed a glance at Grace, knowing that this was another hurdle they had overcome. Owen had always admired well-made property, and once they had viewed the cottage properly, Jassy thought it would be a good idea to take a peek inside Horton's weathered church, which looked as if it had stood there for ever. First of all, though, she wanted to show him around her inheritance, and despite her earlier anxiety she felt her heart give a little leap of pleasure, just thinking of the word. Her inheritance . . . to a girl of twenty years old, it was a dazzling word.

'Hurry up and finish eating, and then I'll show you upstairs.' She couldn't help her eagerness now, considering how grand she felt at the prospect.

The memory of the horrible red paint daubed on the front walls of the cottage hadn't faded in her mind, but for now, she was determined to put it aside. It had to be dealt with, but more important was the impression that the interior of the cottage was making on her family. She could see that Grace was already thrilled with it, but it was her dad's approval she needed most. It was what she had always needed, and so rarely had.

'Not much of a kitchen,' he said, when they had finished the picnic, and carried the mugs and plates out to the stone sink, 'but I daresay it could be extended if anybody put their mind to improving it. You want to be sure that estate agent fellow puts that on the details before he thinks of putting it back on the market for you, Jasmine.'

She didn't rise to the bait, still not sure what she intended to do with it, but not prepared to be pushed into deciding one way or the other just yet. It was practically the first time in her life she was being cautious and not rushing straight in, she realized. Aunt Lucy would have been proud of her.

'Let's see what's upstairs then, Jassy,' Grace said eagerly. 'I'm dying to see the rest of it.'

As they climbed the twisting staircase, Jassy didn't miss the way her father was testing the banister and the stair treads with every step, probably wondering if the woodwork was going to stand up to it. She knew that it would. William Hedges had told her that apart from some plumbing renovations, the foundations and interior were sound. The thatched roof needed patching, but then what was needed was merely cosmetic, he had told her in estate agent jargon.

'This is the back bedroom,' she said, flinging open the door. 'It overlooks the bluebell woods so the view is pretty spectacular at this time of year.'

They could hardly disagree, and she began to feel like an estate agent herself as she tried to boost the finer points of the cottage. But why not, she thought fiercely? It was hers, and she loved it.

'It's really beautiful, Jassy,' Grace said. 'Isn't it, Dad?'

He grunted his agreement. 'It's a nice view, so what about the rest of it?'

Jassy gritted her teeth, and showed them the box room which could easily be converted into another bedroom or a child's room. For a moment, she had a vision of a little family living here, parents and child, and thought how perfect it would be, with the woods all around them, and the village nearby. It hadn't been so perfect for that other couple, she thought swiftly, and was thankful she hadn't mentioned them to her own family. Owen wasn't a superstitious man, but it could be the lever he needed to persuade her that there was a bad feeling about Blackthorn Cottage. Though how anybody could think such a thing, on such a lovely day . . . but somebody did, with their obvious attempt to keep her away, she thought with a shiver, remembering the red paint . . .

After a look around the main bedroom at the front of the cottage, Owen went over to the latticed window to see where it overlooked the garden, the church spire and the roofs of the village beyond. After a moment or two the girls heard his voice practically explode with rage.

'If that young devil's come to do more of his handiwork he's going to get a good thrashing from me,' he bellowed, and before anybody knew what was happening he had gone crashing down the stairs again, leaving Grace and Jassy momentarily frozen with shock.

If it was one of the local lads, curious at having seen strangers driving through the village, Jassy thought frantically, it wasn't going to do her reputation much good to have her father ranting and raving and accusing him. It wouldn't do the cottage's reputation much good, either, if the report went around the village that there was a madman there now.

As the sound of shouting reached her ears, Jassy rushed to the window herself to see what was happening outside. Her father was waving his arms about and gesticulating wildly to the paint-daubed cottage walls at the casually dressed man standing by the gate with his arms folded tightly, a furious expression on his face, a bucket and cleaning materials on the ground beside him.

'Oh no!' Jasmine screeched, clapping her hands to her mouth. 'Why on earth did Dad have to rush out like that?'

'Well, you might have expected it if he thinks it's some local chap coming to snoop around,' Grace defended him. 'He's only thinking of you, Jassy, and the chap does look a bit disreputable, you must admit. It looks as if he might have intended getting up to his old tricks again, and he's hardly the local vicar, is he?'

Jassy almost choked. 'No, he's not. But your disreputable chap has probably still been doing some work on a neighbour's fence, and he'd hardly be dressed in his Sunday best for that, would he?'

'Do you *know* him?' Grace said.

As the two men in the garden below turned to look up at the window, Jassy drew back, her face red and humiliated.

'Of course I know him,' she snapped. 'That's William Hedges, the estate agent, and now he'll think I'm a complete nitwit bringing my father down here to inspect the cottage without letting him know, and then having Dad hollering at him like that. And he calls *me* impulsive!'

'Well, how was he to know who it was?' Grace said, but she was already talking to thin air, because Jassy had gone rushing down the stairs and into the garden, to try to make peace between the two men. In a gossipy village like she firmly suspected Horton to be, the last thing she wanted was for William Hedges to report back that the sooner this place was on the market again and out of the hands of raving lunatics, the happier they would all be.

Four

By the time the girls reached the two men, Owen was looking as red-faced as his younger daughter. Blustering now, his awkward attempt at an apology seemed to be ignored as Jassy ran outside to confront William Hedges, knowing it was up to her to make the peace. Her voice was wild and distracted, and totally unlike the sophisticated city girl she was supposed to be.

'I'm sorry, Mr Hedges. I should have warned you we were coming, but when we saw what had been done to the cottage, I'm afraid my father just saw red.'

She stopped, realizing the incongruity of her words, and both men turned and stared at her for a moment before they started laughing.

'It's all right, Miss Wyatt, I think we were all feeling a bit heated earlier, but sometimes it helps to see the funny side,' William said.

'I don't see anything funny about it,' she snapped, not caring to be patronized, even though she was aware that her father was frowning at her now. 'If you had kept an eye on the cottage for me you'd have seen what some local louts have done here. I'd have thought it was in your interest as a *salesman* as well as in mine as the owner, to see that no damage is done to an unoccupied property.'

She paused for breath, knowing she had meant to insult him by using the word 'salesman', and that he was perfectly aware of it.

'Jasmine, my dear,' her father began, but William didn't give him a chance.

'If you would permit me to speak, madam,' he said coldly, 'you would know, as your father now knows, that I came here this afternoon with the sole intention of removing the

38

offending paintwork from the walls of Blackthorn Cottage. This is not the way I would normally choose to spend a Sunday afternoon, and nor is it my job to keep an eye on a client's property.'

Grace was hovering behind her sister now. She put her hand on Jassy's arm in an attempt to calm her down as Jassy noted the contents of the bucket properly, and she saw that he was speaking the truth. Aghast, she knew what a spoiled brat she must have seemed just now – and very much the product of a headstrong father. Until that moment she had never realized how alike they were in that respect.

'I'm sorry. I didn't know. None of us did,' she muttered.

In the awkward pause that followed, when nobody seemed to know quite what to say next, and the silence was only broken by her father's heavy wheezing, Grace decided it was time she intervened. She spoke directly to William Hedges.

'I'm Grace Wyatt, Jasmine's sister, and I'm very pleased to meet you, Mr Hedges, despite the rather unfortunate beginning. I've heard so much about you from Jassy that I feel I know you already.'

She hadn't heard that much, and none of it had been particularly good, but it was a polite thing to say, and Grace had always been polite, having the knack of saying the right thing as opposed to Jassy, who invariably said the wrong one.

'I'm pleased to meet you too, Miss Wyatt,' William said, giving her the smile that could probably sell a hothouse to an eskimo, Jassy thought. She hoped Grace was suitably impressed by that smile. 'But since this is clearly a family day, I think it's best if I come back tomorrow and attend to the cleaning up. I didn't want you to see it like this, and be assured it will be done before your next visit,' he added, turning to Jasmine.

'Did you walk here, young man?' Owen said, seeing the absence of a car.

William smiled somewhat sardonically. 'We country-folk are well used to walking, sir, and it's hardly any distance from the village.'

'Well, nearly a mile,' Jasmine said, elaborating.

'Anyway, since we've just about finished here, allow us to give you a lift back to the village,' Owen went on, attempting to make amends for the way he'd bellowed at William earlier.

'There's no need, and having abandoned this cleaning job for today I shall call at the church to walk back with my aunt instead. She'll have finished arranging the flowers and hymn numbers for this evening's service by now.'

'The ride is settled then, since Jassy suggested we should take a look at the church, and I would like to see it myself,' Owen said.

Grace sighed. 'You might as well give in, Mr Hedges. My father always gets his way.'

'Then I'll leave my equipment around the back of the cottage,' William went on. 'And don't worry, the next time you come here, it will look as good as new.'

As he disappeared around the back, Jassy hissed at her father. 'Why did you invite him to come with us? The less I see of him the better, and now he'll think we're a crazy family, with both of us shouting at him.'

'It's a good thing he can see that Grace is the sane one then, isn't it?'

They had no chance to say anything more as William appeared again, and as they climbed into Grace's car, Jassy was embarrassed to find William squeezing in beside her in the back.

'This is cosy, isn't it?' he said with a mocking grin, as if knowing exactly how uncomfortable she felt.

By the time they were nearing the church Grace had done most of the talking, since Jassy hardly knew what to say in this far-too-intimate situation with William Hedges. It was surely better to keep their acquaintance on a businesslike footing, but on the other hand, if she was going to think of William Hedges as a suitor for Grace, she could hardly keep him at arm's length. Already, she was starting to think it may not have been such a good idea after all. He probably had someone of his own anyway. He might be engaged, or even married, for all she knew.

She didn't really know the first thing about him, except that he was an estate agent, he had an aunt who ran the village post office and did occasional duty as an undertaker's assistant and arranged the flowers and hymn numbers in the church. In other words, she knew more about his aunt than she did about him! Oh yes, and he had a young cousin who had discovered the dead bodies of the couple in Blackthorn Cottage five years ago.

She shuddered, remembering, and then came an uneasy thought as to how her father would react if he knew the background of this cottage she had inherited. Those earlier tenants probably hadn't been welcome in Horton, if they had kept themselves strictly to themselves and been unwilling to join in any local activities. And it had just been made very clear to Jasmine Wyatt that she wasn't going to be welcome here either.

'Are you all right?'

She heard William Hedges's voice as if through a fog, and realized she had been breathing very quickly. She nodded, ignoring her fears as his face came into focus properly, very close to hers. Her voice was clipped, more with the imagery of that poor couple than with anything else.

'I'm fine, thank you, just a little claustrophobic inside the car.'

'Then it's just as well we're here,' he said, moving away from her.

'Good,' Owen said, attempting to be more jovial now that the incident at the cottage was behind him. 'I've always been partial to looking around old churches, especially out of hours, so to speak, when I don't have to listen to vicars spouting on. I prefer learning about their history, if not touring around old churchyards,'

No, there was only one churchyard he cared to visit, Jassy thought, and even that had become a once-yearly visit of late, since it was apparently too painful for him. And for her too, since it was always on her birthday. She could feel resentment if it didn't seem too shameful an emotion. But sometimes there *was* a sense of resentment in her mind, because it was hardly her fault that her mother had died giving birth to her ... and almost immediately, she knew that it was. Of course it was her fault, and it was a burden she had to bear all her life.

'My aunt could tell you far more about this church than I could, but I do know that it has stood here since the twelfth century,' William was saying. 'It's a very fine old building, isn't it?'

Owen agreed. 'They don't make buildings like that these days.'

'They don't make them at all, but unless you've got a few hours to spare you'd better not get Aunt Kate started on about churches, Mr Wyatt. She gets quite passionate about them, especially if they start to deteriorate, but she reckons it takes wars or earthquakes for folk to turn to God and think about rebuilding a church.'

'It's a good thing there aren't likely to be any earthquakes here then,' Jassy muttered, thinking he was back on his pompous high horse again.

'Let's all pray that there aren't going to be any wars, either,' her father said.

Jassy didn't want all this talk of wars and earthquakes, nor thoughts of dead people in her cottage. She had wanted this day to be wonderful, with her father and sister overcome by the beauty of the area and her picturesque cottage, and for them to be as delighted in it as she was, but somehow those feelings were slipping away from her. As she followed the two men towards the door, Grace grabbed her.

'What's wrong with you? You've been a grouch ever since we left the cottage, and William's being perfectly charming.'

'Oh, it's *William*, is it? Well, it's easy to see he's charmed you!'

She flounced away from Grace and stepped inside the coolness of the church, standing still for a few moments to let her eyes adjust to the dimness. Wasn't this what she wanted – for Grace to find William perfectly charming? Wasn't it the most desirable thing that it had happened so quickly, if her own matchmaking ideas were to come to fruition? She looked ahead, to where Grace had caught up with the others now, and where the middle-aged woman she remembered from the post office was greeting them. For a moment Jassy had a ridiculous feeling of being the outsider, the cuckoo in the nest, as the four people chatting quietly together now formed such a complete unit.

And she was the village idiot, the childish twenty-year-old who was being even more stupid in thinking such idiotic

42

things. She moved quickly towards the group, and Mrs Lester turned to her with a pleasant smile.

'How very nice to see you again, Miss Wyatt – or may I call you Jasmine? It's such a pretty name.'

'Oh – please do,' she said, taken aback for a moment.

'I'm so sorry about what happened to Blackthorn Cottage, but William has assured me he'll sort it all out for you, and I'm sure the culprit will soon be found. I promise you we don't treat all our visitors in this way.'

But Jasmine wasn't merely a visitor. She was the owner of Blackthorn Cottage. She caught Grace's warning glance, and managed to stop herself giving a smart reply that would antagonize her father all over again.

'It's very kind of Mr Hedges – er – William, to take the trouble.'

'Well, that's what village folk do. We all help each other. Now then, I'm sure you don't want to hear me prattle, so William and I will leave you to look around the church. I hope I'll meet you and your lovely daughters again, Mr Wyatt.'

'I'm sure you will, ma'am,' Owen said magnanimously.

She nodded to them all, and as she and William took their leave, Grace gave a small chuckle.

'I reckon you've made a bit of a conquest there, Dad,' she said, teasing him in a way Jasmine never would, or could.

'Don't be foolish, girl,' he replied. 'She's a nice little woman, I grant you, but at my time of life there's no call to be talking about conquests, even if I had the inclination.'

'And how patronizing is that?' Grace whispered. 'I don't imagine Mrs Lester would care to be called a "nice little woman", do you? Not if she's made of the same stuff as her nephew.'

'He's not her real nephew. I told you she adopted him after his parents died,' Jasmine said, remembering the potted family history she had heard around the tea table on her first visit.

'Well, if she brought him up, her influence would have rubbed off on him. I thought she was quite a strong-minded woman, and an enterprizing one too, if she does all the things you told me she does. But I don't know what you've got against William, Jassy. I liked him.'

That was the first hurdle, then. She liked him. Jassy made a mental note of it as they followed Owen around the old church as he studied the organ and the intricate wood carvings on the pulpit and on the ends of the pews, and finally the beautiful stained glass window with the afternoon sunlight sending shafts of light and mote dusts through its multi-coloured facets.

'It's a beautiful old building all right,' he said finally. 'If I come here again at any time I'd like to learn more about it. I once toyed with the idea of scribbling a few notes about the history of old churches and seeing if I could get them published, just as a hobby when I retire.'

'You could certainly start with this one,' Jassy said. 'Of course, you'd have to come down to Horton a few times to study it properly.'

Her voice was innocent, but it didn't fool her father.

'And you, young lady, have all the subtlety of a bull in a china shop. I didn't say I was thinking of doing it yet, any more than I'm thinking about retiring. It's just a vague idea for the future.'

'Well, you know what they say about the future, Dad,' Jassy went on.

'No, but I'm sure you're about to tell me.'

'It starts right now. It's like a clock ticking away. One minute you're in the present, and once that minute has gone it's in the past, so the present and the past have already become unalterable facts. The only thing that's alterable is the future, and if we don't grab it with both hands and take every opportunity that's offered to us, then it's wasted.'

'I knew it was a mistake to educate you so well, but who the devil put such rubbish into your head?' he said.

'It's not rubbish. It's a theory I read in one of Mr Devenish's books. He had a great interest in such things and he often talked to me about them – and I don't think you should mention the devil when you're inside a church, either.'

Now why on earth had she said that? It was enough to make him rant and rave at her next . . . but to her surprise she merely saw his eyebrows raise.

'There's something of the amateur philosopher inside that scatterbrain of yours, Jasmine, but you're wrong about not

44

mentioning the devil inside a church, or thinking he has no place here. If it weren't for the devil, we'd have no need to revere God. And don't give me that cynical look, girl. Just because I don't care for too much preaching, it don't mean I can't believe in the Almighty. It's a case of good balancing evil, so just like your past, present and future, everything has its place in the great scheme of things.'

Grace spoke up. 'This is all getting too deep for me, so I'm leaving you to it. I'm going to have a look around the churchyard and then we'd better think about starting for home.'

'Wait for me,' Jassy said quickly. 'I've had enough philosophizing for one day too. Are you coming, Dad?'

'I'll stroll along to the village and sit on one of the benches on the green until you've finished prowling about. You can collect me there,' he said, predictably.

They went out into the warm sunshine and the girls wandered around the old churchyard as Owen made his way along the street towards the village.

'You shouldn't have said all that about past, present and future, Jassy. I'm sure it upset him,' Grace said at once.

'Why should it? He can't live in the past for ever, even if it's what he really wants to do. Mum's never coming back, so how many years is it going to take for him to get over her?'

Grace looked shocked. 'That's a beastly thing to say. You can't measure grief in a year or a lifetime, and I hope you never let him hear you say such a thing.'

'Of course I won't. What do you take me for?'

'Well, somebody who's young and foolish and talks far too much before she thinks, if you want my opinion.'

Jassy stopped walking. 'Is that what you really think of me, Grace?'

Grace turned around, seeing the shine of tears in her sister's eyes. She put her arm around her shoulders.

'Only sometimes, darling. But it's true that you don't always think before you speak, do you? Although I must admit that Dad seemed to enjoy that little bit of deep discussion with you, even if I didn't. It rather took me by surprise.'

'Why? Because you don't think me capable of having

deep discussions? I may be younger than you, Grace, but I do have a brain, even if it is a bit scatty at times, like Dad said – and I'm capable of using it too.'

'I know you are, otherwise you wouldn't be considering living in Blackthorn Cottage all by yourself, would you? That *is* what you're considering, isn't it?'

'I haven't decided yet.'

She moved quickly away from Grace, and back towards the car. If the truth was told, she'd had enough of churches and churchyards and deep discussions right now too. Nor did she want to think of making any decisions about the cottage, and especially not the thought of living there by herself. The enormity of Giles Devenish's generosity, and the charm of the cottage itself, had blinded her to anything else. She had more or less taunted her father about clinging to the past and not facing the future, but for now it was essentially what she wanted to do. Blackthorn Cottage was her doll's house, her plaything . . . but she knew it couldn't stay like that for ever. There was a lot of work to be done on it, and then she would see what she wanted to do. Until then, the final decision could wait.

Her heart felt considerably lighter, realizing that of course she had this leeway. If she eventually chose to sell, then the cottage had to be in pristine condition before she could ask William to bring any potential buyers to look at it. The thatch needed attention, the indoor plumbing had to be looked at and the gas lighting checked. The interior could do with a touch of paint, and the garden was more like a wilderness. But it could all be fixed.

'Come on, love, let's not quarrel on this lovely day,' she heard Grace say as she caught up with her. 'For what it's worth, I think the cottage is adorable, and the natives are friendly, so I can't say fairer than that, can I?'

Jassy flashed her a smile. 'Your opinion is worth a lot to me, Grace, and I promise to try to be more grown-up in future.'

Grace laughed. 'Don't grow up too fast, then. I like you the way you are.'

They drove companionably towards the main part of the village and by the time they saw Owen he was deep in conversation with several old men on one of the shady benches on the green.

'Look at him, sitting there as if he's been around here for ever, and I bet he'll be putting them all to rights by now,' Grace said sagely.

'Either that or they'll have been filling his head with all sorts of local nonsense,' Jassy replied, suddenly apprehensive.

'What local nonsense?'

Jassy didn't answer as she left the car and waved to her father. He merely nodded and continued talking to the old men, heads close together in the way old people did when they were sharing gossip. She had no idea what tales her father could be hearing, but it was a fair guess that once they knew who he was, he would have been ghoulishly informed about the tragedy at Blackthorn Cottage and the horror of the young boy who had found the dead couple. He finally acknowledged that his daughters were waiting, and he stood up stiffly as Jassy came near.

'We'll have another yarn next time and maybe a jar or two in the local pub if I'm ever here on a weekday,' he told his companions, loud enough for her to hear.

'You're planning on coming here again then, Dad,' she commented.

His voice was grim now. 'I think I'd better, if only to stop you from doing something as reckless as the previous inhabitants of your cottage did. Did you know they were found dead after eating poisonous mushrooms?'

'I did hear something about it,' Jassy muttered.

'But you didn't think to tell your sister or me. Did you think we wouldn't find out that the place has supposedly got a bad reputation?'

'I don't believe in places having bad reputations,' she said.

'Neither do I, so let me tell you something I do believe. You've been busily telling me about past, present and future, and I've told you how good always balances evil. I also believe it's what you bring to a house that builds a good aura around it. Those people were foolish and unfortunate, but a new owner is just as likely to fill it with love. A house will respond to that.'

47

She was astonished. She had never heard him speak like that before. She had never known him have so much heart, nor to reveal it. And then she heard him give an embarrassed laugh.

'Oh, don't take any notice of my ramblings. If your mother could hear me she'd probably say I was going soft in my old age.'

Hearing him refer to her mother so naturally and so rarely, was the second shock in a few minutes. Jassy swallowed the lump in her throat and spoke quietly.

'I'm sure she hears it and approves, Dad.'

He didn't reply and Jassy hoped she hadn't gone too far. For her to mention the mother she had never known sometimes seemed oddly like an intrusion into another world, one that she didn't know, and yet one that was so very much a part of her. She was glad to get back to the car where Grace was waiting to begin the journey home, thinking that this day had turned out to be a far more extraordinary one than she had expected after all. The awful shock of the paint-daubed cottage, and then William turning up like that . . . the animated talk she and her father had had in the church, and now a rare reference to her mother . . . maybe there was more to this talk of a house giving off a good aura than she would have believed. Maybe it was a sign that Blackthorn Cottage was welcoming the new owner, Jasmine Wyatt, and drawing her in. And if she was starting to get such fanciful ideas, she was definitely going potty, Jassy thought, slamming the car door shut behind her.

'I'm going to telephone William's office and tell him I'll be in Horton next Sunday,' Jasmine announced a few days later. 'Grace has agreed to drive me again, and we're going to tackle the garden. If I decide to put the cottage up for sale, it'll be the first thing people see, so it has to make a good impression. We want to get a good few hours in, so we won't be going to church on Sunday morning, either.'

She held her breath. Missing church himself wouldn't be any big loss to Owen, but he had brought up his daughters to attend regularly, knowing it was Celia's wish. After a moment he shrugged.

'I'd better come with you then. That cottage garden's seen better days, and I don't want Grace serving in the shop on Monday morning with blistered fingers. It'll look bad for business. I'm sure the vicar won't be sorry to miss my voice bawling out the hymns on Sunday.'

'Can I use the shop telephone then, Dad?' Jasmine asked tentatively, since they rarely had cause to use it for personal business.

She had avoided looking at Grace, knowing her sister would think the same as she did – that this visit to Horton provided a wily excuse for Owen to miss going to church, which he did as a duty rather than with any great conviction.

When he nodded assent to her request, she didn't intend to waste the advantage and she went downstairs to the shop, picked up the telephone and asked the operator to put her through to the number on the property details William had given her.

It seemed a very long time before she heard his voice. When she did, it was businesslike and efficient, in perfect Estate Agent tones.

'Is that Mr Hedges – William?' she asked, finding to her annoyance that her mouth was suddenly dry.

'Yes, this is William Hedges,' he repeated, having already given his name. And then his voice changed. 'Good Lord, it's Jasmine, isn't it?'

Without intending to, she caught her breath. There was a strange familiarity in hearing his voice on the telephone that she hadn't expected, especially when he used her first name. His voice might be disembodied and far away, yet at the same time it was intimately close.

'I'm afraid it is, and I just thought I'd let you know that we'll be in Horton again next Sunday. I don't want to give you any more shocks like the last time.'

He spoke teasingly. 'Then I'll be sure to keep well away.'

'Oh, I didn't mean that!' She bit her lip, because that was surely a daft thing to say, and nor did she mean to imply that she wanted or needed him at the cottage. She spoke more firmly. 'We're going to tackle the garden. Making a good first impression for prospective future clients and all that.'

'Good idea. And you'll find all the offending red paint has been removed.'

Was there a hint of coolness in his voice now? Or was she hearing things that weren't there? It would be what he wanted, wasn't it? What the village wanted. To be rid of outsiders who thought they could turn into country dwellers overnight. On the other hand, if Blackthorn Cottage had a bad reputation, which of Horton's natives would be brave enough to buy it?

'Thank you for that, and maybe we'll see you on Sunday then,' Jassy finished lamely. She put the telephone back on the hook before he could answer. She stared at it for a few more seconds until her heart stopped thudding, unaware that it had even been doing so, and then she went back to the flat to tell her family that it was all arranged.

Five

'You wouldn't catch me among the crowds in London next month when the new king is crowned. You won't be able to move for people and vehicles. But at least it will put an end to a bad affair,' Owen said after supper an evening or so later, scouring the newspapers as he usually did at the end of a day's work.

The girls knew at once to what he was referring. The whole country had been caught up in the affair between Mrs Simpson, the American divorcée, and King Edward, culminating in his abdication. Some still saw the whole thing as romantic, while others were completely scandalized by it. And now they had a new king who had never expected to be pushed into the limelight, but at least he was a decent family man with a wife and two young daughters, Owen said grimly. A comment that made his daughters smile, finding it impossible to think of a king and queen and two young princesses as anything like an ordinary family.

'I bet the coronation will be a marvellous occasion, and so exciting for the little princesses,' Jasmine said, trying to imagine how it must be to live in a palace with people waiting on you day and night. 'Anyway, as far as the old king is concerned, you can hardly condemn him just for falling in love, Dad.'

'You can when he was the king of England and the country's honour is at stake, my girl. The woman is divorced, and that's something this country hasn't approved of since the days of Henry the Eighth, and we all know what a roguish fellow he turned out to be.'

Grace sided with her sister. 'But you can't have it both ways. You can't be stuffy and self-righteous about King Edward in one breath, and more or less applaud old Henry for being a roguish fellow in the next.'

As usual Owen began to get heated. 'You know very well I never meant that I approved of his goings-on. A marriage should be for life, and whether you're a pauper or a prince you have no business standing up in church and vowing to be faithful in the sight of God, if the marriage is just going to be dissolved by a piece of paper whenever you feel like it.'

'But Henry had his reasons,' Jasmine said. 'He needed an heir, and it's important for royalty to provide one. You've always said they're not the same as ordinary people in that respect, Dad. They have to do what's right for the country, and in the end, that's what King Edward did. I know Henry had a lot of wives, and he couldn't have been the most romantic of figures, but do you seriously believe a person can only fall in love once in their lives?'

The moment she had said it, she knew she was on dangerous ground. Her father had never looked at another woman since his beloved Celia died, and he was clearly seeing this as a more personal comment, even though she knew he would never refer to it out loud, especially to his daughters. But his face had darkened, the veins standing out in his neck.

'Well, miss, since you have reminded me quite rightly that I believe those in high places aren't the same as ordinary people, what I also believe is that they shouldn't change the course of history for the sake of a dalliance. The royal blood-line is what makes this country great, and has done so for centuries. You know your history, and it's always been a great pride to me that you girls studied it properly and are capable of having a sensible discussion about it, but don't throw my words back at me with modern ideas of your own.'

Jasmine wasn't aware that she had done any such thing, but as he became more worked up in the argument, he began to cough and wheeze and to breathe with more difficulty, and Jassy restrained herself from reminding him of the royal bloodline that had always included foreign princes and princesses and the German cousins who had proved to be their enemies in the Great War. This wasn't the time.

Grace listened to him hacking in some alarm. 'Where's the medicine Doctor Macleod gave you last time, Dad?'

He waved her away. 'I don't want his blasted medicine. It does me far less good than a drop of brandy, so if you want to pour me a dram, that'll do fine.'

By the time he finished speaking, the wheezing was worse and his voice was rasping. It was always the same when he got agitated over something, especially something he couldn't control, and his daughters frequently became exasperated when it was something in the newspaper that was no concern of theirs at all. Owen called it keeping his brain alert over current affairs, but wars and illicit affairs and government scandals might as well wash over all their heads, for all the good it would do them to try having their say.

'I don't care what you say, Dad, I'm sending for the doctor,' Grace told him a while later, when it was clear the brandy was doing no good whatsoever. His obvious discomfort had gone on too long and showed no sign of abating.

'You'll do no such thing!' he wheezed. 'I don't want the old fool here.'

'You'll end up seeing him in hospital if you don't take his advice,' Grace said sharply. 'Just look at you now. Your hands are shaking so much you'll drop your glass in a minute.'

He glared at her while Jasmine stood silently by, letting these two sort it out between them. She too was alarmed by the dramatic change in her father's appearance, and upset that she had unwittingly caused it. By now his face had become drawn, the direct effect of trying to get his breath properly.

'Can I make you more comfortable, Dad?' she said anxiously. 'Do you want to put your feet up on the sofa?'

'I do not, girl!' he almost shouted, then began coughing again from the effort, 'I'll be all right in a minute if you'd both stop fussing. And where's Grace gone to now?'

He had hardly noticed his elder daughter slip out of the room to go downstairs to the shop. At that moment she was asking the telephone operator to put her through to the family doctor. It was time Owen recognized that he was no longer a young man and took his medicine regularly, instead of when it suited him. It was time he slowed down, though she knew better than to suggest it, knowing his response would be that it would be a long time before he was ready to be put out to grass.

By the time she rejoined the others, Owen's face was dark with rage.

'You take too much on yourself, girl,' he rasped. 'I'm not heading for the knacker's yard yet.'

'I should hope not, but we'll see what Doctor Macleod has to say about that.'

'If we can understand anything that idiot has to say it'll be a miracle,' he muttered. 'I wish he'd go back among the heather where he belongs.'

Despite her worry, Jasmine couldn't suppress a smile. It was an ongoing battle between her father and their Scottish doctor, who wasn't old at all, to see who could hurl the most insults at one another. Owen saw no reason to show deference to a man of the medical profession the way most people did, especially one considerably younger than himself, and secretly, Jassy thought both men quite enjoyed the verbal sparring. Whatever her father thought she was glad Grace had taken the initiative and sent for the doctor. It was time he realized his limitations. Their father's health was more important than anything else right now.

Her heart gave a sudden jump. They had been so concerned with Owen in the last half hour, that, depending on the doctor's findings, Jasmine hadn't given a second thought to the implications this might have on their trip to Horton on Sunday. Owen had agreed to come with them, and to start tackling the overgrown garden of Blackthorn Cottage with his daughters.

It seemed unlikely now, and in any case, Jasmine wondered how wise it would have been. He wasn't a man who enjoyed physical exercise. They didn't have a garden here, only a small yard with a washing-line at the back of the shop. For a man with a history of chest problems, unused to the effort that would be needed to put the cottage garden into shape, it could be the worst suggestion. Her heart was beating uncomfortably fast now, as if she was staring his mortality in the face.

'What's wrong with you, Jasmine?' she heard him say irritably. 'You've been gaping at me for the last few minutes as if I'm about to breathe my last. I assure you I'm not, no matter what that old fool Macleod has to say.'

'I should hope not,' she almost gasped. 'I wasn't thinking any such thing.'

The truth was, it was exactly what she had been thinking. And with the thought came another. How tragic it would be for a man to go to his grave never knowing how much a daughter loved him. Before she could stop herself, she had flung her arms around his neck and hugged him.

'I do love you, Dad!'

He disentangled her as best he could. 'For God's sake, girl, are you trying to strangle the last breath out of me now?' he said, red with embarrassment. 'Go and make some cocoa to keep your hands occupied and stop talking so daft.'

She fled out to the kitchen and put the kettle on the stove with shaking hands. It may have been a rash and foolish thing to do, but she was defiantly glad she had done it. No matter what happened, and even if he never said it back, she had told her father she loved him.

'What on earth made you say that to him?' Grace hissed in her ear. 'You know he can't bear it when people show their feelings so brazenly.'

'Perhaps he should realize that other people do *have* feelings, then. We're not all made of wood like he seems to be.'

Grace's voice softened. 'He does have feelings, Jassy. He just hates to show what he calls being sloppy. I think he sees it as a sign of weakness in himself, but it doesn't mean he cares for us any the less.'

Jassy sniffed. 'He certainly cares for you, but I'm just a nuisance, especially now I've got the cottage to think about. He doesn't want to come there at all, and Sunday's going to be out of the question now, isn't it?'

'Not necessarily. He can always direct operations and tell us exactly what we're doing wrong!'

That brought a half-smile to Jassy's face. 'In any case we'll have to wait and see. He may be perfectly all right by Sunday.'

She crossed her fingers as she spoke. When the doctor arrived the girls retired discreetly, but they couldn't miss the rumble of voices from the other room, nor the way they

55

frequently became raised. Finally, Owen called out to them to come in, and it was easy to see he wasn't pleased with what the doctor had told him.

'This jackass wants me to take a holiday. When did a shopkeeper ever take time off to go on holiday like rich people?'

Doctor Macleod intervened, his eyes glinting with annoyance, his short red beard almost bristling.

'If you don't do it, man, you're in danger of shortening your life. And if you don't want my advice, then you shouldn't waste my time in asking for it.'

'I didn't ask for it,' Owen shouted. 'These girls of mine seem to take matters into their own hands whenever they feel like it, and I don't take kindly to having a father's authority undermined.'

'You should be grateful to them for having more sense than you do, then,' the doctor retorted. 'For the life of me, I can't see why they'd want an irritable old fool like you around any longer, but apparently they do.'

Jassy gasped, not sure how her father was going to take this. But to her surprise his face relaxed and he began to guffaw. It was unfortunate that the laugh ended in another bout of coughing that had the doctor folding his arms and looking at him with a face that said I-told-you-so.

'You said that deliberately,' Owen gasped now. 'You knew it would start me off again.'

'It'll finish you off if you don't do as I say,' the doctor snapped. 'Now then, what are the objections to your taking a holiday? These girls can manage the shop without you, I'm sure, and I can recommend a nice little bed and breakfast hotel on the coast where you can enjoy the sunshine. There's nothing at all to stop you taking a few weeks off, and I'll be happy to make the arrangements for you as soon as you say the word.'

'A few weeks?' Owen spluttered, ignoring the rest. 'I've never been away from my shop for more than a day or so in my life, and I'm not going to start now.'

The doctor looked at the Wyatt girls, standing silently by now, and not daring to intervene as the men wrangled.

'Well, lassies, the time may come when we'll be thinking

of making a different kind of arrangement for this old goat if he doesn't ease up. I'll give you the name of a good undertaker to keep in mind.'

The girls gasped at such insensitivity.

'You're scaring us now!' Grace burst out.

'I mean to scare you, and you needn't bother to call me out again if it's going to be a complete waste of my time.'

Jassy swallowed hard. 'In any case, I don't think a bed and breakfast place at the coast is the right place for Dad to take a holiday. I know he'd absolutely hate it. He prefers to have the people he knows around him.'

'That's the first sensible thing anybody's said yet,' Owen growled, 'and I refuse to consider such a daft suggestion.'

'Do you have a better one, Jasmine?' the doctor demanded, clearly displeased at having his advice overruled.

'I do, as it happens.'

As they all looked at her with varying expressions, she felt her mouth tremble. She knew she risked another outburst from her father, but it had to be said. There was an alternative, and it was in her hands.

'We can take Dad down to my cottage in Horton. The idea has only just come to me, but it will be the perfect place for him to relax.'

'More like stagnate, you mean!' Owen snapped. 'Have you lost your mind, girl? The place is a shambles, and you were expecting me to go there with you this weekend to tidy up the garden, remember, and now you're suggesting leaving me there to twiddle my thumbs.'

'You're not digging any gardens, nor going there on your own,' the doctor said firmly. 'So tell me more about the cottage, Jasmine. Is it easily manageable?'

She looked at Grace, her heart sinking as the drawbacks became obvious. She had said it spontaneously, because an idyllic cottage in the country had seemed the perfect solution for her father to regain his health, but of course it wasn't easily manageable, certainly not for a man such as Owen, and the quiet would probably drive him mad. Having lived in a city all his life, and been in the hub of things with his shop, he would simply hate it. As usual, she hadn't stopped to think.

Grace spoke quickly. 'It would be manageable if you and Dad went there, Jassy, and left me to manage the shop. Even if it was only for a few days, it would make all the difference, wouldn't it, Doctor?'

It was hard to see who was the more horrified – Owen at the very thought of living in the country; or Jasmine, at the thought of sharing the precious cottage with her father and knowing they would be at each other's throats in minutes.

'It wouldn't do!' they both said at once.

'Why not?' the doctor said. 'It seems a very sensible solution to me, and Grace here is a canny lass, and perfectly capable of running the shop by herself. She practically does it now from what I've seen.'

'Why, thank you!' Grace said, feeling the heat in her cheeks at the unexpected compliment.

Nobody spoke for a few seconds, and Jasmine had the strangest feeling about the way her sister and the doctor were looking at one another and then looking away. Had she been missing something here that was right under her nose? But it couldn't be. If Grace had ever had any kind of a crush on the doctor she would surely have mentioned it. But she wouldn't, would she? Have a crush on him. She had always said she wasn't interested in men. Jassy glanced at the doctor surreptitiously again. He wasn't married and he was good-looking enough in a rugged, Scottish way . . . and Grace did see more of him than anyone else, always fetching her father's medicine and discussing Owen's problems with him . . . but if Jassy's suspicions weren't totally absurd, then it would squash any hopes she had of matchmaking her sister with William Hedges!

'Well, Grace?' Owen said. 'Don't you have anything to say about this idea?'

She flinched. 'I don't really know what you want me to say. Would you be willing to stay at the cottage with Jassy for a few days if I looked after the shop?'

'Or a few weeks,' Doctor Macleod reminded him.

Owen snapped, 'I doubt that Jassy would want me there. We'd soon get on each other's nerves.'

'Well, then, we'd just have to come home again,' she said, forcing herself to sound bright. 'I'm willing to give it a try if you are, Dad.'

The last thing she'd intended was to move into the cottage so soon, if at all. Especially not just herself and her father. It was heading for certain disaster . . .

'Well, I'll leave you to make up your minds,' the doctor said as they all seemed to hesitate, 'but please keep me informed. I haven't lost a patient through stubbornness yet, and I don't aim to lose one now. Goodnight to you all.'

'I'll see you out,' Grace spoke before Owen could react to this, and she followed him quickly out of the room.

Owen turned to Jasmine. 'Before you say another word, I'm going to my room. This needs thinking about. And before you ask, yes, I'll take my medicine. I swear it's like being mollycoddled by two old washerwomen, to say nothing of that young whippersnapper of a quack.'

Jasmine watched him go. She hadn't intended saying another word about the cottage anyway. She was more concerned by the startling thoughts that had come into her mind concerning her sister. Had she been so blind all this time? Had something been there under her nose? It was always Grace who consulted Doctor Macleod about their father, and who telephoned him whenever she thought it was necessary. It was always Grace who collected Owen's medicine from the doctor's dispensary, and Grace who seemed willing enough to have far more of the doctor's time than the patient himself. And even now . . . how long did it take for someone to see a professional man out of the house?

'What's going on?' she said flatly, as soon as Grace re-appeared.

'What do you mean?' Grace said.

'Oh, I think you know what I mean. Your face is flushed and you have a certain look in your eyes. In fact, you've had it ever since Doctor Macleod arrived.'

'You're being ridiculous, Jassy.'

'Am I? I don't think so.'

There was an uncomfortable silence between them and then Grace burst out, 'I don't know why you think it's so unlikely that I should be attracted to Alec. You're the one who always said I should find a young man when I've always said I wasn't interested – unless the right one came along.'

'And is *Alec* the right one? I presume you mean Doctor Macleod!'

Grace became even more flushed. 'We've got to know each other rather well lately. It doesn't mean anything.'

'Enough to be on first name terms with the doctor! I'd say that means something. Is it serious?'

Her own plans for Grace would be in danger of falling apart – not that they had been much more than an idea so far. But in the back of her mind, Jasmine knew she had rather fancied herself as the saviour of her sister's spinster life . . . and now it seemed that Grace had ideas of her own about that!

'Of course it's not serious. It's friendship, that's all,' Grace said crossly, 'so please don't read anything more into it. And not a word to Dad about it, either.'

Neither of them had heard Owen come back until his harsh voice startled them both. 'Not a word to Dad about what, may I ask? If you two have been cooking up something more about what to do with me, you can just forget it. I'm going nowhere, and that's that.'

He stumped out again, slamming the door behind him.

'Now look what you've done,' Grace said angrily. 'All this silly talk about me and Doctor Macleod has finished any hope of getting him down to the cottage to take things easy.'

'He'll probably come round, but I can see why you're so flustered about it. It will suit you better when he's not around, won't it? You won't need to make excuses on Dad's behalf to see Alec again, will you?' she taunted.

'Perhaps I needed those excuses,' Grace retorted, and for the first time Jasmine recognized genuine distress in her sister's eyes.

'You mean you and he aren't –'

'We aren't anything, and if you took the trouble to listen to what people say instead of putting your own interpretation on it, you'd understand that.'

'You aren't anything, but you'd like to be something, is that it? And I always thought you were the great man-hater!' Jassy persisted.

'I never said that, and you're being silly, so just leave it alone, will you, Jassy? There are more important things to think about, like worrying over Dad.'

As if to emphasize what she was saying, a few minutes later they heard an almighty crash from Owen's bedroom. The girls rushed into their father's room to find him lying on the floor, his face ashen.

Jasmine gasped at the sight of him. 'What happened, Dad? Did you fall? Let's help him up, Grace, quickly.'

He shook his head, waving his arms feebly.

'Pain,' he gasped. 'Chest. Can't breathe. Get that fool doctor back here.'

'Oh God, I think he's having a heart attack,' Grace said wildly. 'You sit with him, Jassy, and I'll run after Alec. He won't have got very far, and he sometimes calls at the Dog and Drake on his way home, then walks back by the river.'

Jasmine didn't ask how her sister knew all that. She was more concerned with the way her father's lips were now a greyish colour and how his breathing was so shallow and laboured. His eyes had closed, as if it was too much of an effort to keep them open. He was sweating profusely.

'Please don't die, Dad. Please don't die,' she whispered, kneeling beside him and taking his limp hand in hers.

His eyes flew open. 'I'm not dying, girl. It's just a touch of dyspepsia.'

His hand squeezed hers for a moment and then relaxed.

It seemed an age before she heard Grace and Doctor Macleod come upstairs again. One look at Owen and he told them he would telephone for an ambulance immediately. Grace looked at her sister with frightened eyes.

'He thinks it could be a heart attack. He's sending him straight to hospital, so we'll know more then.'

'I'm still here,' Owen grated, 'and no hospital.'

He was clearly finding it difficult to talk, and a short time later the doctor came back upstairs to say the ambulance was on its way.

'I said no bloody hospital!' Owen said with a great effort.

'And I say that's exactly where you're going, man,' he was told. 'I'm taking charge now, and you'll do as you're bloody well told.'

It was so unlike their father to swear, and so unexpected for the doctor to swear back at him, but the girls could see the flicker of respect in Owen's eyes.

61

'Can one of you lassies put a soft pillow beneath his head?' the doctor went on. 'Not too high, or it will restrict his breathing, and then I'm going to turn him gently on to his side. And I apologize about the language just now. Sometimes men's talk is necessary.'

It hardly mattered. All that mattered was getting Owen to the hospital where they both prayed that this attack was not as serious as it looked. In so short a time, the priorities of all their lives had shifted. Nothing was more important than their father's health now. Grace did as she was told and gently placed a thin pillow beneath her father's head. Jassy sat down heavily on her father's bed, hardly knowing what to do or think as these two seemed to take control now, and she had never felt so helpless nor so racked with guilt in her life.

Logically, she knew she had no need to feel guilty, but she couldn't hep thinking that all this had been brought about because of Blackthorn Cottage. If she hadn't been so keen to show it off and made such a fuss about it all, her father would never have got himself in the state he was now in. Perhaps it *was* unlucky, after all, and it hadn't just been their own stupidity that caused the deaths of the previous occupants. Perhaps it was cursed, because outsiders had dared to make it their own instead of leaving it in the care of country folk.

She found herself shivering with nerves as the crazy thoughts came crowding in on her, and the next minute she found someone's hand firmly on her head as it was thrust between her knees, and Doctor Macleod's voice floated in her senses.

'Take a few deep breaths, Jasmine, there's a good lass, and you'll soon feel better. I'm not planning on losing one patient here tonight, let alone two. The old man's probably not as bad as he looks, you know, so keep your pecker up.'

It wasn't the way a doctor normally spoke to a patient, but Jassy had already gone far beyond thinking of him merely as a doctor. She wouldn't go so far as considering anything romantic between him and Grace, but she knew that in all the time he had attended her father he had become more a good friend than a stiff and remote physician. The fact that the two men often argued and bawled at one another merely showed a healthy respect for one another.

By the time the ambulance came, Owen's breathing was marginally easier, and he was already blustering about not going to the blasted hospital to be messed about by nurses and wired up to any of their contraptions. It didn't do the slightest bit of good and within half an hour they were on their way.

Six

The girls weren't allowed into the ward until their father had had various tests done. They had no idea where Doctor Macleod had gone, but they both missed his familiar presence as they sat in the cold, impersonal corridor while hospital staff in clinical white uniforms swished by on rubber-soled feet. Walking through the endless maze of the hospital to the ward their father had been taken to on a trolley, there had been an overpowering smell of antiseptic and other odours that they couldn't identify, and didn't care to either. None of it made the waiting any more comfortable.

Jassy sat with clenched hands, her whole body rigid. All her life her irascible father had been there, and now there was a distinct possibility that she was going to lose him. No matter how much the doctor had told them otherwise, she couldn't control her fears. In so short a time she seemed to have changed from the confident property owner she had revelled in being, to the small girl who had always clung to her older sister for reassurance.

Knowing of her background, her one-time sweetheart, Freddie Patterson, had told her she had emerged from that state like a chrysalis turning into a beautiful butterfly. Head-turning, treacherous words that he had no right to say, attached as he was to another girl. Without warning, she felt a sob rise in her throat. She had really loved him, with a young girl's first, innocent love, and he had let her down, just as her father was about to let her down too, by dying before they could really be a proper father and daughter . . .

She felt Grace's arms go around her shoulders. 'Don't worry, Jassy. Alec was fairly confident that this wasn't as bad as it looked to us. It may not have been a real heart attack at all, but just a warning. That's what he said, remember?'

Jassy couldn't remember him saying any such thing, but that was probably because she had had her head stuck between her knees at the time, trying to fend off the shaming nausea. She was further ashamed to think that at that precise moment her thoughts had drifted off to Freddie Patterson, and the fact of how two very different men letting her down had affected her own life. She must be a really shallow person, she thought miserably.

'You don't think he's going to die, do you, Grace?' she mumbled.

'I think we should wait to hear what the experts have to say, darling. For heaven's sake, people come to hospital to get better, don't they?'

She tried to coax Jassy into a more cheerful frame of mind, the way she used to do when they were children – which was just the way Jassy felt now, leaning on her sister, letting her put things right – but if her father's health really was in danger, it would take more than words to put things right.

It seemed a very long time before the door of the ward opened again, and the hospital doctor appeared with Alec Macleod. They were talking quite seriously, and both girls felt their hearts jump. By the time Alec had shaken the other man's hand and come over to them the girls were holding one another's hands tightly. Then he smiled and sat down beside them.

'You can relax, lassies. It's not a heart attack, just a few nasty spasms, but your father's been told to take this as a warning to slow down. To make sure he does just that, it's been decided to keep him in hospital for a few days for observation, while he gets used to some new medication. So you can both rest easy in your beds tonight.'

Jasmine burst into tears and turned away in embarrassment as she fumbled in her pocket for a handkerchief, hardly noticing that it was Doctor Macleod – *Alec* – who was comforting her sister. In those first emotional moments, all Jasmine could think about was that she and her father had been given a second chance to put things right between them, and to show the love that must surely exist between father and daughter – if they chose to.

But soberly, as her sobs subsided and common sense took over, she knew it would take even more than a fright like this one to change her father's ingrained ways. He'd be more stubborn than ever now to carry on as he had always done and prove the doctors wrong. Working himself into an early grave, her Aunt Lucy used to say ... well, that had never happened, but it still could. Her heart gave a small flutter of its own, realizing that for all his bluster, her father was no longer a young man and really should take more care of himself.

'Can we see him now?' she stammered, although she wasn't sure how to face the thought of seeing him wired up to any contraptions. Obviously, it would be far worse for him, and she knew how he would hate to appear so vulnerable and helpless.

'Of course you can,' Alec said at once, and released Grace from his hold more reluctantly than a doctor should, in Jassy's opinion. But doctors had feelings too, didn't they? And not only with a professional regard for their patients!

He led them into the ward where Owen was lying in bed, his head resting on the pillows as if he was exhausted. With relief, Jassy saw that he wasn't wired up to anything now, and although his face was drawn, he had a little more colour in his cheeks than before. He gave his daughters a grim smile.

'You can get that anxious look off your faces, and I've told this old fool that he needn't start measuring me up for my box yet,' he said, his voice weaker than usual, but still with underlying determination.

Jassy gasped at such an insensitive remark, but Alec knew him too well to take offence, while Grace rushed forward at once and hugged her father. Jassy wanted to do the same, but Owen had already waved Grace away and told her not to make such a fuss over a bit of indigestion.

'It was more than that and you know it, man,' Alec snapped, 'and if you go straight back to work you'll risk it happening again, and next time you may not be so lucky. You need to take it easy for a while.'

'I suppose you think a shop runs itself, do you? I may not be as clever as a doctor but my customers rely on me.'

'What I think is that you're not indispensable.'

As her father glared back, Grace could see this escalating into one of their usual arguments, and if Alec said scathingly that a small haberdashery shop was hardly big business, her father would probably have a fit.

'I think it's time we left Dad to have some rest, since that's what the hospital doctor has ordered,' Grace said quickly. 'We'll come back tomorrow, Dad.'

'Just get the shop open as usual, Grace,' he said, 'and don't go blabbing about why I'm not there, either. I don't want the do-gooders sending me messages of sympathy.'

'All right,' she said, her own voice choking now.

She bent and kissed him, and Jassy followed suit, feeling her heart swell at the way, even now, her father was unable or unwilling to unbend enough to accept the good wishes of people who would be concerned to hear what had happened. Alec was right, she thought irreverently. He was as stubborn as a mule.

They went home in a sombre mood, despite their father's relatively good diagnosis. As Alec told him, it was a warning, and he should slow down. It was about as likely as asking the sun not to rise every morning, but now that the imminent worry had passed, Jassy also had other things on her mind.

'We shan't be able to go to the cottage this weekend, will we, Grace?'

The minute she had said it, it sounded so awful. It was as if she thought the visit was much more important than her father's health, which wasn't what she meant at all. She muttered an apology to her sister.

'It's all right, darling, I understand. It's a pity, but if you really wanted to go down there, you could always catch a bus in a day or so as you did before.'

'I wouldn't dream of it until Dad's out of hospital,' Jassy said quickly, 'but once we're sure there's no chance of a relapse, maybe then he'll agree to come with me for a few days, as we'd half-planned.'

And how would they both cope with that, with her father in an even more scratchy and unpredictable mood than normal, and with herself being ever-watchful and nervous of the slightest change in his health! Jasmine shivered, wondering uneasily if it seemed such a good idea after all, yet hardly knowing how she could get out of it if Owen decided it was what he wanted to do. Knowing him, he would probably be cantankerous enough to agree, just to get away from Alec Macleod's well-intentioned nagging!

'It would certainly do him good to go away and relax, once Alec gives him the all clear,' Grace replied, determinedly not considering any other possibility. 'Providing he *did* relax, of course, and we both know how alien that is to him.'

They stared gloomily at one another. The flat seemed empty without their father's reassuring presence, whatever mood he was in. Larger than life was an apt phrase to apply to him, and each of them seemed at a loss to know what to do next. Jassy made up her mind.

'I'm going to telephone William Hedges and tell him what's happened. I said we'd be there on Sunday, and now we won't, so it's courteous to let him know.'

Whether it was courteous or not, it would be good to hear another male voice to cover the void right now, and she sped down the stairs to the telephone. It took a while before he answered, and when he did, Jassy found her tongue sticking to the roof of her mouth, and he repeated his name impatiently.

'I'm sorry,' she said huskily. 'It's me, Jasmine Wyatt.'

His voice changed instantly. 'What's wrong?'

Did he have a sixth sense, or was her voice so full of anxiety that he just knew? She gulped, blinking back the tears as she told him the news.

'I'm really sorry to hear that,' William said, real concern in his voice. 'Please give my regards to your father and I hope he recovers very soon. Don't worry about the cottage, Jasmine. I'll keep an eye on it for you.'

'You don't have to do that. It's not your problem, is it?'

'Well, I'm making it my problem.'

Jasmine gulped again, forcing herself to think of practical things. Even if she couldn't be there herself for the time being, there was work that needed to be done.

'The thatch needs repairing. Do you know anyone who could do it? I'm sorry. This is putting too much on you, and of course I'll pay for your services, William.'

As the words left her lips, she thought with a groan how patronizing they sounded, as if she was the lady of the manor, instead of the owner of a near-ramshackle little cottage in the wilds of the country. She heard the amusement in his voice then, and was relieved to realize he hadn't taken it the wrong way.

'Oh don't worry, Miss Wyatt, it will all be on the final bill. There's a good local thatcher in the area, and I'll get it organized for you right away. I'll telephone you in a few days to see how things are, and you just take care of yourself. Your father seemed like a pretty tough old coot, as we say around here, and I doubt that he's ready to give up the good life just yet.'

She found herself staring at the wall in astonishment at his playful words. She had thought him cold and distant from the moment they met, looking down on her for being a townie who thought she could move into Blackthorn Cottage and become an instant countrywoman. But now . . . she might have been listening to her father and Doctor Macleod having their usual banter, and such familiarity only existed between people who knew one another very well. And she didn't know William Hedges at all. Not like that. Strangely, the very fact that he could be so easy with her sent a warm glow through her veins, the first warmth she had felt since the moment she and Grace had found their father on the floor of his bedroom.

'Thank you, William,' she said, her voice still husky. 'I'll look forward to hearing from you.'

She replaced the receiver carefully and stood quite still for a few minutes, aware that her heart was beating too fast. Aware that while they had been speaking, she had pictured his face in front of her, imagining the way his eyes could light up when he smiled. Aware of the deepening of his voice when he showed concern for her . . . for her father, she amended. She swallowed. This wasn't the time to be imagining things that weren't there, or things that she didn't want. He was simply a good man who was doing his job, and part of the job he seemed determined to undertake, was to see that Blackthorn Cottage was restored to a good condition should Jasmine Wyatt decide to sell it.

'Jassy, don't let your tea get cold,' she heard Grace call out from the flat above, and she turned away from the telephone and ran upstairs to join her sister.

'Sorry to interrupt,' Grace went on. 'I thought you might have needed rescuing from too many questions.'

Jassy defended him. 'He sounded very nice, actually, and he's going to call again in a few days to see how Dad's getting on.'

'That's rather above and beyond the call of duty, isn't it?' Grace said, busying herself with putting a tray of tea and biscuits on the sitting-room table.

Jassy laughed awkwardly. 'I think he's making sure the cottage doesn't get even more neglected so that I get a good price for it if and when I decide to sell it.'

'But you're not going to, are you? Sell it, I mean?'

'I don't know. I haven't made up my mind yet. And if Dad really has more serious health problems than we think, it may change things, anyway.'

'Don't let it do that, Jassy. You have your own life to live, and if fate has decided that you should live in the country, then that's what you should do.'

'Are you trying to get rid of me now?' Jassy said, taking a sip of tea that was too hot, and drawing in her breath at the sting of it.

'Don't be silly. I'd miss you like crazy if you left here, but things can't stay the same for ever, can they, darling? We all have to move on to do what we think is best for ourselves.'

'What – even becoming a doctor's wife instead of a shop assistant in a haberdashery shop?' Jassy teased her, and had the shock of seeing her sister's face go a brilliant red. 'Good Lord, that's what you *have* got in mind, haven't you?'

'Now you're being really silly, so let's change the subject. What shall we have for our dinner? Shall I make a mince and potato pie?'

All the same, the fact that she refused to talk about it and went into the kitchen to prepare the meal, made Jassy think there was more to it than her sister let on. And the more she thought about it, the more she could see Grace in the role of the doctor's wife. She had the perfect temperament, and even though Jassy had never thought of Alec Macleod in any way but that of the family doctor, she could see that he could be very attractive to women who were slightly older than herself. Women like Grace. Well, well.

Owen was going to be allowed out of hospital in three days' time, providing he behaved himself, didn't do too much, and regularly took all the medicine he had been prescribed. According to Owen all the nurses were dragons, and the indignity of having to be washed by some young whipper-snapper hardly out of the nursery did nothing to improve his temper. But he was gracious enough to thank them all on the day he went home.

Before then, William telephoned. Jasmine flew down the stairs to grab the receiver before the ringing stopped, and she was breathless as she answered.

'He's coming home tomorrow,' she told him. 'I want to bring him down to the cottage for a few days if he'll agree to it, but I haven't had the nerve to ask him just yet. I'm impatient to come down myself though – to see what I can do in the garden and so on,' she added hastily. 'And what about a thatcher? Did you find someone, William?'

'It's all in hand, don't worry.'

'You're not doing it yourself, are you?' she asked suspiciously.

He laughed easily. 'I may be handy with a paintbrush, but I'm not a thatcher, sweetheart. It's a skilled job, but it'll all be done to your satisfaction, I promise you. Meanwhile —'

'Yes?' she prompted as he hesitated, refusing to admit to the thump of her heart from the fact that he'd called her sweetheart. It didn't mean anything, of course. It was just an expression, nothing more. She certainly didn't want it to mean anything. That would be one complication she could do without.

'I have to be in Bristol on business in a week's time. If you wanted to come down to the cottage then, with or without your father, I could pick you up in my car. If you didn't want to spend the night alone in the cottage I'm sure my aunt would put you up for a night or two, and I'd be happy to run you back again.'

71

'That's very kind of you. Can I think about it?' Jassy said faintly, unable to forget Grace's words, that this was surely above and beyond the call of duty . . .

'Of course. Just give me a call and let me know. You know where I am.'

She did, and for a moment it had seemed as if he was standing right beside her, offering to be more of a friend than an estate agent who had had her business dumped on him by Giles Devenish. She liked the thought of him as a friend.

Even more, she liked the thought of him taking her down to the cottage so that she might spend a few nights there alone – which she would have to do if she moved in permanently – and if she didn't care to do that, to stay with his aunt. But right now there were other things to think about, and once her father was safely home again, predictably he had nothing good to say about his stay in hospital.

'Those damn fool doctors can say what they like. I'm not ready to sit twiddling my thumbs all day while someone else takes care of my shop and probably makes a hash of it,' he groused.

'Customers have been asking about you, Dad,' Grace told him serenely, trying not to fuss around him as she brought him his welcome-home cup of tea. 'As for making a hash of it, everything's been run as smoothly as ever – and I hope you don't think I can't cope for a few days on my own!'

'I don't think that, girl,' Owen said. 'Besides, you've had your sister helping you, I trust?'

'Jassy's been doing the books, and she has far neater handwriting than yours or mine,' she said, refusing to let him rile her. 'You'll be impressed.'

He glared at her, not prepared to be impressed by anything. If the truth were told, he'd been more scared than he let on and his nerves had been shaken, but he wasn't going to lose face by admitting it to his daughters.

'I don't doubt that Jassy can read and write and do her sums, since she was employed by that Devenish fellow and got ideas above her station,' he snapped. 'It's a pity she can't take a proper interest in the shop instead of wasting her time and money on that old cottage.'

'That's not fair, Dad,' Grace said at once, not letting him get away with this. 'Jassy has always taken a pride in everything she does, and if her interest doesn't lie in serving customers with their ribbons and fabrics, that's up to her.'

'And just where does your interest lie lately, Miss?'

Grace stared at him. 'Why, here with you, of course. When have I ever said otherwise? You know I enjoy meeting people in the shop.'

'And admiring their infants too, I've noticed.'

Grace banged her own cup on the table. It wasn't often she allowed herself to get angry with her father, particularly today when he had just come out of hospital, but he seemed determined to provoke her.

'Well, why shouldn't I? Do you intend to put a ban on preventing me chatting to the customers now?'

Owen grunted. 'Of course I don't, but I had a bit of time to think while they kept me incarcerated in that damned hospital. Don't you ever think about having a life of your own, and finding a good man to have your own infants with, Grace?'

Her mouth fell open. He had never spoken to her about such things before. They weren't living in the Victorian Age, when the oldest daughter was expected to devote her own spinster life to dutifully caring for her parents, but neither had the subject of Grace wanting to be married and have children ever come up between them.

'Has Jassy been saying something?' she asked suspiciously.

'What about?' Owen replied.

'I don't know. Perhaps about some daft idea she has in her head that I'm not too old to be married, even though I always said I was never interested.'

'Of course you're not too old to be married! What a stupid remark to make. Why shouldn't you be interested? You're a handsome, red-blooded young woman that any man with eyes in his head would admire.'

Grace stopped bristling. Instead, she found herself laughing at the sudden indignity on his face that said he'd be insulted if any man should ever think one of Owen Wyatt's daughters wasn't a red-blooded young woman, worthy of marriage and children. She bent and kissed his forehead.

'When the day comes when I'm more interested in a young man than working in the shop, you'll be the first to know, Daddy dear.'

He caught at her hand. 'Don't leave it too long, girl. I didn't exactly get a glimpse of my own mortality when I was in the hospital, but it made me think. A man would much prefer to go to his Maker leaving grandchildren behind than just a noble saint of a daughter.'

'Well, you've got no fear of me being that, and nor Jassy, I'd say!' she told him, suddenly choked at his clumsy attempt to give his approval on his girls finding love and marriage and not being a slave to an old man's needs.

She repeated the conversation to Jassy word for word that night when she sat on Jassy's bed for a late night chat the way they always did.

'Good Lord, the next thing you know, he'll be starting up a marriage agency,' Jassy said, laughing. 'Or putting cards in the shop window, advertising for any lonely bachelor to look no further than Wyatt's Haberdashery for a suitable mate!'

'It's not funny,' Grace said, although her mouth was twitching at the picture Jassy was painting. 'I think what he was trying to say in his usual garbled way, was that he'd like to see us both happily settled before he died. It was sweet, really.'

'Well, you don't have to look any farther! You've already found your Doctor Right, though I don't know what Dad would say to having his sparring partner for a son-in-law. He might quite like it, of course, if it meant they could have their little arguments more frequently, as they could if Alec was permanently on the scene.'

'You do talk rot sometimes, Jassy,' Grace said crossly as her sister prattled on. 'I told you all this because I wanted you to realize how vulnerable Dad was feeling today, even though he'd never admit it. I suppose all parents want to think there's somebody left to carry on, and Dad's no different in that respect.'

'You'd better get a move on and provide him with some grandchildren then. Even if I found someone, I doubt that he'd look any more kindly on any infant of mine than he does on me.'

It was a depressing thought, but it was one that she couldn't even imagine. Firstly you had to imagine a husband before any babies, she thought ruefully, and that dream had gone when Freddie Patterson had revealed his true colours. She wished she still didn't think of him now and then, but he had become the untrustworthy yardstick by which she measured all men. She wished it wasn't like that, but it was. The only good thing was that she would never have to see him again. He was probably married to his girl by now, and she was welcome to him.

'Jassy? Where have you gone?' She heard Grace's voice as if through a mist, and she gave a shaky laugh. It was one thing to be thankful she had found out about Freddie's deceit before she did anything rash . . . it was another to forget just how charming he could be, and how nearly she had forgotten all her inhibitions and succumbed to that charm . . .

'Nowhere,' she answered quickly. 'I was just thinking how glad I am that Dad's back home, and that the attack wasn't any worse than it was. And if anyone's going to give him grandchildren, it'll probably be you, not me!'

She had never confided in Grace about the way she had felt so let down and humiliated by Freddie Patterson, and she wasn't about to start now. She kept her voice light and teasing, speculating on whether the babies would start talking with a Scottish accent, until Grace started laughing and threw a pillow at her.

'If you're going to talk such nonsense I'm going to bed,' she said, but her eyes sparkled in a way Jassy had never noticed before.

Talking about the person you loved did that for you, and she found herself fervently wishing Grace all the luck in the world with her doctor. And once she was alone, she snuggled down in her bed, smiling at the thought of Grace finding love at last, and of her father's reaction on eventually being told the news. It would be enough to give him another seizure, Jassy thought, and her smile abruptly faded, because, as the doctors had told them, it was a warning, and all such warnings should be heeded.

Seven

Alec Macleod was making one of his routine visits to Owen, and was quite capable of overlooking his patient's moods.

'I'm telling you I feel fine, man,' Owen swore. 'You know damn well I've never been one to pamper myself, and I don't intend to start now.'

Sitting at the living-room table in the Wyatt flat, Alec ignored the other man's words and continued writing on a piece of paper. Owen looked at him suspiciously.

'If you're thinking of prescribing more pills or foul-tasting wallop to shut me up, then I refuse to take it. You're not my keeper and you can't force me to do it.'

Alec looked up, his voice cool and unruffled.

'I can't force you to kill yourself, either, but if you don't slow down and face the fact that you're not as fit as you once were, you'll probably do that all by yourself. For God's sake, man, start looking after yourself properly, and be told.'

'I had the all clear from the hospital, and that's what matters.'

'I see. So you're saying you don't think I'm a competent doctor, are you?' Alec said, his eyes glinting now.

Owen snorted. 'I'm not saying that at all.'

'You're implying it if you refuse to take my advice.'

Owen sounded exasperated. 'What is it you want of me? To wrap myself in a tartan blanket and be wheeled about in a wheelchair? If that's what you've got in mind, you've come to the wrong house, mister!'

Alec laughed. 'You're a damn fool, man, but we both know that, don't we? I certainly don't see you being wrapped up in a tartan blanket and being wheeled about in a Bath chair, and nor would I wish such an ordeal on either of your

76

bonny daughters. I know you've been back behind the shop counter for a few hours each day – if not more – but if you won't take care of yourself for your own sake, then do it for your girls.'

Owen glared at him. 'So what have you been writing there all this time, if it's not another of your damn prescriptions?'

Alec handed it over silently, and despite himself, Owen gave a grunt as he read the instructions.

'This is your idea of a joke, I suppose. I always thought you fellows from north of the border had a perverted sense of humour – if you had any at all.'

They heard the sound of footsteps on the stairs, and Grace and Jassy came into the room, having closed the shop for the day. Jassy didn't miss the smile her sister exchanged with the doctor, before Grace addressed her father sternly.

'We could hear you two shouting in the shop, Dad. I don't know what the customers must have thought.'

Before her father could open his mouth to say he didn't care what the customers thought, she had picked up the piece of paper he had thrown back on the table and started to read it aloud.

1) Stop worrying about the shop. It will still be there when you've gone.
2) Look at your most important assets – your health and your daughters.
3) Get away for a few weeks to recover and give us all some peace.
4) Mix all the above together and come back refreshed.
5) Don't be pig-headed enough to ignore this timely advice.

Both girls were laughing by the time Grace had finished reading out the list of instructions, and Owen was finally shrugging his shoulders and letting a smile play around his mouth.

'It won't do you any good to gang up on me,' he said. 'I'll make up my own mind about what's best for me, the same as I've always done.'

Alec stood up to go. His voice was brisk. 'Then don't

bother to send for me the next time your daughters find you on the floor – and if that's your intention, you might scribble out a note absolving me from my duties as your doctor, just so that everyone's clear on the matter.'

Their eyes clashed for a moment and then Owen's voice crackled.

'What, and miss my regular spats with you? It's the one thing that lets me know I'm still alive, man. As long as you keep nagging me and I give as good as I get, I know there's still breath in my body.'

Jassy decided it was time she intervened between these two stubborn men. Alec might be Grace's fancy, but in his own way, he could be as obstinate and contrary as her father.

'How soon do you think Dad would be able to come and stay in my cottage in Horton, Doctor Macleod? It's not ready yet, but when it is, do you think it would be a good idea?'

'Of course I do, providing you don't get him digging the garden. A bit of pottering in the sunshine and a few walks in the country will do him a power of good. I presume there's a doctor in the area, and when it's all arranged, I'll give you a note for him, explaining the previous symptoms, just to be on the safe side.'

'And I'm perfectly capable of taking care of the shop while the two of them are away,' Grace said quickly. 'It would give me a chance to do some spring cleaning in the flat too.'

'I am in the room you know,' Owen roared. 'When you've all finished deciding my future, let me remind you that I'll have the last say on it!'

To his fury he began to cough, and immediately waved them away. None of them said anything until he had finished spluttering. His voice was hoarse now.

'All right. If and when that blasted cottage is fit for human habitation, I'll think about it. And I only said I'd *think* about it, mind, so don't think you've won.'

'I wasn't aware that this was some kind of competition,' Alec said coolly. 'But it's good to know that at least there's a wee bit of sense in that mad dog head of yours. I'll be on my way to see some patients who really need me now, and I'll look in on you again in a couple of days.'

He was out of the room before Owen could draw breath to tell him he needn't bother, and Grace followed him quickly down the stairs. After a few silent minutes, her father looked at Jassy uneasily.

'Do you all think I'm being that much of a fool to myself?'

She resisted the urge to tell him exactly what she thought, and spoke carefully. 'I think you've been in control of your life for so long that you find it hard to accept when other people are trying to help you, Dad.'

He looked at her steadily, and then nodded reluctantly.

'You're probably right,' he said wearily. 'I know you mean it for the best, girl, but do you honestly think we could live together in your cottage for more than a couple of days without half-killing one another?'

'I don't know, but I'm willing to give it a try if you are.'

Mentally, she was crossing her fingers as she spoke. It was probably the very worst idea, but she wouldn't be anything of a daughter if she didn't make the gesture. Alec said her father needed to get away and relax, and she had the means of giving him a restful place in the country to do it – providing the work was done to her satisfaction.

Owen told her he was going out for a bit of fresh air to think. Before he left the room, he paused and stroked Jassy's hair for a moment.

'You're a good girl, Jassy. Sometimes I forget to tell you.'

As he left the room, she felt her eyes blur with tears. He so rarely said anything to make her feel she was important to him, and she cherished any small crumb of comfort he gave her. She resolved right there and then, that no matter how irascible he became when or if they shared the cottage for few days – or a few weeks – she was going to hold her tongue and remember that he really did love her, no matter how hard it was for him to show it.

She had been out buying groceries when William Hedges telephoned again, and she was putting them away in the pantry when her father called upstairs to tell her that her young man had called.

'Freddie?' she whispered before she could stop herself.

She was thankful that her father hadn't heard her breathe

his name when he yelled back that it was the estate agent chap calling about the cottage, and that he'd call again later.

'He's not my young man,' she said crossly, even though there was no one to hear.

She continued banging down packets and tins on the pantry shelves, annoyed with herself for even thinking it could have been Freddie, and even more annoyed at the *frisson* of disappointment that it hadn't been him. Considering he didn't know where she lived now that she had left Giles Devenish's estate, it would have been the least likely thing to happen. And one that she didn't want to happen, since he was probably married by now, she thought, unable to deny the pang in her heart at the thought.

She ran down the stairs when the phone rang again, not wanting to irritate her father more by taking personal calls – although they were so few that the idea was almost laughable. The telephone was strictly for business – and in recent times, also for the doctor. As expected, it was William Hedges.

'I'll be in Bristol tomorrow. If it's convenient for you to come down to Horton I could pick you up around two o'clock. My business should be concluded by then. That's always assuming you're happy to leave your father for a few days.'

He was brisk and efficient, reminding her that he was doing her a favour, and that she had to fit it in with his business dealings. She understood that. She was no more than a client who was proving a bit of a nuisance, but she wanted to see this through, and unconsciously she lifted her chin as she answered him coolly.

'My father is well, thank you, and that will be very convenient.'

'Good, and since the work has begun on the cottage, my aunt says it would probably be more comfortable for you to stay with her. She's on her own since my cousin moved into Cooper's Farm to get out of the village, but it's your choice.'

She could imagine why the cousin would want to move away . . . and there were always choices, thought Jasmine. She could dig her heels in and say she was staying at the cottage, regardless of any work going on; she could probably book a room and breakfast at the local pub; or she could stop being so stuck-up and accept Mrs Lester's kind offer.

'Please thank your aunt for me, and tell her I'll be glad to accept,' she said quickly before she changed her mind, even though she had no idea how they would get along, being virtual strangers.

'Very wise. Then I'll see you about two o'clock tomorrow.'

She hung up slowly, suddenly anxious. She didn't really know the woman or the village . . . but she supposed this would also be a very good time to get to know more of it, and she smothered her brief attack of nerves.

Her father told her it was the most sensible idea she had had yet.

'You don't mind my going off for a few days then? You will be all right, Dad, won't you?'

'If you're suggesting that I think you're deserting a sinking ship, then no, I don't, my girl. This old ship is far from sinking, and how do you think we managed without you when you were off working with your toffs on the Devenish estate? Besides, Grace is always here, isn't she?'

'Dad's right Jassy,' Grace put in. 'I'm always here.'

Was there the tiniest bit of resentment in her sister's voice as she repeated his words? Or was Jassy hearing more things that weren't really there? For the first time she thought of the different directions their lives had taken them. She had gone away from home to work for Giles Devenish, branching out in a way many young girls of her age never did. She had learned how to be independent of home ties. Grace had always cared for her father and herself from the day Jassy was born, and had always seemed perfectly content to work in the shop alongside him.

But what if all that was changing? What if Grace really had fallen in love with Dr Alec Macleod, and he felt the same away about her? What if they eventually decided to marry? As a busy doctor's wife, Grace could no longer work in a haberdashery shop, and the time may come when they would have a family of their own . . . would Jassy be called upon then to fulfil the role that Grace had always taken? And if so, how could a dutiful daughter refuse?

'Sometimes I think the girl goes off into a trance whenever

you try to talk to her,' she heard her father say irritably. 'We've both agreed it's a good idea for you to go off and see if anything's been done to the cottage, Jasmine. In my opinion, the best way to get workmen working is to keep your eye on them, and you can't do that from forty miles away.'

'Stop worrying about it, and go and pack some clothes, Jassy,' Grace added quickly, 'and remember you can always keep in touch by telephone. It's not as if we're on the other side of the world.'

It seemed as if everyone was urging her to do it; Grace and her father; William Hedges and his aunt. And of course, it was what she wanted to do. It was part of the great plan . . . but it was one thing to talk about living an idyllic life in the country, it was another to be taking the first step, even if she would be living with Mrs Lester on this first proper visit. She still hadn't really thought any farther ahead than that, but if she eventually decided to move into Blackthorn Cottage, she would need to get a job. She had always been a busy and active person, and at nearly twenty-one years old she could hardly spend the rest of her life sitting around all day like the proverbial lady of the manor in her country retreat. She would go slowly mad – and not so slowly at that.

Lying in bed that night, with her small suitcase ready packed for tomorrow now, she thought of the options that were open to her regarding the cottage. She admitted that at first she had been dazzled and stunned by the legacy that Giles Devenish had left her. It had felt so grand and important to think she was a property owner at such a young age. It still felt a bit like play-acting, having a doll's house big enough to live in and fill with whatever she wanted.

Did she really want to live there by herself, cut off from her family, and knowing nobody in Horton except the estate agent and his aunt? They could hardly be counted as friends yet, if ever. Did she want her father to live with her, even temporarily, leaving Grace behind in Bristol? Or did she want to sell the cottage and keep the money as a nest egg for the future?

She remembered the kindly Giles Devenish and how much she had enjoyed working for him and listening to his wisdom. He always said that life was for living and should never be wasted. He hadn't been a particularly religious man, but he'd also said that wasting a life was throwing God's gifts back in His face. Giles's gift to her had been the cottage, and she knew in her heart that he hadn't meant her to sell it. But now that the decision came nearer, nor did she know if she could really live in it permanently.

There was another alternative that had been playing around in her mind occasionally, even if it was something that she hadn't thought seriously about yet. It was a sort of safety net, and she felt a bit like a conjurer keeping something up her sleeve until the moment was ripe to reveal it to her astounded audience. She wasn't sure that would be the right word to apply in this case, but for now, it was an idea that she was keeping strictly to herself. She buried her head beneath the bedclothes and made her mind a blank in an effort to sleep.

She waited impatiently for William Hedges to arrive the following day. When he hadn't turned up by two thirty, she felt alternately annoyed and frustrated. Owen came up to the flat for an afternoon cup of tea and told her he'd probably forgotten.

'Well, thank you, Dad! As if I'm not on edge enough!'

'I didn't mean to upset you, girl. I only meant he'll have forgotten what time he told you, that's all. What are you on edge about, anyway? Afraid the curse of the couple who poisoned themselves in Blackthorn Cottage will rub off on you?'

She groaned, wishing those old men who yarned their time away on the benches of Horton Green hadn't informed him so readily. She would have preferred to keep such knowledge away from him. She was still technically a minor in the eyes of the law, and aware that she still needed his approval before she did anything permanent about the cottage. He might well decide it was an unsuitable place for a young and impressionable girl to inhabit, especially after someone had made it plain by their daubing that they didn't want strangers there. She wondered if that had been accounted for yet. Certainly she had heard nothing since.

Owen snorted. 'I'm sure you don't forget the day me and

Grace went down there with you, and the old boys I was talking to on the village green. There's always plenty of gossip and old legends to be found in such places, and they were full of old yarns, especially about the young couple who'd been found dead by a local lad. I'm surprised such a tale didn't put you off.'

'Well, it didn't,' Jassy said stubbornly.

To her surprise he gave a short laugh. 'Good for you. I wouldn't want to think any daughter of mine was lily-livered enough to be put off by old folks' tales – even if they're true.'

Jassy supposed this was a compliment of sorts, but she wished he hadn't added the last part. She couldn't deny it, anyway. It had happened, and everyone in the village knew it, including the vandals who had violated her cottage walls. She tried not to shiver, not wanting her father to reverse his opinion of her being strong willed.

Then, to her relief, she heard Grace talking to someone downstairs and the next minute William Hedges came into the flat. She turned to him almost eagerly, glad to get her thoughts away from past events in the cottage. She was startled when she saw him. Until now, she had only seen him in casual or working clothes, but here was the smart businessman in a suit and crisp white shirt and tie. He looked very different now, and Jassy was aware of the imperious way she had sometimes spoken to him – very much as if he was the local yokel and she the smart city girl, she thought guiltily.

'You look as if you've seen a ghost,' he said easily. 'Am I that much of a shock to you?'

'Of course not, but I've only seen you splattered in paint before now.'

William laughed. '*Touché*, but it wouldn't go down too well with my colleagues in our Bristol office to appear like a country bumpkin, would it?'

Suspiciously, she sensed that he was mocking her to provoke some cute remark, and she felt her face go hot. He was anything but a country bumpkin, and how she could ever have thought so was beyond her now when she was faced with this elegant man seeming to take up so much space in the sitting-room. She quickly remembered her manners.

'Would you like some tea before we leave?' she said.

'I'd rather get on the road if it's all the same to you. I've had a word with your father and he seems his usual self, so I assume there's no need to worry about leaving him with your sister for a few days. My aunt is perfectly happy for you to stay as long as you wish.'

'Thank you. Dad refuses to allow himself to feel ill, so Grace has suggested that they come down to Horton to collect me on Sunday afternoon.'

That would give her three days to find her way around the village a little more. Three days to see what work had been done on Blackthorn Cottage. Three days to gauge what she really thought about Horton and the countryside. Three days to get to know Mrs Lester, and to see more of William Hedges.

'Right. Have you got everything?' William said briskly.

She picked up her suitcase and as he took it from her their hands brushed. It was only for a moment, but it was the kind of thing that romantic novels, from tuppenny paperback stories to *Jane Eyre*, made such a big thing about. The fleeting touch . . . the feeling of electricity between two people . . . the warmth that flowed between their fingers . . . Jassy frowned as the stupid phrases surged into her head so annoyingly. There was nothing of that feeling between herself and William Hedges, nor ever likely to be.

Ten minutes later, they had said goodbye to Owen and Grace, and were driving out of the city. It was a clear, late April day and the sun was still high in the sky as they headed west. People had long since shed their heavy coats and boots and were looking springlike in bright, fresh colours, reflecting the season.

'I love this time of year,' Jasmine said, trying to think of something to say in the first awkward intimacy of William's car. 'Even the river winding through the city doesn't look so bleak and gloomy when the sun shines down on old Brunel's wonderful suspension bridge.'

'Cities are still cities, though, and this is the best time in the country,' William commented. 'The spring lambs are arriving, and the grass is sweet and new.'

Jassy laughed in surprise. 'My goodness, that was almost poetic. Are you a bit of a poet, Mr Hedges?'

'I shouldn't think so, although you might say an estate agent needs to have the knack of addressing words attractively for their clients.'

'Making a tumbledown cottage appear on paper as a desirable country residence, for instance,' she couldn't resist saying.

'Something like that. But in the end, beauty's in the eye of the beholder, isn't it? Or some such rubbish.'

'I've just said you were a bit of a poet and now you've spoiled it.'

'Sorry, but if we're talking in business terms, it's not really an estate agent's intention to fool a prospective client, just to make a property sound as attractive as possible so that they view it in the first place. Then they make up their own minds about it.'

'That sums it up a little cynically, if I may say so. But I was never a prospective client, was I? Blackthorn Cottage was mine, whether I wanted it or not!'

'And do you want it?'

For the first time, he glanced away from the road ahead of them and looked directly at her. She wished he hadn't asked the question because she was as undecided about it now as she had ever been. And for someone who always thought herself capable of making strong decisions, she didn't like the feeling.

'I don't know. I think so. It would be mean to throw such a gift away, but it's a different way of life in the country and I'm not sure I'm ready for it.'

'Like all young girls, you prefer the bright lights, I suppose.'

He was giving all his concentration to his driving again, although they were out of the main part of the city now and there was relatively little traffic ahead.

Jassy flushed at his words. 'Do I seem so frivolous to you? I'd like to remind you that I worked for several years on a busy country estate – and you're not exactly Methuselah, are you?' she finished.

'A country estate is like a little self-contained town in

itself, isn't it? Besides, I'm old enough to know when someone isn't suited to village life – and it's very different from working in a big house among so many other people.'

Her mouth fell open. 'Is that what you think of me, then – that I'm not suited to village life?'

She felt unaccountably dampened at this swift assessment. She may not have expected or wanted Blackthorn Cottage, but she was darned if she needed some village person telling her she wasn't suited to be there.

His hand reached out and covered hers for a moment. 'I'm sorry. That was clumsy of me, and I didn't mean to upset you. I think you could adapt to anything you set your mind to, Jasmine.'

She stayed with her lips clamped together for a while, watching the countryside begin to unfold in front of her as they passed through the various villages and hamlets along the way to Horton. It was truly in its full glory now, she thought, the burgeoning leaves on the trees a delicate network of spring green against the backcloth of fields and sky.

'Why are you doing all this for me?' she asked finally, turning to look at William's profile as he drove. 'You don't have to take such an interest in my business, and I can't imagine you do this for all your clients. So why me?'

He gave an imperceptible shrug. 'Firstly, I thought you were an impossible client, tottering through the village on those high heels. Secondly, my aunt thought you had the look of a bewildered fawn that needed looking after.'

He ignored Jassy's gasp of indignation at such a description. 'And thirdly, she liked your father and was very concerned to hear what had happened to him. My aunt is the kind of woman who takes an interest in people, whether they're friends or strangers. You'll discover that for yourself.'

The words 'village busybody' came to mind, but Jassy wisely kept them to herself. Besides, she admitted that she had liked Mrs Lester too.

'And fourthly,' William went on, glancing her way again, 'I liked you.'

Now she really didn't know what to say, and she gave a stifled laugh, finding her breath coming much too fast.

'Good Lord, I hope you don't act like this with all your

lame duck clients, or you'd never get any work done at all.'

'Not all of them. Just those who I think are going to be a bit of a challenge.'

And if that didn't put her in her place of being no more than a challenging client, she didn't know what would!

Eight

Kate Lester lived above the post office in the centre of the village. Although Jasmine had been there once before, it felt different to be entering it now, knowing she was going to live there for a few days. She found, almost to her embarrassment, that William had been invited to stay for an early supper, and in her opinion it was far too cosy round the table that mealtime. They should have kept things on a businesslike footing from the start, but it had seemingly been impossible to do. It was almost as if William and his family were encroaching in on her, just as the weeds around Blackthorn Cottage were in danger of choking it. She tried to ignore the thought.

She had left her things in the pretty back bedroom where she was going to sleep, and once the meal was over she spoke directly to William.

'If it wouldn't be too much trouble, I'd like to see what progress has been made on the cottage this evening.'

'It's no trouble,' he said at once, 'and I think you'll be pleasantly surprised. The thatch wasn't as bad as it appeared, and has patched up very satisfactorily.'

'Jim Granger is a good workman,' Mrs Lester put in. 'You couldn't ask for a better thatcher. He's done some work on Cooper's Farm recently and they're very pleased.'

'Isn't that the name of the farm where your horse is stabled?' Jassy asked William, remembering.

'It is, and it's where my cousin Ted works as well,' he said. 'I've no doubt you'll meet him sooner or later.'

'Oh, I'm sure he'll be along on Saturday evening as usual to bring me a load of his dirty washing and take back his clean pile,' his aunt said dryly.

'You spoil him, Aunt Kate,' William said sharply. 'He's

eighteen now, and old enough to look after himself. You shouldn't have to do everything for him.'

Mrs Lester gave a heavy sigh. 'I don't do everything for him, and don't you go putting bad thoughts in Jasmine's head before she's even met the boy, William. Ted's over his wild days and he's a reformed character now.'

'So you say, but I can't say the same for the company he keeps.'

Jassy began to feel like an eavesdropper at this little exchange. It had nothing to do with her . . . and yet it could have a good deal to do with her, she thought suddenly. If you scratched beneath the surface of what they were saying, Ted Lester had obviously been a bit of a tearaway, even if he wasn't now. He didn't keep the best company, and what was more, he'd been the child who found the dead couple in Blackthorn Cottage all those years ago and been so traumatized by it. What more obvious candidate was there for the vandalism to the walls of the cottage?

Her eyes glazed slightly, remembering that she was a guest in this house, and that she was letting her imagination run away with her. The very worst thing she could do right now would be to name Ted Lester as a suspect in front of his mother and cousin, especially when she had no evidence of any such thing. It began to feel increasingly suspicious, though, that no culprit had been found. Or if they had, no one had told her about it. *It had been dealt with*, were the words she remembered William saying. And why wouldn't he, if it was his own cousin who had done it!

Of course, her father's illness had taken precedence over any interest she had taken in the cottage in recent weeks, but all the same, if any real news had emerged, she should have been told. Seeing the troubled look on Mrs Lester's face now, she knew that this was not the time to bring it up. But it wasn't going to wait long. The outrage she had felt on that day was still simmering, and once they had finished supper and she and William were on their way to the cottage, she couldn't hold back the questions any longer.

'Have you found out who daubed that red paint on the cottage walls?' she burst out. 'It seems strange that I haven't heard anything.'

'Would it be any use to you to hear any names?' he countered. 'Those responsible have been severely cautioned by the local bobbies and are unlikely to bother you again.'

'I don't think that's good enough. Is there any reason why I shouldn't know their names, even if I've no idea who they are?'

'Well, only that it may prejudice you in future, should you happen to meet them, and the police were satisfied that it was only high jinks.'

'And that's it? I'm supposed to forget it, am I?'

'Jasmine, they were young lads out for a lark. They've been given local punishments to do and they're carrying them out to everyone's satisfaction. I'm told that they're suitably ashamed of their actions, and I've no doubt their fathers would give them a good thrashing if such a thing occurred again.'

'Was your cousin one of them?' she asked directly.

He snorted. 'Good God, no. Ted wouldn't go near the place if you paid him a fortune. He's a brawny chap now, but as far as Blackthorn Cottage is concerned, it's strictly taboo.'

'Then I'm sorry I asked, but after the way you and your aunt were talking about him, it made me start wondering.'

'Oh, neither of us are too keen on the company he chooses to call his pals, that's all.'

They had arrived at the cottage now, and Jassy looked at it in surprised delight. To her inexperienced eyes, the thatch looked completely renewed, even though William said it had merely been patched wherever it needed it.

'You'll find the plumbing's up to scratch now as well, and if you want some inside painting done to brighten it up, I can recommend someone in the village.'

'Thank you, but I shall do that myself. I am capable, you know,' she added, seeing his raised eyebrows. 'It's not exactly a Rembrandt job to put some whitewash on the walls, is it?'

'Let's go inside and take a look then,' he said, amused.

It was what she wanted to do. This time, she was assessing it with a view to actually living here for a few days or weeks with her father. Before that, there were things to be done, and things to buy. New bedding, of course. The beds themselves were sound, and so was the basic heavy furniture that went with the cottage, but Jassy wanted soft furnishings that were fresh and new and to her own taste, and the anticipation of shopping for such things was more exciting than she had imagined. Downstairs she would need new cushions to brighten up the place, and even though all the pots and pans and cutlery in the small kitchen had been left exactly as before, she decided she would throw everything out and begin again.

Oh yes, it was definitely like playing house . . . and just how a bride must feel on planning her first home. Even if she and her father were only here for a short time, she thought hastily, it should all be made pristine and comfortable, and if and when she decided to sell it, any new owners could be proud of her excellent housekeeping.

'You've got a very determined look on your face, and something else that I can't quite define,' William told her, when she had made a silent inspection of every room in the cottage. 'You're almost glowing!'

She laughed, aware that she certainly felt more alive than at any time since the awful moment when she and Grace had found their father on the floor of his bedroom. She could make things good for him here, and it would be like a temporary haven in his busy life.

'I don't know about glowing, but I was just wondering whether your aunt would come shopping with me while I'm here,' she said. 'I don't mean for food and vegetables, but for furnishings for the cottage. There's a lot that I'll need and I shall start making a list tonight. I don't suppose there are any shops big enough in Horton to supply everything, though – and now that I stop to think about it sensibly, your aunt couldn't leave the post office, could she?'

'What a lot of objections you make. Why don't you simply ask her? She's not tied to the post office twenty-four hours a day, and she always has Monday off when an assistant takes over. I'm sure she'd quite enjoy an afternoon shopping in Taunton, and you'd get everything you need there.'

'Well, that's the end of that, then, since I'll be going home on Sunday.'

'You don't have to, do you? Why not stay another few days? If you buy anything for the cottage, I'm sure you'll want to see how it looks. Besides, you can always get a bus back to Bristol, or I could run you back one evening. It's hardly the other end of the world.'

'I don't know. I'll have to think about it,' she said, thinking again that, kind though the offer might be, he was intruding far too well into her life. 'I still want my dad and Grace to come down on Sunday, though, to see how things are getting on.'

'Of course. And by the way,' William said, 'forgive me for asking, but you're no longer a working girl, so are you sure you can you afford all this?'

She flushed. 'Probably not by the time I've finished, but I was able to live frugally while I was working for Mr Devenish. I had no living expenses, so I got into the habit of saving most of my money. I'm sure that's something you approve of, Mister Estate Agent!' she added mockingly.

William laughed. 'Oh yes! And my aunt is a canny shopper, so I'm sure she'll see that you get value for your money.'

It seemed to be cut and dried already, but she still had to ask Mrs Lester if she would be willing to spend her day off traipsing around the Taunton shops. Jassy felt another surge of excitement at the thought. There didn't seem anything else to do at the cottage, and even if she had wanted to linger and envelop herself in its atmosphere, she had no wish to do it with William Hedges. They were necessary business acquaintances, no more.

'Do you want a drive around the countryside before I return you to Aunt Kate's?' he asked suddenly. 'If you're going to live here, no matter how short a time it may be, you might as well see what it has to offer.'

She started at the unexpected offer. 'Well, if you don't think she'll consider me rude, then yes, thank you.'

'We'll go over to Cooper's Farm and you can meet my horse and my cousin.'

'In that order?' she grinned, not missing the fact that he'd put his horse first.

'In that order,' he said grimly.

Cooper's Farm was a few miles away from Horton, and as soon as the village was behind them they were enveloped in a rolling Somerset landscape that seemed different with every turn in the road, a gentle evening panorama of spring green, the hedges bursting with all kinds of blossom, and contented cows grazing in the fields. The occasional isolated cottage and farmhouse only added to the pastoral scenes unfolding in front of them.

'It beats anything the city has to offer, doesn't it?' William said, when she had been silent for too long.

If he was mocking her she was more than a match for him.

'I notice you spend some of your time in the city so it can't be that distasteful to you.'

Or had he invented the business trip to Bristol simply to bring her here? Whatever she might have thought of such an idea was instantly dismissed.

He shrugged. 'That's of necessity. I merely control a small branch of the main estate offices which are in Bristol and Taunton. Believe me, I'm always glad to shed my city image and get back where I belong.'

'Well, maybe I shall be just as glad to shed my country image and get back where I belong!'

She didn't know why she had said it or where the words came from. It was a shame when they had been getting on reasonably well, because she saw how his hands tightened on the car's steering wheel and knew he was seeing her words as an affront to the country way of life. Actually, she was finding it far more alluring than she had ever expected . . . the way so many people did when they came for a short holiday and then couldn't wait to get back to civilization again. But she had worked on a country estate before, so she wasn't an out-and-out townie, as he seemed to think.

'I didn't mean that the way it sounded,' she added defensively.

'No? Something said impulsively can reveal quite a lot about a person's real feelings, Miss Wyatt.'

'Why do you keep using my full name whenever you're annoyed with me? You sound just like my father.'

He laughed, reaching out his hand for a moment to squeeze hers. 'I assure you I don't feel in the least fatherly towards you, and I'm not annoyed with you, Jasmine – Jassy. In fact, I shall make it my mission to change your mind about the charm of the country as opposed to the town. Take your first look at Cooper's Farm and tell me, if you can, that you don't find it enchanting.'

If that was estate-agent speak, then she couldn't deny the truth of it. He had stopped the car now, and they were gazing down into a valley between softly rising hills. A sprawling farmhouse and outbuildings nestled comfortably in the valley, and the cows and sheep dotted about in the surrounding fields looked like children's toys from this distance. It was an idyllic picture that should be on canvas, she thought instantly, beautiful and timeless . . .

'It's perfectly lovely,' she gulped.

His laugh was more gentle this time. 'Round one to me, I think. Remind me not to bring you here when the rains come, or you'll change your mind about its loveliness when you're wallowing in mud.'

'You've spoiled it now!' she said, as the unwanted image came into her mind. 'If this is how you go about selling properties, I wonder you ever sell anything!'

'Ah, but I'm not trying to sell you Cooper's Farm, just reminding you that it's not always as perfect as it looks. Nothing ever is,' he added.

'Really?' she said, twisting round to look at him. He didn't answer, just continued driving down the winding road to the farm, and she had to make up her own mind whether his words were enigmatic or just damned annoying.

The family at Cooper's Farm greeted them warmly, including the two large dogs leaping all over William, who were obviously glad to see him. That had to be in his favour, Jassy thought dryly. At least the dogs loved him. The farmer and his wife could have come straight off the pages of the same picture-book as their farm, she thought. They were round and jolly, pressing the visitors to sit a while and have a slice of home-made ginger cake and a large mug of dark, evil-looking tea. It was hard to refuse, and in the end it was simpler not to try.

'You'll be finding it restful down here in Horton, Jasmine,' Mrs Cooper said, cutting across any formality.

'And mighty different from the stink of the city, I'll be bound,' her husband said in his booming voice. 'I could never abide cities myself. Nasty, busy places, full of folk rushing hither and thither and getting nowhere.'

'Oh yes,' his wife agreed. 'If it's God's clean fresh air that you're looking for, then the country's the only place you'll find it.'

'Mother won't hear a word against it,' Sam Cooper said with a grin.

'I only went to the city once, and that was enough for me. I felt as if I couldn't breathe again until I got back to the familiar old farmyard smells,' his wife agreed, leaving Jassy wondering if they ever let other people get a word in, or if they continued every conversation between themselves and left the rest of them as onlookers.

William was clearly used to this, sitting back and grinning over his mug of tea at Jassy as she tried to make sense of anyone preferring the all-pervading farmyard smells to the varying smells of a city. He could have warned her what these farmers would be like, she thought indignantly. They were what Grace would call 'real characters', she supposed, but the more she listened to them she realized what good hearts they had and how affectionate they were towards one another, and her small sense of putting them into a stereotypical mould faded. What right did she have to feel superior to anyone here?

'You'll be wanting to take Jasmine out to see Raven, I daresay,' Sam went on. 'He's been a mite fretful of late, William, and although Ted's been giving him some exercise, I reckon he's missing his boss.'

'Raven's my horse,' William managed to breathe in Jassy's ear.

'Where is Ted?' Mrs Cooper said. 'It's not like him to miss out on company, especially if he heard William's car.'

'I sent him and the other lads over to the end field to repair the fences if you remember, Mother. They'll be back soon and clamouring for their supper as always. Young 'uns are always hungry, and I'm sure Mother can rustle up a bit extra for the two of you if you want to stay.'

'No, we won't do that,' William said quickly anticipating Jassy's dismay at staying too long. 'Aunt Kate will be expecting us, so we'll just wait long enough to see Ted after we've been out to the stables if you don't mind, but thanks for the offer.'

'Well, you know you're always welcome, William,' Mrs Cooper said comfortably. 'You and your young lady.'

'Why didn't you correct her?' Jasmine demanded as she strode along beside William *en route* to the stables.

'What, and miss your outraged expression?' he said with a grin. 'Don't worry, Mrs Cooper knows exactly who you are, just as the whole village does, but if she enjoys her bit of mischievous matchmaking, who am I to deny her?'

Jasmine digested the fact that the whole village knew exactly who she was, and knew that it was more than likely. Any newcomer would be a novelty, and everyone seemed to know everyone else's business in a small community like this one, compared with the more impersonal ways of a city. It struck her how few real confidantes any of her family had, other than the constant stream of customers who came to the shop. Most of Jasmine's friends had been at the Devenish estate in recent times, and she quickly veered her thoughts away from that, knowing that Freddie Patterson had been far and away the most important of those friends.

'Have you gone into a fit of the sulks now?' William enquired.

'No, I have not,' she flared. 'What a perfectly quaint thing to say!'

'Being perfectly quaint down here in the sticks is supposedly one of our country charms, in case you hadn't noticed,' he replied mockingly.

'Look, William, let's get one thing straight.' She had stopped walking, and he had no option but to stop as well. 'I don't despise anything about the country. I like it here. If I didn't, I wouldn't keep coming back, would I? I wouldn't ever have considered moving into Blackthorn Cottage, even for a short while.'

'So you are going to move in then. Even for a short while.' He made it sound like a statement, but his eyes challenged her, and her chin lifted.

'Probably. We'll see.'

She was the one who strode ahead then, but she guessed that he was smiling behind her back, as if he'd won a small battle. As if he *wanted* her here. Which was absurd, because it shouldn't matter a fig to him whether she moved in or not.

Except, of course, that if she did put the cottage back on the market, he'd have to go about finding another buyer for it, which would probably suit him from a business point of view, of course.

They had reached the stables while she was still debating this. She was also trying to ignore the indignant feeling that it was for his own benefit that he wanted the business with Blackthorn Cottage over and done with as painlessly as possible. Putting it on the market again would doubtlessly be a tiresome affair. It wasn't herself that he wanted here, just the simplicity of having to do no more work in selling the property. It didn't do much for her self-image to know it.

'This is Raven. Hello, old boy,' she heard him say, a new and almost caressing note in his voice. 'Isn't he a beauty, Jasmine?'

The gleaming chestnut horse whinnied softly as if in appreciation of the compliment. Jasmine had no experience of horses, and his head seemed alarmingly large as he leaned forward over the stall towards the visitors.

'He seems very nice,' she murmured.

William smiled. 'You can stroke him if you like. He won't bite.'

She gingerly put out her hand and stroked the horse's nose and was relieved that he didn't flinch from her touch.

'Ted's been doing a good job of grooming and exercising him,' William went on. 'The Coopers hire out horses on a regular basis, but nobody rides Raven but Ted and me. I pay for private stabling and ride him when I can. He particularly enjoys the fete when we have a competition for the best-dressed horse and cart. I told you about that, didn't I? It's always held here on Cooper's Farm.'

'On Midsummer Day,' she said flatly, remembering.

By which time she wouldn't be here. He detected the slight change in her voice without knowing why it had happened.

'Absolutely. It's the best time of the country year in many ways. The village women display their home-made jams and honeys and compete for the best tasting cakes, and everyone feels a great sense of well-being. You'll love it. Though I always enjoy harvest time more, when we also

98

have a celebration. August and September are lovely months in the country.'

In an instant he seemed to have reverted from big businessman to enthusiastic countryman. And for no reason at all, just as instantly his complacency turned Jassy's mood to one of pent up fury.

'How do you know I'll love it, or if I'll even be here then to watch you prancing about in a horse and cart! You know nothing about me, and anyway, the last place I'd want to be in August is away from home and my family.'

To her horror she burst into tears, and she was almost unaware of the moment when his arms went around her, holding her tight.

'Do you want to tell me why?' he said quietly. She could feel the rumble of his voice from deep in his chest, and she pulled away in embarrassment from this unexpected embrace.

'I'm sorry,' she gasped. 'You must think I'm a total idiot and very ill-mannered into the bargain to speak to you like that.'

'Well, I may know nothing about what goes on in your head, Miss Wyatt, but I think I know a damsel in distress when I see one, so if you want to tell me why you don't think you'll be here in August in particular, I'm willing to listen.'

It was the craziest place to be spilling out all the hurt she had ever felt because she had done the unforgivable thing and caused her mother to die in childbirth, therefore giving her father the deepest grief any man should have to bear. Somehow William's arms had gone around her again and she was sobbing silently against his accommodating chest as she tried to explain the way she could never reach her father in the way that Grace could, that she had always felt second best in every way, and she did love him, she did!

'It seems to me you've got a huge case of jealousy towards your sister,' William said eventually, and kept hold of her as she made to pull away from him again. 'It's not just your father's lack of loving that you resent. Even though you love her, you found it hard to accept the fact that Grace was such a competent little mother to you instead of your real one. Was it August when your mother died?'

'The first. It's when she died and when I was born,' Jassy said bitterly. 'And when did you become so wonderful at understanding human nature?'

'When I had to deal with a young boy who had just witnessed a terrible scene in a cottage, and felt incapable of talking to anyone but me.'

Knowing he was referring to his cousin Ted, Jassy was shocked into silence by his answer and didn't know what to say. She felt limp with emotion, and was still standing there, apparently locked in his arms while she tried to get her breath back, when they heard the scuffle of feet on the gravel nearby.

'Hey there, cuz! It looks as if old Ma Cooper wasn't wrong after all when she said you were out here with your young lady. Are you going to introduce us or are you keeping her all to yourself?'

Jassy felt William stiffen as he released her, and she looked at the dishevelled young man who had appeared as if from nowhere. He was a young man with a look of William about him, but none of his finesse. Dressed in working overalls, there was nothing smart about him, from his swaggering walk to his bold eyes that looked Jasmine over in a far too familiar way.

'Jasmine, meet my cousin, Ted Lester,' William said.

The thoughts whirled around in Jassy's mind. Seconds before there had been real compassion in William's voice when he spoke about the trauma his young cousin had gone through. But that was a different time, and the boy was now a man, and there was no doubting the annoyance William felt towards him now.

'I'm pleased to meet you,' she mumbled.

'The feeling's mutual,' Ted said, his mouth widening into the sort of smile that could make any gullible girl's heart lurch.

With his rugged looks, he could probably have his pick of the village girls, Jassy thought, and that could bring another sort of trouble to his family. But she chided herself for making a quick assessment which may or may not be true, and smiled back at the boy. If such an action annoyed William still further, that was his problem, not hers.

Nine

The three of them walked back to the farmhouse together, with Ted doing most of the talking. When he discovered that Jasmine was staying with his mother, he told her he'd see her on Saturday night when he brought his washing home. Predictable, she thought, just as his mother had said.

'Well, I must say Ted didn't seem bothered to meet me, knowing that I'm the new owner of Blackthorn Cottage,' Jassy said, once she and William were driving back to Horton.

'No, but I doubt that you'll see him anywhere near it, even though thinking it's jinxed is stupid. Other people have lived there since that time and no harm has come to them, but you didn't hear him talking about it, either. He prefers to shut it out of his mind.'

'Is that a good idea? I always thought people should face their fears.'

She bit her lip as she said it, wishing he hadn't mentioned that Ted thought the cottage was jinxed, and hoping he wouldn't turn the tables on her and suggest that she examined her own mind over her feelings towards her sister. Not that there had ever been any doubt until he said it, she thought indignantly. She loved Grace. In any case, he didn't comment, and the last thing she wanted was to argue with him. Back at the village she assumed he would come into the house with her, but he merely opened the car door for her and told her to enjoy her stay with his Aunt Kate.

'I'm sure I'll see you around while you're here,' he said. 'Horton's too small a place to miss people.'

He was gone before she could say anything more, leaving her slightly piqued, but she chose to ignore his lack of manners. Mrs Lester was a friendly woman, and glad of the company, she told Jasmine. They settled down with cups of cocoa before bedtime, and Jassy ventured to ask a bit more about the cousins who seemed so unalike, despite having been brought up together.

'It's like any two siblings, which is how they always saw themselves, Jasmine. The older one looks after the younger one, but in time they each find their own feet and become less dependent on one another. There was the usual bit of healthy rivalry between my boys, of course.'

She went on talking almost to herself.

'Of course, there was also the incident at Blackthorn Cottage, which neither of them can quite forget. I'm sure that for some silly reason Ted resents the fact that he was once so vulnerable and clinging to William, and in an attempt to prove his independence, I suppose, he's become far more aggressive as a young man. He's still young, but in time I hope he'll find a nice girl and settle down.'

As she gave a deep sigh, Jassy wished she hadn't been so nosey. But there was something else she dearly wanted to know, and Mrs Lester had unwittingly led her into it.

'And has William found a nice girl to settle down with? I know it's none of my business, but my dad said I was born curious,' she said with a small laugh.

'There's nothing wrong with that, my dear, and I'm sure your dad meant it kindly. Such a nice man,' she added. 'But William had a bad blow several years ago. He was courting a lovely girl from one of the farms around here, and she was struck down with German measles. They thought she was getting better, but she died in her sleep during the night, and it was learned that she'd had a heart defect from birth that would have killed her sooner or later. She was weakened by her illness, and apparently that was enough to trigger it. It was a terrible shock to her family, and you can imagine the effect this had on William, and he's never got serious with any girl since then.'

'What a dreadful story,' Jassy said, her voice catching, 'and I'm sorry for stirring it all up for you again, Mrs Lester.'

'Oh well, it was a long time ago, but some things stay in the memory longer than others, don't they? I'd like both my boys to find a nice companion to settle down with, but Ted prefers going out with his pals, and William's too busy with his work, more's the pity.'

She was visibly getting gloomy, and Jassy knew she had brought it about. She changed the conversation hastily.

'Mrs Lester, I want to ask you a favour, and please refuse if it's impossible. You've been so kind, and I know I'm taking liberties, but—' she hesitated.

'Well, I'll never know if you are or not unless you spit it out, girl,' the woman said briskly. 'What is it you want?'

Half an hour later it was all arranged, including Jasmine's phone call home to Grace to say that Mrs Lester had suggested she stay for a whole week to get her shopping organized and to get herself acclimatized to the village, as she put it.

She spoke animatedly into the phone. 'You'll clear it with Dad, won't you, Grace? And you'll still both come down here on Sunday afternoon, won't you? Mrs Lester has invited you both to supper before you drive back to Bristol. Please say you will, and that you'll fetch me the following Sunday.'

She was taking liberties with everyone's good nature now, she thought, but Grace was laughing at her enthusiasm and saying she was sure it would be all right with their father.

'It'll do him good to have two days out in the country, and he can't refuse when I tell him you're staying down there for a week, can he?'

'Well, he could, but I know you'll win him round the way you usually do.'

And there wasn't an ounce of jealousy in the comment, no matter what Mr amateur psychiatrist William Hedges thought!

On Saturday evening, when Ted came home to bring his dirty laundry, he didn't miss the chance to flirt mildly with Jassy, and while his mother was busy elsewhere, he said that if she wasn't going to be hob-nobbing with William next week, he'd be willing to take her out.

'There's the monthly village dance in the church hall next Friday. I'm not much cop at dancing, but we could jig around the floor if you're game.'

She was taken aback. She was a few years older than he

103

was, and to her, he was just a boy. But it would probably be tactful not to let him know it.

'I'm not much cop at dancing, either, Ted, but if you're so keen to spend some time with me, I could lend you a paint brush to do some whitewashing in my kitchen one evening next week.'

Her eyes challenged him for a response. By now, he must know that she had heard the story behind his reluctance to go anywhere near Blackthorn Cottage. For a moment she thought he was going to snap at her, and then he shrugged.

'What's it worth?' he said.

Jassy hadn't anticipated this. She had expected a flat refusal and she gave an uneasy laugh.

'A few jigs around the floor at the village dance?'

'I'll think about it.'

Long after he had gone back to the farm, Jassy was trying to sleep in the unfamiliar bed with none of the city noises she was used to. She thought about his response, and about something else too. Mrs Cooper had referred to her as William's young lady, and Mrs Lester had said there was always a bit of healthy rivalry between her boys. What would be more natural for Ted to ask Jassy out to a dance with the daft idea that he was scoring over his cousin? There wouldn't be an ounce of truth in it – except in Ted's mind. And she would supposedly be the prize in whatever silly contest he seemed to have conjured up.

She thumped her pillow into a more comfortable position beneath her head and tried to ignore her annoyance. She hadn't asked to come here before Giles Devenish had decreed differently, and she certainly didn't want to be caught up in any competition between cousins. She'd hold Ted to it, though. If he turned up at the cottage to help her paint the kitchen, she'd go to the village dance with him. And from what William had told him of Ted's refusal to go near Blackthorn Cottage, she was fairly confident that it wouldn't be necessary.

She put it out of her mind. She had already explored the village on foot, wearing the kind of sensible shoes she was sure William would approve of. That afternoon the maypole had been erected on the green and draped with garlands, in preparation for the local children who would celebrate May Day around it with songs and dances. She had had an animated conversation with some of the old men on the benches who said they looked forward to having a yarn with her dad again, and acquainted herself with the local shops.

She had walked to the church with Mrs Lester on an unusually warm Saturday afternoon, and browsed around the churchyard while her hostess and the vicar discussed parish affairs.

'Come and meet the vicar, Jasmine.'

She heard her name called a short while later and turned around from marvelling at how many ancient gravestones there seemed to be in such a small place, as Mrs Lester and a round, white-haired man approached her.

'This is Mr Barnes, our vicar, dear.'

The man shot out his hand and took Jasmine's in a firm grip.

'Delighted to meet you, Miss Wyatt. It's good that you're going to live among us. The village can certainly do with more young folk to liven things up.'

'Oh, but I'm only here for a short time,' Jassy said, confused that he seemed to assume she was moving in for good.

'Well, let's hope that you'll take such a liking to us that you'll want to stay for ever, my dear. Don't you agree, Kate?'

'I do indeed,' Mrs Lester said with a smile.

The day was getting hotter, and Jassy felt the sun burning down on the back of her neck, making her skin prickle. Or maybe the sensation had more to do with the fact that she felt she was being drawn inexorably into Horton's rural life, whether she wanted to or not. It was nonsense, of course. She was a modern young woman with a mind and will of her own, and yet as these two smiled at her with those oddly complacent smiles, it was as though they knew something she didn't.

She was angry with herself for such imaginings. Horton had no history of sorcery or witchcraft as far as she knew ... and if it did, she didn't want to know, either! It was simply a pretty little Somerset village, like so many others. She forced herself to smile back and to speak hastily.

'It's a lovely thought, I'm sure, but I doubt that my father would agree to it, and now that he's not in such good health, he needs me to help him at his shop.'

It was hardly blasphemous to say a half-truth in a vicar's hearing, and it was hardly tempting fate to say it, either.

She felt Mr Barnes tap her hand as if she was a child. 'Then let's all pray for his return to perfect health, Miss Wyatt.'

She nodded meekly, her eyes lowered. When had she become such a hypocrite, she wondered! If she wanted to stay in Horton, she would stay . . . and once she was twenty-one, her father would have no say in it, anyway. Apart from the fact that she would never want to hurt him by openly defying him – well, only if it was absolutely necessary. She found herself crossing her fingers behind her back, with the ludicrous thought that she hoped it wasn't a pagan superstition that would damn her when she was in the vicinity of a church!

'We'll see you in church tomorrow morning, Vicar,' Mrs Lester said next.

'And William too, I trust. It's good to know that one of your brood still attends, even if Ted is always too busy these days. But a farmer has the good of the land in his heart, and a staunch upbringing will always see him through. I know he had that, dear lady.'

He had become so gushing that for a horrible moment Jassy thought he was going to kiss them both, but as she and Mrs Lester walked back to the village she was assured that it was only his way. The older woman chuckled.

'He never misses a chance to comment on Ted's defection from the church, even though he never thinks of it as more than temporary.'

'Is that what you think as well?'

'Oh yes. One thing the young eventually learn, is that when all else fails, the church is always there. But before we get too gloomy, Jasmine, tell me what you're going to buy when we go shopping on Monday.'

Before then, there was church to attend on Sunday morning, and Jassy found herself sitting between William and his aunt in their regular pew. If she had always thought it mildly embarrassing to sing in the presence of strangers, it was even worse now, with Mrs Lester's stringy voice on one side of her, and William's fine baritone on the other. She didn't have a bad singing voice herself, and at the end of the service when they all spilled out into the clear spring air, Mrs Lester commented on it.

'If you came to live here permanently, Jasmine, you should think about joining the Monday Club. They always welcome new blood.'

'What's the Monday Club?' Jassy said.

'It's a small group of people who enjoy singing for their own amusement, and sometimes put on a show for the village at Christmas,' she was told. 'William's one of the organizers, and a real asset to the group with his voice. I'm sure he'd take you along on Monday night if you fancied it, Jasmine, and I think you'd enjoy it.'

Jassy wasn't at all sure that she would. Nor did she want to be included in too many village activities when she was only here on a temporary basis, at least, so far. She wondered if it was a necessary requisite of all aunties to have a subtle or blunt way of persuading you to do something. It was almost as if she could hear the echo of her Aunt Lucy's voice, asking why she was hesitating, when she normally rushed into things . . . no doubt her ethereal opinion would be called reverse psychology.

She was saved from giving any answer when several of Mrs Lester's acquaintances joined her for a chat. William grinned at her.

'I'm sure you'll find a way of getting out of it, Jasmine. You won't want to get enmeshed too deeply in village life, will you?'

'Why wouldn't I?' she said perversely, wondering if he was reading her mind. 'Your cousin's asked me to the dance next Friday night, and I said I'll go if he helps me do some painting at the cottage one evening.'

She couldn't have shocked him more if she'd danced naked on the village green.

'I think hell will freeze over before then,' he said brusquely. 'So what about the Monday Club then? Do you want to come to see what we rustics are all about?'

She studied him briefly. In his Sunday clothes he was handsome all right, and he'd be a catch for any girl, but he was so often stiff and starchy, and sometimes she just couldn't fathom him. His question made her angry.

'Why do you always say such things? I don't think of the people here as rustics, so why do you have to put such words in my mouth? But if it proves a point to you, yes, I'll come to the Monday Club.'

'Then it's a date. I'll pick you up at seven o'clock on Monday evening.'

He was gone while she was still mulling over the unlikely fact that she had a date with William Hedges on Monday evening, and a possible date with his cousin on the following Friday, and still not quite sure whether or not she had been goaded into either of them.

There were more important things to think about today. In a couple of hours Grace and her father would be here. She felt her heart leap with anticipation, glad that it was such a beautiful day, and that the cottage would be looking its best.

'You'll be missing them, I daresay,' Mrs Lester remarked later as they waited for them to arrive.

'I'm anxious to see that Dad's all right,' Jassy admitted with a smile. 'But it's only been a few days, and I lived away from home for some time until Mr Devenish died, so I don't get homesick.'

She almost surprised herself as she said it, knowing it was true. Inevitably, working at the Devenish estate for all that time, she had grown apart from her family, physically, if not mentally. It didn't mean she loved them any the less, it was just part of life. Staying here in Horton for a few days or a week, wouldn't be any great hardship, nor would it affect their strong relationship with each other. In fact, now that she had made up her mind, she admitted how much she was looking forward to being here a little longer. She could visit the cottage as often as she chose, pottering about and re-arranging things ... *playing at house again* ... the words slid into her mind and she gave a small shrug of defiance. Well, why not? Why the dickens not?

She was watching out of the window of Mrs Lester's

sitting room for Grace's car to arrive, and she ran down the stairs and across the green, meeting her father and sister halfway and hugging them both.

'It's really good to see you!'

Grace laughed. 'For heaven's sake, it's only been a few days, Jassy.'

'I know, but I was anxious to see how Dad is.'

'Dad's very well, thank you, Miss,' Owen retorted. 'And also thanks to this one's eagle eyes on me all the time, and that fool of a doctor calling in every five minutes, I'm being wrapped in cotton wool and it's stifling me.'

Jassy linked her arm in his as they walked towards the post office. 'Oh, come on, I'm sure it's not that bad,' she said, not missing the fact that Alec Macleod was calling on him every five minutes. Him – or Grace, she thought.

'Anyway, Mrs Lester's preparing some tea and cakes before we go to the cottage. You'll offend her if you refuse.'

'We wouldn't dream of refusing, and perhaps it would be courteous to ask her to come with us,' Owen said.

Grace and Jassy exchanged glances. This was a turn-up. Owen never encouraged any middle-aged women in his company, for fear they would get that settling-down gleam in their eyes as he put it. But he and Mrs Lester had had a pleasant rapport on Owen's first visit here, so it was a relief that he wasn't averse to spending a little time in her company.

'That would be nice,' Mrs Lester said, her cheeks faintly pink. 'Jasmine and I are going shopping for a few essentials tomorrow, so it might be useful to have an older woman's eye on what's needed.'

'Digging yourself in, aren't you, girl?' her father asked his daughter archly.

'Well, if I decide to sell the place, it won't hurt to have it looking fresh, will it? I wouldn't want people to see shabby cushion covers and old pots and pans, so I've decided to buy all new.'

She let him digest what she'd said about possibly selling the cottage, and told Grace instead that she was going to the Monday Club with William. As her father frowned, she knew it hadn't been the most tactful thing to say.

'Like I said, digging yourself in,' he grunted.

Mrs Lester took charge of the small atmosphere that had suddenly come out of nowhere. 'Well, before you two go back to Bristol tonight, I hope you're all partial to leek and potato pie with a good helping of mince to go with it. We all have healthy appetites down here.'

'It sounds wonderful,' Grace said. 'And you must have second sight, Mrs Lester, because it's one of Dad's favourites.'

'Oh well, I think it's something that everyone enjoys,' she replied, flustered.

Jassy had already abandoned any matchmaking plans for Grace and William now that it was obvious that Grace had eyes for no one but Alec Macleod. But as they drove through the village towards Blackthorn Cottage, she found herself musing on the almost impossible situation where two middle-aged people found themselves attracted to one another. Impossible, since one of them was her own father, who had never allowed himself to look romantically at another woman since his beloved Celia had died. And a highly unlikely situation, with one of them dedicated to his shop in the middle of a city, and the other an out-and-out countrywoman. There was also the question of the physical distance between them.

But that was something else that could be fixed . . .

'I don't know what's going through your mind now, Jasmine, but I can feel your eyes boring into the back of my head,' Owen said as they neared the cottage.

She laughed. 'You wouldn't want to know!' she said gaily.

He was undoubtedly feeling better and in a good mood as he took in the fresh thatch on the roof of the cottage, and the way the sun glinted alluringly on the white walls and windows. There were birds singing in the trees, and Jassy thanked her lucky stars that it hadn't been raining to spoil this new vision of her property. It would be anybody's dream cottage, even dedicated city dwellers . . . and although at first she had thought it was completely isolated, there were other cottages within throwing distance – providing you had a good throwing arm. There was nothing to be scared about here.

'I'm going to do some painting indoors this week, and

110

maybe do a bit to the garden as well,' she announced quickly, before she began dreaming too many dreams. 'And before you get that startled look on your face, Dad, Mrs Lester's son Ted may give me a hand, but if not, I'm sure I can manage.'

'She's probably got all the local young men at her feet by now, offering their services,' Grace murmured.

'Only two,' Jassy replied lightly, somewhat surprised at the remark. If she hadn't known how ridiculous it was, she could have sworn there was a hint of jealousy in Grace's voice. But there was surely no need – even if it was true. Grace had her Alec . . . But maybe Grace was finally waking up to the fact that she had spent all her life caring for these two and she was still a young woman who deserved a life of her own, and hopefully she was going to get it.

They went inside the cottage, and the musty smell it had when she first arrived had dispersed now, after the comings and goings of various workmen. There were no ghosts here, she thought at once. And if there were, they were only loving ghosts who would welcome caring tenants. She blinked, wondering where such daft thoughts came from, but by now, Grace was saying it was all just as perfect as she remembered it, and Jassy felt a stab of pride, as if she had personally built the place herself!

'And you're going to buy new bedding and kitchen stuff tomorrow, are you?' Owen said. 'It will cost a pretty penny, Jasmine. Do you need any money?'

She gulped. She hadn't expected him to make such an offer. It was as good as endorsing what she was doing – and it would be just like him to do it in this obscure yet practical way.

'I don't think so, but thank you for the offer.'

'Well, don't skimp on cheap goods. As a shopkeeper I don't believe in buying shoddy products in order to make ends meet. It's a false economy in the end. So ask if you need anything – just as long as you don't break the bank.'

He didn't usually speak in clichés, and Jassy knew it was to cover his slight embarrassment at talking about money, especially in the company of strangers. But before she made any reply, Mrs Lester spoke approvingly.

'There speaks a man who knows the value of money. It's all too easy for young folk to let themselves get carried away by the sight of pretty things in shop windows, isn't it?'

'I'm sure you'll see my girl gets the best value,' Owen agreed. 'I'm glad of your support, Mrs Lester.'

He didn't say it was what a mother would do, and Jassy knew he never would, but the smile that passed between the older couple was a comfortable one. They had both seen more of life than she and her sister, and it was an odd moment when the four of them seemed to divide into two small groups.

'Why don't you call me Kate, Mr Wyatt?' Mrs Lester said hesitatingly.

'Kate it is, then, and I'm Owen.'

They shook hands solemnly, and it seemed so absurd to be standing here like the performers in a play that they all burst out laughing, and then there was an awkward moment when nobody quite knew what to do next.

'Shall we go upstairs, everybody?' Jassy said quickly. 'I want to make a list of what I want to buy tomorrow. Mrs Lester's borrowing William's car, so we can bring everything back without having to carry too many parcels.'

By the time they left to stroll back to the village, the list was complete, and despite Jassy's protests, her father had slipped some money into her pocket, saying she could call it part of an early birthday present. And an hour or so later, when they were all replete with Mrs Lester's wonderful cooking, the time to say goodbye seemed to come all too soon. Grace hugged Jassy and spoke cheerfully as they walked back across the green towards the family car, leaving Owen to chat for a few minutes with the inevitable group of locals on the benches under the oak tree.

'Well done, darling,' Grace said. 'Today has perked him up no end. I think he'll be almost eager to come again next Sunday. And will you be just as eager to come home?'

'After a week of rusticating I probably will,' she grinned. 'Then again, I may not. This place has a habit of creeping up on you, whether you want it to or not. I thought it was a bit unfriendly at first, but if you smile at people, they usually smile back.'

'Profound as ever,' Grace laughed. 'I bet that was one of your Giles Devenish's sayings too.'

'I think it probably was. He's got a lot to answer for, hasn't he? But never mind me. What about you and the great romance?'

'What great romance is that?' Grace said innocently.

Ten

M onday couldn't have been more satisfying. Mrs Lester was a determined driver, clutching the steering-wheel as if her life depended on it, but they reached Taunton safely, bought everything they needed, and were back in Horton by the middle of the afternoon. They merely dropped everything off at the cottage, deposited William's car at the edge of the green, and tottered into Mrs Lester's flat to kick off their shoes and rest their feet. Jassy smiled at the older woman gratefully.

'Thank you so much for helping me, Mrs Lester. I could never have found the best shops by myself.'

'Nonsense. I think you could do anything you set your mind to, my dear. For such a pretty young woman, you've got a capable head on your shoulders.'

Jassy took it as the compliment it was meant to be, even though she could never see why being pretty meant you didn't have a brain as well. As Mrs Lester went to the kitchen to put the kettle on for what she called a reviving cup of tea, Jassy gave a small groan, remembering she was going out that evening to the Monday Club, when she'd far rather stay in and listen to the wireless or read a book. How staid and 'capable' that sounded for a girl of not yet twenty-one years old! And not for a moment would she give William Hedges the satisfaction of thinking she couldn't cope with a day's shopping and an evening at his Monday Club, when his sprightly aunt looked less exhausted than she did.

He called for her after supper, and they walked the short distance to the church hall where the Monday Club was always held. It felt odd to be going somewhere with him which had nothing to do with any business arrangements, and she began to wish she hadn't agreed to it.

'What are you thinking about so deeply?' he asked.

'I'm thinking this is weird,' she said honestly. 'We're business acquaintances, that's all, and I'm sure I was nothing more than a nuisance to you at first, and here we are, going out on a – a date!'

She wished she hadn't said the word, even though he had used it in the first place. It made it sound as if she was thrilled at the thought of being on a date with him, when she was quite nervous at being thrust into the company of strangers. It made it sound as if she fancied William Hedges, when she didn't, not at all. Well, . . . maybe she could if she tried, just a tiny bit, but she had no intention of pursuing that feeling!

'What's wrong with that?' He tucked her hand in his arm as she stumbled a little. 'And why are you wearing those ridiculous shoes again? Don't you know you're a country girl now?'

'I'm wearing these ridiculous shoes as a change from the sensible ones I've been wearing traipsing around the shops all day! As for being a country girl, I doubt I'll ever be that.'

'Do you want to take a bet on it?'

He was laughing at her now and she found herself smiling back.

'No thanks. My instincts tell me you're in the habit of winning your bets.'

'Then it's already round one to me, isn't it?'

They had reached the church hall now and there was a lot of noise and banter going on between the dozen or so people inside. William introduced her to them all, and she knew she wouldn't remember half their names. One or two stood out, like Jim Granger, who played the piano for the group, and had done the thatching on her roof. A glamorous fair-haired girl called Esme Dunn looked as if she should be on the stage already, and made no secret of the way she was eyeing up the newcomer, and registering how William was taking care of her.

Jassy remembered how his Aunt Kate said he hadn't been serious about any girl after the sad ending to his previous romance. So it was amusing to note Esme always seemed to be at William's side during the evening, sometimes infiltrating herself between him and Jassy. It was interesting to be an observer, and know that the lovely Esme almost certainly had no chance with him at all!

'We're doing Noel Coward this year,' Jim Granger told her enthusiastically. 'After the initial warm-up to get our voices in trim, we only have four songs to practise tonight, and I hope you'll join in, Jasmine. Later on we're going to sort out the soloists and duetists. William will almost certainly be one of them.'

'Well, I'm happy to join in any group singing, but I'm only here for a few days, so I wouldn't be eligible for any major parts,' she said quickly.

'Unless she decides to stay longer,' William put in.

She ignored that. Nor would she want to upset the regulars, thought Jassy, seeing the cool expression on Esme's face, and being perfectly sure that Esme would angle her way into singing a duet with William.

He was looking very spruce tonight, wearing an open-necked shirt and slacks, and less like the starchy estate agent she knew he could be. Although the first time she had seen him he had been even more casually dressed, she remembered, with splodges of paint on his shirt and skin, and impatient at being interrupted by a nuisance client who hadn't bothered to make an appointment.

She hadn't realized she had been staring at him until he spoke.

'Have I got a smudge on my nose or something?'

She felt herself blush. 'I was just thinking how easy it is to get a wrong impression of people. There's always more than one side to everything, isn't there?'

'I'm not sure what I'm supposed to make of that remark, but we'd better line up, or Jim will be getting impatient. He's got a new wife and a cosy fireside to get back to later.'

It was a lovely image, and one that Jassy couldn't quite get out of her head as she listened to the balding Jim playing the piano so expertly. He wasn't as old as she had thought at first, probably in his mid-forties, and with a broad mid-Somerset accent that was sometimes difficult to follow.

Someone was handing out song sheets, and she took hers

automatically. The songs they were going to practise were all familiar Noel Coward ones she had heard on the wireless many times: *A room with a view*; *I'll see you again*; *I'll follow my secret heart*, and *Mad about the boy*. The sentiments were all romantic, and reinforced Jassy's guess that Esme would be hoping to sing a duet with William.

But before that, they had the initial warm-up Jim had referred to . . . Jassy had wondered if it was all going to be a session of *Doh – ray – me* up and down the scales, but instead, Jim started thumping the piano for *Knees up Mother Brown*. In Jassy's view it could hardly be called a warm-up session to lubricate their singing voices, but it certainly livened up the atmosphere, with a few of the older members putting actions to the words, and all of them ending up flushed and laughing.

'I told you it would be fun,' William whispered in her ear.

She wasn't sure he had used those words, but she was certainly enjoying it. And then, from being a pseudo pub piano player, Jim reverted to an exquisite rendition of *I'll see you again*. He played it unaccompanied at first, to let everyone get their breaths back, and so that they could read through the words silently to absorb the phrasing, and then he invited everyone to start singing.

Jassy was mightily impressed. They might be a totally amateur group in a sleepy little country village, but encouraged by a good pianist and voice coach, they could work magic. Jim was such an unlikely person for either of those things, but he clearly enjoyed what he was doing and had everyone's respect because of it, since he was the undoubted leader of the group.

Her heart jumped when she realized Jim was looking directly at her now.

'You've got a good voice, Jasmine. Would you like to try a few bars of the song on your own?'

'Oh, I don't think so,' she said in a mild panic. 'There's no point, really – as I said, I'm only here for a few days. I'm unlikely to come to the Monday Club again.'

'I'd still like to hear you sing solo, and I think we all would, wouldn't we?'

This wasn't fair! By appealing for the group's opinion, he

got their immediate assent, and before she knew what was happening, Jim had struck the opening chords of the song again, and unless she was going to stand there like a complete dummy, Jassy knew she had no option but to start singing. The music didn't stop after a few bars, and at the end of the song there was spontaneous applause.

'Beautiful,' Jim said. 'How about making it a duet, William? I know this is one you particularly like. Jasmine can sing the first two lines, then you do the next two in a lower key to suit your voice. She does the third part, and you harmonize the last section with Jasmine sticking to the melody. You'll see how it divides on the song sheets.'

'Look, I didn't expect to be doing this,' Jassy said, in a real panic now, and aware of the fury on Esme's face. 'You should give this to a regular member.'

Jim smiled. 'I suspect that you've found a few folk around here suspicious of strangers in their midst, Jasmine, but in this club we've always welcomed newcomers, especially those with talent. Give it a try. If you never come here again, at least we can have the benefit of hearing you and William sing together.'

She looked at William now. She couldn't tell from his expression whether he was pleased about this or not, but he wasn't objecting. And short of throwing a childish tantrum, she knew she had better agree. If it meant creating good village relations for as long as she were here, it would be worth it.

They moved to stand together in front of the group, and followed the instructions Jim had given them. It worked spectacularly well, and there was more applause at the end. One of the older ladies whispered in Jassy's ear, 'As well as being wonderful, you also saved William from Esme's unwanted attentions, dear, and I hope you'll be here often enough to join us on Mondays.'

She murmured that she didn't know about that, and then she felt William's hand press hers for a moment.

'My goodness, Miss Wyatt, you sang those words as if you almost meant them,' he said, half-mockingly. 'Well done.'

If that was praise, it didn't sit too well with her, and then he turned away and discussed some of the finer points of the song with Jim, virtually ignoring her. Esme sashayed across to her, smiling sweetly, the smile of a crocodile. Jassy got the ridiculous phrase out of her head and smiled back.

'You've got a nice little voice, Jasmine. How long are you staying?'

'Not long – this time.'

She didn't know why she'd said it in that airy fashion, but she didn't miss the narrowing of Esme's eyes.

'You've been left Blackthorn Cottage, I hear. Do you know it has a bad reputation?'

'Such things don't worry me, Esme. Besides, I don't believe houses can have bad reputations. It's only people who give it a bad name, and I think the cottage is absolutely beautiful.'

'Oh well, people who live in cities often think that until they move to the country, thinking it's such a wonderful life. Most of them get bored very quickly, and they never stay long.'

'Really?' Jassy wasn't going to rise to such unsubtle bait, and merely stared back at the girl unblinkingly.

'Come on, everybody,' Jim called out. 'There's time enough for gossiping, and I've got a home to go to, if the rest of you haven't.'

They reverted to what they were here for, and Esme was given the solo of *Mad about the boy*, which was just perfect for her, Jassy thought in amusement, since it enabled her to be provocative towards William while she was singing, which went down well with the members, since it gave added punch to the song.

She had a good voice, Jassy conceded, and no doubt when it came to any show the Monday Club put on later in the year, she would probably be singing the duet with William too, since Jassy would be long gone by then. It gave her an unexpected twist of envy to think of it. She had enjoyed it, she admitted.

When the group broke up, she and William walked back to the village companionably. He insisted on seeing her right back to his aunt's home, and said he might as well come in for a cup of something before going back to his own house.

'Singing is thirsty work, isn't it?' he said.

119

'It certainly is, and it was fun too, just as you said. But I wish I hadn't been pushed into doing the duet with you. There's no point really, is there?'

'I thought there was every point, especially when the words are so apt. We haven't known one another very long, Jassy, but I'll remember this particular spring for a long time.'

'Why? Because you had such an annoying client?' she said with a laugh.

'Something like that.'

There was no reason to muse over what he had said, but the words of the song kept running through her head all night. They were still there when she told Mrs Lester she was heading for the cottage that morning to put some of her new purchases in place.

'I'll buy a pie in the village and have it for my lunch,' she said, 'so don't worry if you don't see me again until this afternoon.'

'There's no need for you to buy anything, my dear. Once I've gone down to open up the post office, you can make yourself a sandwich to take with you, and anything else that you please. While you're here, I want you to feel at home.'

She was so nice, thought Jasmine, doing exactly as she was told once she was alone in the flat. It wasn't home, but she was made very welcome. She glanced out of the window as she was ready to leave, and caught sight of William striding across the green to the small building that she now knew was the estate agent's office.

As if he knew he was being watched he looked up and waved, and she automatically waved back, feeling her heart lurch absurdly as she did so. It was absurd, because he meant nothing to her, other than as a business acquaintance, but the words of that wretched song were still spinning around in her head. 'I'll see you again . . .'

Mad, she thought. Completely mad. The sweet memories between herself and William were non-existent, and destined to remain so – unless Jim Granger had his way and she remained in Horton, and the song she and William had sung together became firmly on the agenda. But she wasn't, and it wouldn't, and she turned away from the window in frustration and annoyance, and determinedly put her sandwiches and a piece of Mrs Lester's fruit cake into a paper bag.

She rammed a straw hat on her head to keep off the sun that was quite strong today, and set out for Blackthorn Cottage, deliberately keeping the words of *Knees up Mother Brown* in her head to ward off that other one.

By now she knew people, and people knew her, and she passed the time of day with quite a number of them on that Tuesday morning. She didn't plan on doing any painting today. She intended to hang her new curtains and put the new covers on the old cushions, throw out the old pots and pans, and replace them with her gleaming new ones.

She looked around her with great satisfaction and pride when it was all done. She was surprisingly hungry, and it was time for her sandwiches. She put out a chair at the front of the cottage and with the hum of insects and twittering of birds, she could almost imagine it was a summer picnic. The only drawback was the state of the garden in front of her, and when she had finished eating, she decided she was definitely going to tackle the weeds. They were so high and so thick it spoiled the look of the cottage, and all the tools she needed were in the small outhouse.

An hour later she was hacking away with a spade when she heard the sound of a motor bike approaching. For a moment she wondered if it was Ted's mode of transport, and although she had practically given up on the idea, wondered if he had some time off and had come to offer to help with the interior painting after all. The motor bike slowed down, and she shielded her eyes against the sun to see the rider.

And then she dropped her spade in shock, her heart beating so fast it made her head spin.

'Hello babe,' the man said easily. 'Found you at last.'

'*Freddie!*' Jasmine stuttered. 'What are you doing here?'

He got off his machine and came walking towards her. He was every bit as dashing as ever, and she felt her mouth go dry at the unexpected sight of him.

'It took a while to find out where this blasted cottage is,

but I had a bit of time off, so I thought I'd come and look you up. Nice place you've got, kid, courtesy of old man Devenish. I always thought he took a real shine to you.'

'Don't be so daft. He was old enough to be my grandfather.'

Freddie Patterson laughed. 'When did that ever put a bloke off? When I'm too old to stop looking, they can put me in my box.'

Jassy didn't like what he was implying, especially as Giles Devenish had always been impeccably polite towards her, but silver-tongued or not, Freddie had always had a crude streak about him as well. She decided it was best to ignore it.

'How's your wife?' she said pointedly instead. 'I presume she *is* your wife by now?'

He shook his head. 'Didn't work out, babe. That's why I thought I'd come and find you. We always had something going for us, didn't we?'

He was so arrogant it took her breath away. To think she had loved him with all the sweet passion of a young girl's heady first love. At the time she thought he had broken her heart, but clearly he hadn't, because she was still here, still breathing, and still furious with him for deceiving her – and his real sweetheart – the way he had. A man like that didn't deserve a second chance, and if he thought she was going to forget all the heartache he had caused her, he could think again.

He was leaning on the fence now, clearly expecting her to invite him inside. When she didn't move, seemingly transfixed, he shrugged and nodded towards the patch of weeds she had hardly disturbed as yet.

'You need a real gardener to tackle that little lot. I've got a couple of hours to spare, so how about if I give you a hand?'

'It's all right, I can manage,' she said jerkily, wondering how something that had once seemed so magical could seem so shabby now. He had done that to her, she thought bitterly, demoralizing her with his lies.

'Come on, Jassy, there's no need to be stand offish. I'm only offering a bit of help from an old friend,' he said coaxingly. 'I won't try anything on, honest!'

He had come nearer, and he was still as charismatic as ever with his tousled hair and bohemian clothes and leather gloves. He picked up the fallen spade and told her he wouldn't say no to a cold drink, and he promised to stay outside while she fetched it. Making her feel foolish, idiotic, as if she wouldn't be able to trust him – or herself – if they went inside the cottage together.

She turned abruptly, and once inside the cottage she shut the door firmly, her hands trembling. She leaned against the door for some minutes until her heartbeats settled down. It wasn't that she had feelings for him any more. It was more the shock of seeing him like this, and even more so, the shock of realizing that, shameful though it was, she had still been harbouring thoughts of him all this time, and now there was nothing. She had no feelings towards him at all.

She poured him a glass of cold water, since she had nothing else to offer, and went back outside with it. His skill as a gardener was evident, because in so short a time, he had already hacked a way through the jungle of weeds. She walked through the long grass towards him, and then gave a yelp of horror as something jumped in front of her, brushing against her leg as it did so. Then there was another, and another . . . the glass of water dropped from her hands, and she was trembling for a different reason now.

Freddie came across to her in a moment, taking her in his arms as she tried to fend him off. He was laughing, she thought wildly. He was actually *laughing* at her now.

'I don't know what you find so funny,' she yelled. 'Something leapt up at me, and if there are unmentionable *things* in this garden, I'm not stepping out here again until this lot's cleared.'

'You'd better let me stay and do it for you, then,' he said, still laughing, still holding her tight. 'But before you start imagining the worst, it was only a couple of frogs. They're good for the garden, and they won't hurt you.'

'They might not hurt me, but I don't fancy finding any more of them,' Jassy yelled, still not convinced it wasn't something even worse.

'Look, darling, I'm quite willing to clear this garden for you in return for a few smiles and a cup of tea. No strings, honest!'

It was tempting. The frogs had shaken her more than she realized. She couldn't help remembering that old folk song about an English country garden harbouring all kinds of horrid things that slithered and stung in the undergrowth. She just hadn't thought about them being here!

'All right,' she muttered, finally shaking herself out of Freddie Patterson's clinging arms. 'But no funny business, mind. This is strictly a friend doing me a favour.'

She was probably being churlish, but as he grinned and gave her a mock salute, she knew he was thick-skinned enough not to notice. And it was a relief to sit outside near her front door and watch an expert at work. She didn't want him to do anything other than clear all the weeds. There would be time enough later to decide what she wanted to plant there. But she might have known Freddie would have his own ideas about that.

'Have you got a plan for the garden?' he asked later, the professional in him coming to the fore when the patch of garden looked amazingly cleared now, and much larger than when the weeds had encroached on it.

'Good Lord no, I haven't thought that far ahead. I'll just put in some shrubs and flowers that will come up every year,' she said vaguely.

'Perennials,' he said approvingly. 'I can help you if you like, bring you down some catalogues and so on.'

'That won't be necessary, Freddie. I don't actually live here, and I don't know how often I shall be here. I can't make any plans like that.'

Nor did she want him to keep turning up, she thought in a panic. Although she had to admit it had been good to see him again, because now she knew for certain that he was part of her past, and she wanted to keep him there.

'Well, that's a pity,' he said with a shrug. 'We had something good once, didn't we, girl?'

'That was before I knew I wasn't your only girl,' Jassy snapped.

'I told you, that's finished, so there's nothing stopping you and me getting together again, is there?'

She had brought him out a cup of tea, and as he removed his gloves to take it, something glinted in the sunlight, something that hadn't been evident before.

'Isn't that a wedding ring on your finger?' she said coldly.
He sighed, but he was as brash as ever. 'All right, so
you've caught me out, but you can't blame a chap for trying,
can you, Jassy? So how about a kiss for old times' sake
before I go on my way?'

He was the giddy limit, but despite herself, Jassy found
herself smiling at his cheek. For all his rough and ready
charm he meant nothing to her any more, and perhaps it had
taken this encounter to finally know it.

'No thanks,' she said airily. 'But you can give me a lift
back to the village on your motor bike if you like. I'm staying
with an elderly aunt for a few days.'

If anything would put him off, that would! And keeping
things light was by far the best way of dealing with philan-
derer Freddie.

She managed to ease him away from the cottage, and
perched gingerly on the back of his motor bike. This had
been fun in the old days . . . and spinning along the lanes
towards Horton gave her the same kind of thrill it had done
then, but not for the same reason. Clinging to Freddie's back
was done out of necessity and common sense, not out of
adoration. He roared the engine a few times when they
reached the village green, which alerted people to their arrival.
He grabbed Jassy's hand before she could get away, and
before she knew what he was going to do he had pressed it
to his lips in an old-fashioned gesture.

'You should have been the lady of the manor when old
Devenish was alive, doll,' he said mockingly. 'You'd have
fitted the part well. Enjoy your country cottage!'

He was gone before she could give him a smart answer
to his snide remark, and she marched across the green to the
post office, very aware of the looks she was getting, and the
fact that William was just leaving his office and must have
seen her unorthodox arrival too.

Eleven

An old friend?' William remarked as they neared one another.

'He was a gardener at the Devenish estate when I worked there. He knew about the cottage, of course, so he thought he'd come and look me up, and he actually did me a favour at the same time, by clearing the front garden.'

She didn't have to explain anything to him, and nor had she needed to sound so quick and defensive. Did he think she had no friends? Men friends in particular? Despite what she thought of Freddie's continuing deceit, it wouldn't hurt William Hedges to know that her world didn't begin and end in Horton, even if his did. But if she had expected some reaction from him, she was disappointed. He merely nodded and said he'd see her around.

He didn't say 'I'll be seeing you', she noted, hardly knowing why the words came into her mind. Except that it was the song they had sung together at the Monday Club. The song she hadn't been able to get out of her mind at first, and now it would be stuck there again, she thought crossly.

She strode on towards the post office with her chin in the air, wondering why men had to be so complicated. And there was no reason for *that* thought, either!

Of course, Mrs Lester had seen her on the back of Freddie's motor bike as well, and since her hostess had become the kind of confidante Jassy would have wished her mother to be, that evening she told her a little about him, and how he had come to be in Horton that day.

'I really thought I loved him once,' she added with a sigh, 'but you never really know people, do you? They always hide something of themselves, and what you do find out isn't always as savoury as you'd like it to be.'

126

She had spoken without thinking, and she saw the concern on Mrs Lester's face now.

'My goodness, Jasmine, he wasn't a criminal, was he?'

'Oh no, it was nothing like that, although in my eyes it was just as bad. He was practically engaged to another girl at the time he pretended to be in love with me, and even today, he said it was all over until I noticed the wedding ring on his finger. He's a rat, and I know I'm well out of it.'

'But you still have some feelings for him?'

'I honestly thought I did, until today. In fact, I'm glad he turned up, because now I know I definitely don't. So he did me two favours. He cleared my front garden, and he showed me what a fool I'd been all this time, still thinking of him.'

She smiled as she said it, knowing it was true. Holding on to something in the past that could never be revived was a waste of energy and emotion. She wished her father could see that after his long futile time of pining for her mother. You never forgot people, but you had to put them in their proper place in your lives, and Freddie was now firmly in the past, she thought, her heart lightening.

'You're bound to find a nice young man soon, Jassy,' Mrs Lester said reassuringly. 'You're a lovely young girl, and I'm surprised they're not chasing you to your door.'

Jassy laughed. 'Well, they're not, and I'm not really looking. In fact, I think it may be my sister who has found her one-and-only, not me.'

'Oh?' Mrs Lester said, perking up. A bit of healthy gossip never came amiss, and they spent the next half hour cheerfully discussing the pros and cons of Grace Wyatt marrying Doctor Alec Macleod.

Ted turned up while they were still contemplating how such a marriage would affect Jassy's father, and whether or not he could still be persuaded to come down to Horton for a stay at Blackthorn Cottage.

'I hear you had company at the cottage today,' he announced to Jassy.

'Good Lord, it doesn't take long for news to spread, does it?'

He smirked. 'I called in on William on the way here. Boyfriend, is it?'

His mother intervened. 'Ted, if you've just come here to be nosey, I'm sure Jasmine has better things to do than explain her business to you.'

That was rich, coming from her, thought Jassy, hiding a smile, but she answered Ted quickly.

'He's an old *friend*, and I've known him a long time,' she said. 'He cleared the garden for me which saves me a job I wasn't relishing. Is there anything else you'd like to know?'

'Yes. If you still want any help with painting the interior of the cottage I'm free tomorrow evening, and the dance is on Friday, so how about it?'

It was hard to say who was the most surprised, Jassy or his mother. It was common knowledge that Ted never went anywhere near Blackthorn Cottage if he could help it, and here he was, offering to go inside it and help paint the walls.

'Are you sure about this?' she said awkwardly, not wanting to let him know how very aware she was of it all.

'About holding you to the promise of the dance – you bet I am!'

'No, about helping me paint the cottage.'

'I've said so, so do we have a deal?'

His mother recovered from her surprise and added her piece.

'I think I'll come with you if Jasmine has no objection. I can be chief tea-maker while you two get on with the work, and I'd like to see how it's looking now with the new furnishings.'

Ted gave a short laugh, seeing right through her. 'There's no need to babysit me, Mother. I'm not going to throw a fit and imagine I'm seeing things. That's long past, and I'm a big boy now, in case you hadn't noticed.'

They had both noticed, and Jassy hoped it wasn't going to cause any trouble, hardly able to miss the way he was looking at her. Reminding her of Freddie . . . and she groaned. Ted had experienced one terrible incident at her cottage, and it would be disastrous if he started flirting with her and got upset and angry when she rebuffed him outright. She had no idea how vulnerable he could still be underneath his boastful outer skin. So she welcomed his mother's suggestion.

128

'I'd like your mother to come as well, Ted. She's had a hand in making the cottage look nice, so fair's fair, isn't it?'

For a minute she thought he was going to give a little boy scowl, but then he shrugged and said he supposed it would be all right. His mother overlooked his grudging acceptance and when she mentioned she'd bake one of his favourite lemon cakes for a snack to keep up their energy, he became more amiable again.

'It never fails,' Mrs Lester said, when he'd gone. 'There's plenty of truth in the old saying about reaching a man through his stomach – or some such!'

As Jassy laughed, she couldn't help wondering if that was why she had promised to make the same meal for next Sunday when her dad and Grace came down to fetch her, since Owen had enjoyed her cooking so much. There was definitely a sense of harmony between them, and it was so lovely to see her father relax with a woman of his own age ... Jassy dismissed the way her thoughts were going. It was none of her business, but she couldn't help indulging in a delicious little bit of 'what if?' ...

The two women set out early the next evening, having arranged for Ted to meet them at the cottage. He was late, and his mother voiced her misgivings.

'I hope he hasn't had second thoughts about coming. It was a real breakthrough to hear him say he agreed to help you, Jasmine.'

'He hasn't really believed that the cottage was jinxed all this time, has he?'

'I don't know. Of course it was a terrible thing to happen to him when he found that couple, but it was one bad incident over heaven knows how many years. The cottage has been lived in since then, and I always thought it a shame to let it stand empty for as long as it has. Personally, I always loved it.'

'Did you?' Jassy was startled to hear a wistful note in her voice now.

Mrs Lester gave a small sigh. 'When my husband was alive the bluebell wood behind the cottage was one of our favourite walks, and we sometimes imagined ourselves living here – so now you'll know why I was so keen to help you, and you'll probably think me a sentimental old fool!'

'I don't think that at all,' Jassy said softly. 'I think it's a lovely story.'

So she was play-acting too, just the way Jassy always felt in making this pretty cottage a happy place for caring tenants, whoever they were.

By the time Ted finally arrived, they had got out the paint-brushes and whitewash, and moved the furniture out of the way, ready to start on the walls. He stood perfectly still for a moment before he came right inside. Nothing could possibly resemble the way it had been on that terrible day so long ago, but this was clearly a rite of passage for him, and neither woman made any comment.

'The front garden looks better now it's cleared,' he said at last 'Whoever did it made a good job of it. I thought I was in the wrong place for a minute.'

'The friend who did it for me is a professional gardener,' Jassy said quickly. 'He worked on the Devenish estate, as I did.'

'Well, this is a man's job too,' he said, coming forward and taking the paintbrush from his mother. 'I thought you said you were going to be chief tea-maker, Mum, and if you forgot to make that lemon cake you promised, I'm going right back out of here again. That's the only thing I came for.'

If it was his way of saving face, it didn't matter. He was here, and he was a reasonable hand with a paintbrush, and a long while later, when they were replete with tea and cake, they all hoped that the ghosts had finally gone.

'I've been an idiot about this place, haven't I?' he said suddenly. 'But it's all over now, so I shall claim my reward. Don't forget your promise, Jasmine. I'll pick you up at seven thirty on Friday night. Now I'm off. Me and the boys have got a card game lined up for later tonight.'

His mother wisely kept her own counsel about his last remark, and she gave a huge sigh of relief when she and Jasmine were getting ready to leave the cottage.

'Well, that couldn't have gone any better, could it? And I've got you to thank for it, my dear.'

Jassy shook her head. 'Ted deserves the credit himself, not me.'

'But if he hadn't taken such a shine to you, he'd never have agreed to come here.'

'Well, I hope it's not too much of a shine,' Jassy said in alarm. 'I'm just being friendly, that's all.'

And if Ted thought there was anything else in it, she'd be sure to tell him there was someone else in her life. Even if she had to elaborate on the relationship between herself and Freddie Patterson ... and if he wanted confirmation, she could always refer him to William, who had seen her arrive back at Horton on the back of Freddie's motor bike. Although there was no reason on earth why she should have to justify herself to someone who was no more than a casual acquaintance, besides being William Hedges's sort-of cousin.

When Friday came, she found she was looking forward to the dance. She had been back and forth to the cottage a few times now, and managed to fork over the front garden now that it was free of weeds, with no danger of frogs leaping about and startling her. She was going to plant some shrubs and roses that would hopefully thrive and appear every year.

By now, she knew she was in danger of falling in love with the cottage and with Horton too, and she was still trying to keep an open mind about everything. She was seeing it at its best, and the cottage wouldn't be such an attractive proposition in midwinter when it snowed, or was lashed by rain and wind. It would definitely be *Hansel and Gretel* time then! But she wasn't thinking of that tonight. Tonight she was wearing her prettiest dress, she had tied a ribbon in her hair, and was awaiting Ted's arrival.

When the allotted time had come and gone, she was starting to feel impatient, and his mother said wryly that he had a habit of being late for everything. Half an hour later it was William who came into the flat, still wearing his office attire, despite the hour.

'Mrs Cooper had just phoned my office to see if I was there, so it's a good thing I was catching up on some paperwork. She didn't want to alarm you by phoning you, Aunt Kate, and she assured me it's nothing serious, but Ted's had an accident on the tractor and he's slashed his arm quite badly.'

Mrs Lester gave a gasp, and Jassy squeezed her hand as William went on quickly.

'He's all right, Aunt Kate, truly. The Coopers took him to hospital and he's had his arm stitched. They would have kept him in but you know Ted. He insisted on going back to the farm. The doctor gave him some sedatives, so I daresay he's sleeping it off by now. He sent a message to say he's sorry about the dance, Jassy.'

He had been talking solely to his aunt, but now he looked at Jassy properly for the first time, taking in the soft blue dress, the matching ribbon in her hair, and the subtle make-up she had applied. She felt her heart thump as she saw the flicker of something that was definitely not the antagonism that had been between them at the start.

'I must go to him,' his mother said, breaking into Jassy's spinning thoughts. 'I must see for myself that my boy's all right. You'll take me, won't you, William? It's a pity about the dance, Jasmine, but I'm sure you won't want to go by yourself. Another time, maybe.'

By the time she had finished talking, she was already halfway out of the room to fetch her coat. William looked at Jassy again.

'It is a shame about the dance,' he said. 'But Ted wouldn't be much good with his arm in a sling, anyway.'

'Can I come with you to see that he's all right?' Jassy said huskily. 'I can't just sit here twiddling my thumbs all evening.'

'Of course you can, dear,' Mrs Lester said as she came back into the room. 'Ted will be touched that you're concerned about him.'

Jassy looked away, not wanting her to think there was anything more than general concern for a young man who had had an accident.

It was Jassy's second visit to Coopers' Farm. Nobody had said very much in the car, but Mrs Cooper assured them that since it had happened while Ted was in their employ, they would give him every care. He wouldn't expect to stay at his mother's flat, as Jassy had been half expecting, wondering

132

if she should offer to move out. Though where she would have gone, she didn't know. But it seemed it wouldn't be necessary. Ted was firmly entrenched at the farm, and it was more home to him now than the village.

It was as William had told them. Ted was already in bed and sedated, his heavily bandaged arm in a sling on top of the bedcovers. He opened his eyes briefly, and managed to slur a few words to his visitors.

'Don't worry about me, Mum. It's only a scratch and Mrs Cooper will look after me. It could have been a lot worse, but they say the devil looks after his own, don't they?'

'Oh, don't say such things, Ted,' his mother admonished him.

He gave her a weak grin and glanced at Jassy.

'Sorry about the dance. Get old William to take you instead.'

His words tapered off and he was asleep, so there was nothing else for them to do but have a cup of tea with the Coopers and go back to the village.

'Why don't you do what Ted said, William?' his aunt said.

'What was that?'

'You know very well what it was. Take Jasmine to the dance. She was looking forward to it, and it would be a shame for her to miss it. I can easily walk back from the village hall.'

Jassy felt her face go hot, embarrassed that everyone was looking at her now.

'Really, it doesn't matter. It's a bit late, anyway, and I wouldn't want to put William to any trouble. I'm sure he's got better things to do this evening.'

'No, I haven't,' he said abruptly. 'If you don't mind waiting while I have a quick wash and shave and change my clothes, we'll go.'

This evening was developing in the strangest way, Jassy reflected, and she wasn't sure she even wanted to go to the dance with William. But she could hardly refuse now without inventing a sudden headache, and how corny would that be! If she believed in fate – which of course she did – she would think that fate was determined to throw her and William Hedges together, whether she wanted such a thing to happen or not. She didn't, of course . . .

She hadn't been inside his house before, but his aunt assured them both she would happily walk home from there, and that she needed the fresh air to calm her down after seeing Ted in such a state.

'You two enjoy yourselves, and if I'm in bed when you get back, Jasmine, make yourself a hot drink or whatever you like, and just feel at home. I shall be perfectly all right on my own.'

William assured her it was the way his aunt preferred to be. She might have a little weep over Ted's injury, but she would want no one to see it but herself. So if she didn't want to appear completely churlish and ungrateful, Jassy had no option but to accept William's offer to take her to the dance.

So now she was waiting for him to get ready. It felt odd to be in someone's house when they weren't there, seeing the way he arranged his furniture, the photographs on the mantelpiece that were mostly of his family and his horse, the pictures on his walls, the books in his bookcase, the magazines he read . . . it was a strange kind of intimacy to absorb it all, and to realize that the man who lived here was a tidy man without being obsessively so; a man who cared for family connections and animals; a man who should be married with a family of his own.

'So let's go and enjoy ourselves,' he said, his voice making her jump, not having heard him come downstairs and enter the living-room.

She gulped. He looked – gorgeous, was the only word that entered her head at that moment, wearing a light grey suit and a white shirt and dark blue tie. Complementing her outfit, she thought in confusion.

'It's not far, but I'd hate to see you fall over in those shoes, so we'll take the car. We don't want to risk another accident tonight,' he went on.

She had to agree with that. She didn't know how much dancing she was ready to do, either, let alone with William Hedges. With Ted, it would have been somehow impersonal. With William, it could never be. She was aware of a different kind of tension between them now, and put it down to the fact that they had both experienced different emotions already that evening. She tried to tell herself it was just an evening dance in a village hall and she might as well enjoy it.

It was in full swing by the time they arrived. She knew a few of the young people there now, and since no one had expected her to be with Ted, no one seemed surprised to see her with William. Why should anyone care . . . except for the jealous flash in someone's eyes on the far side of the room.

'I see Esme's here,' she said casually.

'Esme's always here,' William told her. 'Her father organizes the dances and acts as MC.'

'If you want to have a dance with her, I won't mind.'

'Why would I want to do that? You're the one I came with, not Esme. I can see her any time, but you're a bit like a beautiful butterfly, and I never know when you're going to flit away again.'

'Yes, you do. It's on Sunday,' Jassy said. 'Dad and Grace are coming to fetch me in the afternoon.'

He caught hold of her hand and drew her on to the dance floor as the band began to play a waltz. 'Then I shall have to make the most of you, won't I?'

Probably out of pique, Esme Dunn seemed to decide to ignore the two of them, and threw herself enthusiastically into dancing with various partners all evening. It was a mixture of old-time dances and waltzes to allow people to get their breaths back, and almost before they knew it, the band was playing a last waltz, and then it was *God save the king* and time to go home.

'Did you enjoy it?' William asked as he drove her back to the village.

'You don't need to ask. It was a lovely evening, and although it took poor Ted's accident to bring it about, I'm really glad you asked me, William, even if your Aunt Kate did rather push you into it.'

'Oh, I don't need my aunt to push me into anything I want to do.'

She was digesting this when she realized they had driven the short distance back to the village and he was getting out of the car to open her door for her.

'I'll walk you to the flat,' he said

'Really, there's no need.'

'It's what a gentleman does after taking a pretty girl out for the evening, so no arguments, please. Sometimes I think you must be the most argumentative girl in creation!'

'Sorry,' she said meekly.

'And don't apologize,' he said perversely. 'It doesn't become you. I much prefer the feisty Jassy to the docile one.'

It was amazing that he preferred either of them, she thought dryly. She still thought of herself as a thorn in his flesh, although she had to admit that during this evening, the necessary closeness between them had been more than agreeable. She really *had* enjoyed herself, and, guiltily, she was sure that neither of them had given Ted a single thought as they danced the evening away. She would make up for it tomorrow by sending him a card to wish him well.

'Thank you again, William,' she said awkwardly as they reached the post office. 'I've had a lovely evening.'

'Aunt Kate said something about making yourself a hot drink, didn't she? I'm sure she meant to include me in the invitation.'

'Don't you have a home to go to?' Jassy said, starting to laugh.

'Yes, but I'm sure you wouldn't turn me away on a cold and frosty night, would you?' he said mockingly.

Considering it was late spring and the evening was balmy, he was hardly going to suffer from the cold on his short distance home. But she couldn't rebuff him without sounding like a prim Victorian maiden, either. He followed her upstairs to the flat, and she shushed him for fear of waking his aunt. She felt oddly nervous as she went into the tiny kitchen, as if she was inviting a man into her own rooms late at night, and she had only done that once before.

That occasion had been in her room on the Devenish estate, and the man in question had been her would-be lover, Freddie Patterson. It had all ended with a kind of pseudo-erotic wrestling match between them. Thankfully, as it turned out, she had won, and her honour was intact.

'I'll have cocoa, please.'

She jumped as she heard William's voice right behind her

and her hands fumbled with the cocoa tin. He took it from her and put it down on the table while she set out two cups and saucers on a tray.

'Why are you so nervous, Jassy? I'm not going to seduce you.'

'You'd better not try!' she flashed at him. 'And I'm not nervous at all. It's probably the reaction after this strange evening that's making my hands shake. Poor Ted, and all that,' she finished lamely. 'I thought you'd have spared a thought for him too.'

'I have been. I've been thanking him for being such a damn idiot and getting his arm caught the way he did, so that I had the chance to take out his girl instead.'

Jassy was too busy watching the milk in the saucepan and moving it off the gas before it boiled over, to really heed what he was saying. She made the cocoa, and when she registered his words, she flushed.

'You've got two things wrong there. Nobody's an idiot for hurting themselves, and I'm not his girl.'

'Oh no, that's right,' William said, taking the tray of cocoa into the living-room. 'You're my young lady, aren't you? Or so Mrs Cooper believes.'

She stared at him unblinkingly as they sat on opposite sides of the fireplace. 'Do you make a habit of tormenting all your lady clients, or is it just me?'

'Just you,' he said. He drained his cocoa, making her think he must have a cast iron stomach to drink it so hot, and then he stood up to leave.

He put out his hand and drew her to her feet.

'I also wanted to thank you for being such a delightful companion this evening, Jassy, and to end it in the proper manner.'

Before she could guess what he was going to do he had pulled her into his arms and pressed a demanding kiss on her lips. Even if she had wanted to pull away from him, she was being held too tightly. The masculine scent of him was in her nostrils, the roughness of his skin against hers an excitement she hadn't expected. And in an instant, she knew she didn't want to pull away. Where she was right now, was exactly where she wanted to be.

'Goodnight, Jasmine,' he finally said gravely, as he let her go. 'Sleep tight, and prepare for the onslaught tomorrow.'

She blinked as he let her go, wondering if he had any idea of the tumult going on inside her as the result of that kiss.

'What onslaught?' she stammered.

'It's May Day, in case you hadn't noticed. The whole village will be out to watch the schoolkids dance around the maypole. It'll be just the usual rustic affair, but I think even a city girl will find it entertaining.'

He gave her a mock bow and then he was gone, leaving her fuming. Leaving her with a furious sense of let down. Why did he have to say such stupid things, just when they had shared a lovely evening together, and she was starting to reverse everything she had ever thought about him? Just when she was in great danger of falling in love with him . . . if she hadn't done so already. But it wasn't part of the plan. It definitely wasn't part of the plan.

Twelve

'Did you have a good time last night?' Mrs Lester said companionably at breakfast. 'I must say you look a little tired this morning, Jasmine.'

That could be because she hadn't slept much, trying to sort out her turbulent feelings. But that was something she was keeping to herself. There was only one person she might feel able to confide in, and that was Grace, and Grace wouldn't be here until tomorrow.

'It was fun, Mrs Lester, and I understand that today is going to be a special one for the village too.'

'Goodness me, yes, and what with all the fuss over Ted last night, I'd almost forgotten it. The local school children always put on a display of dancing and singing around the maypole on the nearest Saturday to May Day, and it's fortunate that this year it falls on the very day. It's a pity your folks couldn't be here a day early too. I daresay you won't have seen anything quite like it before.'

'Oh, I think all infant and junior schools celebrate May Day in the same way. I remember in my school playground we always practised dancing around the maypole and the parents were invited to come and watch.'

It was always just her father and her Aunt Lucy in her case . . .

'We're not so different then, are we?' Mrs Lester went on. 'We'll be having a huge village tea party on the green on the day of the Coronation as well. Whatever you're doing by then, Jasmine dear, I hope you'll find time to join us.'

'Well, as it's only twelve days away now, it might be a good excuse to persuade Dad to come and stay with me at the cottage for a week or two then. It would give him something to look forward to.'

The smiles they exchanged were happy ones, each with their own thoughts. Jassy was sure Mrs Lester wouldn't be averse to Owen spending some time in Horton and joining in the festivities to celebrate King George the Sixth's Coronation, and she wasn't averse to spending more time here, either. She told herself firmly that it had nothing to do with William Hedges and that kiss that she couldn't forget. Not much, anyway.

She wondered how things would be between them when they met again. He'd had to go and spoil it last night with his little bit of mockery, of course, but after what his aunt had told her, she was beginning to think it was a kind of defence mechanism, not allowing himself to get too attached to any woman after the death of the girl he had loved. He and Owen were alike in that respect, Jassy thought suddenly. She had never been so aware of it before. But her father had carried his grief for far too long, and seemed unable to let it go, while William was surely too young and personable and virile to let it ruin his whole life.

She blinked as her thoughts ran on. Someone had been talking to her for the last few minutes, and she hadn't heard a word that had been said.

'I'm sorry, Mrs Lester. It was very rude of me, but my head was in the clouds just then. What were you saying?'

'I said, why don't you ask your father tomorrow about coming down to stay, Jasmine? Strike while the iron's hot, as the saying goes. When he sees how smart the cottage is looking now, I'm sure he'll be more agreeable to taking some time off from that shop of his.'

'I think you may be right.'

And if a certain postmistress cooked his favourite meal again, and he saw how relaxing it was here, Jassy had every hope that he would say yes. Two successive Sundays away from the city, and anyone would relish good clean country air. Even the earthiness of the farmyards was honest and healthy compared with some of the smells that wafted in from the River Avon as the summer grew hotter.

But first there was today to get through. The post office would be closed in the afternoon, and there was a huge amount of activity going on all morning as the local teachers and their helpers arrived in lorries to put out folding chairs and benches for the spectators.

'Do you think they'd object if I offered to help?' Jassy asked Mrs Lester.

'I'm sure they'd be more than pleased, dear. You go along and ask, and I'm going to phone the Coopers to see if I can speak to Ted and find out how he is.'

'Good idea,' murmured Jassy, having completely forgotten him for the moment. She stepped out on to the green, feeling the morning sun on her face, and caught the glance of a young woman about her own age.

'Hello,' the woman said. 'I saw you in church last Sunday. You're the new owner of Blackthorn Cottage, aren't you?'

Jasmine didn't bother asking her how she knew. By now, it was immaterial to wonder how news of her arrival and the reason why she was here had filtered through every cottage in Horton and beyond. It was the way of small communities. She smiled back.

'That's right. I'm Jasmine Wyatt, and if you want any help with today's preparations, count me in.'

'I won't say no. I'm Daphne Smith, a local schoolteacher, and partly responsible for the way the youngsters perform today.' She gave a small grimace. 'I just hope none of them get cold feet and go off bawling to their mothers in the middle of it all. They're all very young and nervous as well as being excited, and it can only take a glimpse of a doting parent to start them off,' she added cheerfully.

Jasmine laughed. 'It sounds as if you enjoy it, though.'

'If I didn't, you wouldn't catch me working with kids.'

She was putting chairs in rows all the time she was talking, and Jassy found herself doing likewise.

'What about you?' Daphne said next. 'Didn't I hear that you worked on some big estate or other before you inherited Blackthorn Cottage? Nothing stays a secret for very long around here, by the way.'

'So I've noticed. But you're right again. It was on the Giles Devenish estate, and I catalogued Mr Devenish's books, which probably sounds pretty boring, but actually it wasn't.'

Daphne straightened up. 'You're not looking for another job, are you? We're badly in need of a school secretary since our Miss Oldfield died, and she was about ninety-two by then! We've been muddling along ever since, but it's a full-time job looking after the infants without having to organize the job of ordering books and all the general requirements of a village school as well. If you're interested I'm sure our head teacher would be thrilled to meet somebody with your experience.'

'Whoa, slow down!' Jassy laughed as she paused for breath.

'Sorry,' Daphne grinned. 'My enthusiasm tends to get the better of me sometimes.'

Which was probably what made her a wonderful teacher for the little ones, Jassy thought. But as for getting a job here . . .

'I'm afraid I'm not actually going to live in Blackthorn Cottage. Well, probably not. It's all up in the air at the moment, but I'm hoping my father will join me for a few weeks to recuperate. He had a mild heart scare a few weeks ago, but he's perfectly all right as long as he doesn't forget it!'

And Miss Daphne Smith probably knew all about that, anyway . . .

'I wouldn't mind betting that's just what he wants to do, Jasmine. Forget it, I mean, and not have people fuss over him. Sorry if I'm overstepping the mark by saying that.'

'You don't happen to know him, do you?' Jassy said with a grin.

They discovered an easy rapport between them, and if she ever did want a job here, Jasmine could think of nothing more enjoyable than working in an infant-cum-primary school with this outgoing young woman.

'I think we've done enough for now,' Daphne said eventually, when there were more helpers than necessary and they had begun to get in one another's way. 'Maybe I'll see you again this afternoon when the little dears come out to play. And keep in mind what I said about that job, Jasmine.'

She was keeping it in mind all afternoon while the green was miraculously turned into an outdoor stage with the children dressed in their Sunday best and doing their performance around the maypole. Several teachers, including Daphne Smith, started off the singing, clapping their hands and encouraging the children to keep in time as they performed the intricate movements that were simplified because of the young ages, as they wove in and out of the ribbons around the maypole.

'We don't have a May Queen in Horton,' Mrs Lester told Jassy. 'Since there are only very young children at school here, it was decided long ago that it would cause too much upset among the little girls for one of them to be chosen above the others.'

'Very wise,' Jassy agreed. 'Tell me, do you know Daphne Smith?'

'Yes, of course, and a very nice girl she is too. She went to the Monday Club a few times, but she lost interest. I think that little madam Esme probably upset her, as she manages to do with most people.'

'Daphne said something about a job at the school if I was interested.'

She shouldn't have mentioned it, since it wasn't going to happen, but she might have known Mrs Lester would leap on it.

'What a marvellous suggestion. You'd be perfect for it with your secretarial skills, Jasmine. Miss Oldfield's ideas were so out of date, and I'm sure she caused more of a muddle than anything else.'

'But I'm not staying,' Jassy said faintly, her voice almost lost in the sudden roar of applause as the afternoon's entertainment came to an end.

As everything began to break up, there was further chaos as children and parents were reunited, and the teams of teachers and helpers began to dismantle the maypole and to pack chairs and benches away into the waiting lorry. As Jassy and Mrs Lester made their way back to the flat, William came walking towards them across the green. He smelled of earth and fresh air.

Jassy had realized he wasn't among the crowds earlier or he would surely have joined them, but with so much going on she had forgotten he wasn't there. But now he was here, looking casually fresh and masculine and anxious to let his aunt know that Ted was recovering very fast.

'I've been at the farm all afternoon,' he told her. 'With Ted out of action for a couple of weeks, I need to go over there regularly to exercise Raven. I could ask one of the other lads to do it, but he's used to either me or Ted riding him, so I'll be there every evening until Ted's back to normal.'

'I couldn't get much sense out of him on the phone this morning. I think he'd only just woken up. So how is he really feeling now?' Ted's mother asked.

'Sore – and foolish, but with Mrs Cooper pampering him, I think he'll survive,' William said dryly. 'Sorry I missed today's event. Did it go well?'

From the innocent way he said it, Jassy suspected that he wasn't sorry at all. Watching infants prancing around a maypole probably wasn't his favourite way of having a good time.

'It was absolutely lovely,' she said, as if to make up for any lack of enthusiasm on his part as they walked back to the flat and went inside.

'And Jasmine was offered a job,' his aunt said, going to make the inevitable cup of tea for them all.

Jassy bit her lip. She hadn't intended mentioning it. It was never likely to happen, but she saw the spark of surprise in William's eyes and hastened to put him right.

'It was nothing. I was helping Daphne Smith in the preparations, and she said they're in need of a school secretary, that's all. I told her I probably didn't intend to live here, so that was the end of it.'

'That's a pity. I think you'd be good at it,' he said. 'Daphne's a shrewd judge of character, and I imagine you'd get on well with her.'

Mrs Lester poked her head back through the kitchen door. 'Jasmine would get on well with anybody, even someone as cantankerous as you, my lad,' she told William.

'Who says I'm cantankerous?' he began, and then smiled as the other two laughed. 'Seriously, though, Jassy, you might think about it if you decide to take up permanent residence in Horton.'

'I'm not, actually,' she said delicately. 'I do want to bring my dad down for a few weeks, and I may decide to stay a bit longer for the summer months. But after that, I've been thinking about advertising it for rent, either on a permanent basis, or for seasonal lets.'

His aunt dumped the heavy teapot on the table with a

bang. To Jassy it sounded like a reproach. But it was the obvious solution, and the one she had been keeping at the back of her mind all this time. If she didn't live in Blackthorn Cottage herself, and she didn't want to sell it, then if she rented it to suitable tenants, at least the property would still be hers, as Giles Devenish had intended.

'There goes your dream, Aunt Kate,' she heard William say lightly. 'Just as you were getting used to Jasmine being around, and able to pop in and out of Blackthorn Cottage any time you liked, she goes and throws a spanner in the works.'

'For heaven's sake, William,' his aunt said crossly. 'Jasmine has every right to do as she pleases with her property, and I'm glad to see she's thinking sensibly.'

All the same, Jassy had the uncomfortable feeling that neither of them was too pleased with her for what she had just said. But it didn't really have anything to do with them, she thought indignantly, even though she had grown quite fond of Mrs Lester, and she was sure the feeling was reciprocated. William shouldn't be too displeased, either, since he would find more business coming his way, advertising for new tenants for the very desirable, rural Blackthorn Cottage, surrounded by a bluebell wood, and in easy reach of every amenity in a lovely little Somerset village.

And for goodness' sake, Jassy thought in alarm, she was starting to think in estate agent's jargon now!

She put it all out of her mind, and began to think about seeing her dad and sister again tomorrow. She had a lot to tell them about the happenings of the week. If anyone thought living in the country was dull, and that nothing ever happened, she could certainly tell them otherwise!

They arrived in mid-afternoon, by which time the Sunday ritual had been the same as the previous week, except that William wasn't at church. Presumably he had taken the opportunity to exercise Raven again, but he had promised his aunt that he'd take her to visit Ted that evening when their visitors had gone.

Yes, thought Jassy again, there was never a dull moment – if you chose to make it so. She imagined that you could also make the fatal mistake of retiring to the country and stagnating. Thankfully, she could never think of herself or her father ever doing such a thing. Even if he only stayed here for couple of weeks, she had no doubt he'd re-acquaint himself with the old boys who frequented the benches on the green, and get involved in village life in some way or other.

There was a flurry of excitement when she saw Grace's car pull up on the road, and she flew across the green to meet them and hugged them both.

'It's so good to see you,' she said, as if they had been parted for months, 'and I can't wait to show you how wonderful the cottage is looking now,' she burst out. 'We've been working hard on it, and I had a little help with the garden, so even that looks as if somebody cares for it now.'

She had no intention of telling them who had given her the help with the garden, and it still smarted to think that Freddie thought he could just turn up and she would fall at his feet. She was older and wiser now – and he was married.

Owen was already calling out hello to the locals sunning themselves on the green and Jassy had every hope that he'd agree to come to stay as Grace asked her how the week had gone.

'It's been great. We had the May Day celebrations on the green yesterday. You remember the way we used to dance around the maypole at school, Grace. I helped to get it all ready, and there's going to be a huge party on the green to celebrate the Coronation,' she said as they made their way to the flat. 'I daresay I'll be asked to help that too if I'm here.'

'It sounds as if you've already made up your mind about that, my girl,' Owen commented, catching on to their conversation.

'I rather hope you'll be here too, Dad, but we'll talk about that later,' she said, not giving him time to argue as she pushed open the door to the flat.

The inviting smell of food simmering in the oven was very evident as Mrs Lester came forward with a smile. The kettle was boiling, and there was an overwhelming sense of homeliness and welcome.

'It's good to see you both again,' their hostess said at once, 'and I'm glad to see that you're looking so much better, Owen.'

'And feeling it too, dear lady,' he said expansively. 'I'm sure I'll be even more so with the smell that's teasing my nose.'

Mrs Lester laughed, her face pink from cooking, and possibly something else, thought Jassy. Her matchmaking ideas had switched now from Grace to her father, impossible though it had once seemed. But Giles Devenish had once told her that anything was possible if you wanted it badly enough . . .

'Let's have a cup of tea, and then I know Jasmine's simply dying to show you the results of her hard work this week,' Mrs Lester said.

'It's not only *my* hard work. You've been wonderful in helping me buy the new things I wanted, and even Ted turned up to help paint the walls. And oh, you don't know what happened to Ted, of course.'

She knew she was talking too fast, wanting to tell them everything at once, about going to the Monday Club, and about poor Ted's accident which resulted in her going to the dance with William instead. There were two things she wasn't going to tell them about. One was Freddie Patterson's arrival – although even relating that to them needn't bother her now. He was just an old friend she had known on the Devenish estate who had turned up to lend a hand. The other thing was the fact that William Hedges had kissed her. That did bother her, and she had already revised her idea of discussing it with Grace.

'You'll come to the cottage again, won't you, Kate?' Owen said when they had finished their tea. 'You're as much a part of this venture as anyone.'

'She once had a fancy to live there too,' Jassy put in, not knowing whether the woman wanted it divulged or not.

'That was a long time ago,' Kate said quickly, 'and such dreams are for children,' she finished with a laugh.

'I bet it hasn't changed that much, though,' Owen said. 'If you had that dream long ago, it's probably still lingering somewhere.'

'That's exactly what I told her. It's not only children who have dreams, is it?' Jassy said, not really sure if she had said anything of the sort.

Grace grabbed her arm as they walked across the green to the car.

'What are you playing at?'

'What do you mean?'

'You know very well what I mean. You're embarrassing Dad by all this talk of dreams.'

Jassy nodded to where the older couple were strolling ahead of them.

'Does he look embarrassed? I think he and Mrs Lester are well matched.'

'*She* might think so too, but don't go putting any daft ideas into Dad's head, or he'll back off at once.'

Jassy knew when to keep quiet about something, and this was definitely one of those times. Let Grace think what she liked, but in matters of the heart, Jassy considered herself more experienced than her sister, and there was definitely *something* between her father and William's aunt, even if it was only a *frisson* of attraction as yet.

'How's the lovely doctor?' she asked innocently.

Grace laughed. 'All right, so we're changing the subject. He's very well, thank you. He's still badgering Dad to take time off, even to retire and enjoy life instead of working all hours, and Dad's still ranting and raving at him.'

'It makes sense though, doesn't it? And I really want him to come down here in time for the Coronation celebrations, Grace, to see how we do things down here.'

'*We?*' Grace said, picking up on it at once.

'Let's get in the car,' Jassy said, ignoring the question.

Half an hour later, when they had inspected every bit of the newly decorated cottage, admired the new furnishings and the freshly turned earth in the front garden, Owen sat back with a grunt of approval.

'It all looks very presentable,' he agreed. 'Whatever you're going to do with it, Jassy, anyone would be very comfortable living here, providing they don't get snowed in during the winter. It could be a different picture then.'

'As a matter of fact, we rarely get much snow here, Owen,'

148

Kate said quickly. 'It's different up on the Mendips, of course, but we're quite lucky in Horton, and we escape any real problems.'

'Well then,' Owen said, leaving the words hanging in the air as if he didn't quite know how to continue.

With a flash of intuition, Jassy knew he would never be the one to say he'd like to come and stay for a week or two as the doctor ordered. It had to be up to her. And now was the time to be tactful.

'I'd really like to move in for a couple of weeks to get the feel of the place,' she said with a sigh. 'I'd especially like to be here for Coronation Day.'

Before Kate could break in to say that she'd be more than welcome to stay with her any time, Jassy rushed on.

'I couldn't ask Mrs Lester to let me stay with her again, as Ted may want to move back home for a while after his injury, so I'd have to stay here. I might be a bit nervous on my own at first, though.'

Owen let out a great guffaw that was half a snort and half a laugh.

'You're about as subtle as an elephant, my girl. What with that old fool Macleod urging me to get away from the shop, and you with your pleading doe eyes, I suppose I'd better give in, providing Grace here thinks she could manage for a week or two without me.'

'Of course I could manage,' Grace said crisply. 'Haven't I been telling you that for ages?'

Jassy didn't dare look at Kate at that moment, unsure what reaction she expected to see in her eyes. But she felt jubilant, because now there was going to be the perfect opportunity for two lonely people – if they could be referred to as such – to realize how much they enjoyed one another's company.

As the day went on, it was evident that they did so, and it was just as evident to Jassy that her sister didn't like the idea at all. It astonished her. Didn't Grace want to see her father happy? Or had she been his favourite for so many years that she felt jealous of Kate Lester? It was something that had never occurred to Jassy before. There had been a time when Grace had pooh-poohed any idea of marriage for herself, and had seemed perfectly content to care for her father and younger sister. But surely that had all changed now that Alec Macleod was on the horizon. Or had something gone wrong there?'

'What's wrong, Grace?' she asked, when she and Grace had insisted on doing the washing-up after supper, leaving the other two to take a stroll around the green.

'Nothing's wrong,' her sister said almost viciously.

'Well, that tells me that something definitely is! Is it to do with you and Doctor Macleod?'

Grace paused, her hands plunged in the soapy washing-up water.

'I don't know where I am with him. I thought he liked me. Well, I thought it was more than liking, but now I'm not so sure.'

'Maybe it's because you're his patient. Don't doctors have to be careful of having a close relationship with their female patients? Ask him if he'd prefer you to have another doctor and see what he says. If he agrees, it'll be either because he'll feel free to ask you out – or because he genuinely doesn't like you enough to get involved,' she finished lamely, wishing she'd never been so daft as to put this thought in Grace's head.

'Thank you for nothing, Jassy! Now I feel even worse.'

'Well, don't take it out on Dad and whatever his feelings might be towards Mrs Lester. He has a right to companionship after being alone all these years, and I'd like nothing more than to see him happy.'

She drew in her breath, praying that Grace wouldn't snap back that Owen hadn't been alone all these years. He'd had *her* . . . and Jassy too.

But Grace didn't answer, and only when they had finished and were drying their hands, did she comment.

'I know you're right, and I can't let things go on like this,' she said slowly. 'I feel so awkward when Alec comes to see Dad now, and he must have noticed it. Maybe he thinks I don't like *him*.'

'But you do.'

'Oh yes. I like him a lot,' she said fervently, the expression in her eyes saying far more than the words.

Thirteen

Before they left, it had been arranged that Jassy and her father would move into Blackthorn Cottage on the following Sunday, with the intention of staying for two weeks, and not a second more, Owen declared. He was feeling out of sorts by the time they left Horton, reluctant to admit he had eaten too much of Kate's delicious supper, which resulted in a touch of indigestion.

He assured his daughters it was nothing more than that, and nor was he blaming Kate's cooking. It was his own greed that had brought it on. The consequence was that all the way home to Bristol he was back on his usual form, grumbling about having been coerced into the future visit by scheming females, and not only by two of them, but now there were three! It didn't bode well for what Jassy hoped might become a close friendship between her father and Mrs Lester – if not more. But she wasn't the one who showed her annoyance with him.

'For heaven's sake, Dad, you're perfectly capable of making up your own mind, and of changing it,' Grace said in exasperation. 'If you don't want to do it, then just say no. It's your life, and what you do with it is up to you.'

It was so unlike Grace to be sharp with her father that nobody said anything for a few moments. Then he turned to her, frowning.

'Have I done something to upset you, Grace? I thought you'd welcome the chance to be in charge of the shop while I was away, but if you think it's beyond you then I definitely won't leave you to it.'

'It's nothing to do with the shop,' she snapped. 'Of course I can manage it by myself. In fact I'll probably still be doing it when I'm old and grey! That's the sort of thing dried-up old spinsters do, isn't it!'

151

He was genuinely astonished at the bitterness in her voice. 'What nonsense is this? Nobody could ever accuse you of you being a dried-up old spinster, you silly girl. I want to see you happily settled with a family of your own long before I hang up my boots. That goes for both of you,' he added, glancing back at Jasmine. 'No man wants to leave this world without grandchildren, and since that old goat Macleod is determined to keep me here a while longer, the pair of you had better keep it in mind.'

Grace gave a sniff that wasn't all derisory, and Jassy wasn't too sure whether it was nearer to a sob. She broke in, her voice determinedly light.

'So, Dad, if you think you've got three females coercing you into staying at Blackthorn Cottage, and the wily doctor's determined to put in his spoke as well, what chance do you have? You might as well give in gracefully and let us all have some peace,' she added daringly.

He glared at her. 'All right. You've both had your say, and I suppose I gave my word, so let's not hear anything else about it. We'll go to your blasted cottage, and if we end up at one another's throats, don't say I didn't warn you!'

'I'll remember,' Jassy said with a giggle.

She saw Grace's eyes reflected in the driving mirror as she nodded with relief. They had won, but Lord only knew how scratchy life was going to be for Jassy and her father in Blackthorn Cottage, let alone the whole of next week before they left. It was giving him too long to ponder on it, but there was nothing they could do about that now. And nothing was going to take away Jassy's excitement at the prospect. She could really start to play property owner, and there was no reason on earth why she and her father shouldn't get along if they tried hard enough. Fingers crossed.

Alec Macleod made his usual weekly visit on Monday evening and was told the news by an irascible Owen. He had been living on indigestion remedies all night, he informed the doctor.

'And before you say anything, it was nothing more than that,' he said with a scowl, anticipating what was to come.

'A bit of exercise would do you far more good, man, but

I'm glad you've seen sense about getting away for a while,' he said heartily. 'Some walks in the country will work wonders, providing you don't try running a marathon. It's the best thing for you, and I'll give you another note for the local doctor, in case of any problems.'

'There aren't going to be any problems, damn it. That's the reason I'm going, isn't it – to set myself up again?'

'All the same.' Alec wouldn't be put off, and he continued writing the note before handing it to Jassy for safe keeping.

'You can give me that and stop treating me like a child, you lunatic,' Owen roared. 'The day I allow a daughter of mine to become my keeper I may as well pack it all in.'

'I'm only giving it to Jassy because you're just as likely to tear it up,' Alec said calmly. 'It's only a precaution, so there's no need to get into a fluster about it.'

They clashed for a moment and then Owen shrugged.

'All right. If it makes you all happy, I'll do as you say. I can't be bothered to argue with you.'

That was a first, but they knew it was as much of a compromise as they were likely to get, and a while later when Alec was about to leave, Grace said she would see him out.

She was gone quite some time, and when she returned her face was flushed and her eyes bright. Jassy groaned, wondering which way the conversation had gone – if indeed, there been any conversation between them at all. It could be that Grace had blown any chance of her one great romance, which Jassy was sure was how she saw it now. She didn't get a chance to ask any questions until their father had gone to bed and they were alone at last.

'So, come on. Tell me what happened between you and Alec earlier – or are you going to bite my head off for asking?' she said directly.

For a moment she thought Grace was going to burst into tears. Her face seemed to reflect a mixture of emotions, and then the shine in her eyes gave way to a smile of relief.

'I couldn't leave things as they were, Jassy, so I asked him why he was being less friendly towards me than he used to be. At first he said that simply wasn't true, but that wasn't good enough for me, so I asked him outright if he liked me as more than a friend, and if he felt he couldn't show his

153

feelings, being our doctor. I know it wasn't the right thing to do and it was far too forward of me, but I couldn't help it, so I decided it was now or never.'

She rambled on, as if reluctant to get to the point, leaving Jassy more and more exasperated. Then she swallowed, and Jassy was almost too afraid to ask any more. But Grace was still smiling that wondrous smile . . . and she had to know.

'You can't leave it there, Grace! What did he say to that?'

'He got quite aggressive. He said of course he liked me, and in fact his feelings went far deeper than just liking, but he knew how devoted I had always been to my father. He said he wouldn't be surprised if we all moved to Horton eventually so that we could stay together, and he didn't want to risk spoiling the friendship we had now if nothing could ever come of it. Aren't men *stupid* sometimes?' she finished on an angry gasp.

Jassy didn't dare laugh, knowing how important this was to Grace, but she had a hard job holding it in at the way these two were still fencing around one another. For heaven's sake, it was obvious they were made for one another!

'Did you say that to him?'

Grace began to laugh then, her face relaxing in her excitement, making her look about twelve years old and about to open all her birthday presents at once.

'No, of course not. I said if he thought I was ever going to leave Bristol he could think again. I told him I had a life to live too, and it wasn't my father that I wanted to share it with. I didn't have to say anything more, Jassy, and I think – well, I'm still not sure how it happened – but I think we're sort of engaged. At least, we will be when Alec gets around to asking Dad, and we haven't decided whether to do it now, or to wait until you and he have had your time together in Horton. Alec says that if he says anything about it to Dad now, he may not go, for fear that his little girl's going to be seduced by the big bad doctor while he's away! On the other hand, I think he feels we've waited long enough and wants to get things settled.'

'Good Lord, did he really say all that?' Jassy said, astonished that these two seemed to have come so far in so short a time.

Grace giggled. 'He did, and you needn't look so shocked. Once we started talking we couldn't seem to stop. But not only that. Dad might only think of him as a doctor, and a verbal sparring partner at that, but he's also a man, Jassy, and from the way he kissed me I think it would be a very good idea if we were officially engaged as soon as possible, so that nobody can doubt his intentions.'

Jassy still felt dazzled at how quickly her sister's fortunes had changed. They hugged one another as she promised not to breathe a word of this to anyone. It had to wait until Alec asked Owen for his daughter's hand in marriage – but this was certainly turning out to be the strangest evening, she thought.

Grace spoke almost shyly now. 'I'm going to bed to think about everything that's happened today. After I was so miserable, it's almost like a miracle, and I've got you to thank for pushing me into saying something. I do love him, Jassy, and I've kept my feelings wrapped up inside me for a long time now, but you'll know what I mean when it happens to you.'

'I'm sure I will,' Jassy said.

She'd thought she knew it once, when she fell so heavily for Freddie. But feelings could change and hers had done so with a vengeance on the last occasion they had met. She sincerely hoped it *would* be the last occasion.

Once in her own bed, she couldn't stop thinking about the extraordinary way this evening had ended. Grace and Alec were sensible people, and she expected everything to go smoothly for them, but she had reckoned without Alec's impatience. He was an excellent doctor, and had the patience of Job when it was needed, but she also knew that he could be a hothead from the way he and Owen enjoyed their frequent disputes. Now that he and Grace had an understanding, any idea of waiting to approach Owen at some later date was abandoned when he called round again on the following evening on the pretext of checking that Owen had sufficient medicine to last him for two weeks away from home.

'To what do I owe the dubious pleasure of another visit so soon?' Owen greeted him darkly.

Alec did his professional duty, and then told him he wanted to discuss a private matter. Knowing what the private matter was all about, Grace and Jassy had already made themselves scarce in the kitchen, but they left the door ajar, and since both men had voices that carried, they could overhear everything.

'The fact is, I want to marry your daughter,' Alec said bluntly.

Grace gasped. 'Oh Lord, why couldn't he have led up to it gradually? Dad will throw a fit now.'

Amazingly, after a moment's silence, they heard Owen start to laugh, which ended in a coughing bout. When he recovered his breath, he wheezed out a reply.

'Which one?'

'Don't be so daft, man. Grace, of course.'

'You want to marry Grace!' Owen repeated, his voice rising. 'Is this some kind of a farce? What makes you think I'd ever be willing for my daughter to marry you, even if she wanted to, which I'm sure she doesn't!'

'She assures me that she does,' Alec said evenly.

Owen's voice exploded. 'Oh, she does, does she? Then just what has been going on behind my back? Have you been taking advantage of her? If so, I shall find out, and you could be in serious trouble over this. I thought you doctors were supposed to have ethics.'

It was too much for Grace. She couldn't listen to any more of this without bursting into the sitting-room.

'Why can't you just listen to what Alec has to say, Dad, without always thinking the worst of people? Alec has not been taking advantage of me, and it's absolutely true what he says. We love each other and he wants to marry me, and he's come here to do the decent and honourable thing in asking for your permission.'

Jassy was right behind her sister, and neither she nor her father missed the way the two people in question moved closer together, their hands just touching. Owen's attention turned to Jassy, his brows drawn together in a black line of disapproval.

'Have you been a party to this, Miss?'

It was the final straw, and Jassy wasn't prepared to be the

scapegoat in what should be a wonderful moment in her sister's life. Her temper flared.

'I have not been a party to anything underhand, Dad, and if you weren't so darned blinkered about anything other than yourself and your own narrow outlook on life, you'd have been aware that Alec and Grace have feelings for one another. You said you wanted grandchildren, and pardon me for pointing out the inescapable fact that we do need to have husbands before that can happen! Or maybe you think we're going to be visited by the Angel Gabriel and told that we're each going to have an immaculate conception. Sorry, but that only happened once, and if that's being blasphemous I don't care! All you ever think about is the blessed shop, and you can't accept that other people can fall in love, or even just like each other. You even had to make some nasty, suspicious comments over why Mr Devenish left me the cottage, when he only did it out of kindness and appreciation for my work, and it was nothing more devious than that.'

She raged on, knowing she had ended any chance of him coming to the cottage with her now, but she couldn't stop herself. She had held back for far too long. But her father's face was turning a dull shade of puce, and for a moment she thought he was going to raise his hand to strike her. Or have a proper heart attack.

Alec stepped forward, grasping Owen's arm.

'Sit down and get your breath back, man.'

He shook Alec's hand away and spoke harshly. 'It's that young madam who needs to wash her mouth out and get her breath back, not me. She clearly has some perception of the Bible, but "honour thy mother and thy father" seems to have no meaning for her any more.'

He looked at the three of them, standing close together now, watchful and wary, and then he slumped down in a chair.

'So is what Jasmine said the way you all think of me?' he said harshly at last. 'That I've become too bigoted and self-centred to think of anyone but myself?'

'You do have your moments Dad,' Grace muttered, 'but you've known Alec for a long time, and you know he's a good man. He came here in good faith to ask for your blessing, and you've managed to ruin it,' she finished, her voice choking.

'As usual,' Jassy couldn't resist adding.

Alec decided it was time he took control before they reached a complete stalemate. 'I think we should all take a few moments to gather ourselves and calm down. You lassies go and make us all a hot drink, and since I know you've got a drop of brandy in the house, I'm sure your father and I wouldn't say no to taking a dram or two, and not just for medicinal purposes.'

He shooed them out and closed the door firmly behind them. They looked at one another dismally, and Jassy felt close to tears.

'Well, I made a real mess of that, didn't I, Grace? I'm truly sorry, and I said some awful things to Dad. He'll never forgive me.'

Grace put her arms around her. 'Yes, he will, and despite how it all came about, I think we all know it needed to be said. He has become far too introverted over the years, and getting him away from here for a while is just what he needs.'

'You don't think he'll want to come now, do you? Especially with me!'

'We'll see. Alec can be very persuasive when he wants to be, and he's usually got the better of Dad before, hasn't he? Give him time to sort things out.'

It seemed to take for ever before the door opened again and Alec called them back. They had been sent to make a hot drink, but the mechanics of it had been totally forgotten. In the sitting-room, the roles of the two men had been subtly reversed. They had always relished their frequent arguments, but apart from when he had gone to hospital, the honours had really been fairly even. Now, Alec was acting like the man of the house, and the girls noted that the bottle of brandy that had emerged from the sideboard was open and two glasses of the golden liquid were already half empty. But Owen wouldn't relinquish his position that easily. He cleared his throat and spoke shortly.

'So, now that we've all had time to clear the air, I think

we should all begin again. Macleod, I think there was something you wanted to ask me.'

His eyes flickered for a moment, and his daughters knew him well enough to know it was important for him to keep his dignity now.

Alec took a small box out of his waistcoat pocket. He opened it and looked at the object inside for a moment before he spoke.

'This was my mother's engagement ring,' he said directly to Owen. 'She left it to me to give to the woman I loved and intended to marry. For a long while I thought I would never find her, but I have, and I am sincerely, and with all my heart, asking your permission to marry your daughter Grace.'

It was hard to say which of the Wyatt girls felt more touched at that moment. It was a sweet, beautiful and simple speech, and it was clearly said from the heart. Owen too, was momentarily taken aback by the sincerity of the man's words, and it was Grace who broke the silence. She clutched her father's arm.

'Oh, for goodness sake, Dad, hurry up and say yes, or the anticipation will be too much for us and Alec and I will both burst!'

He paused for no longer than a heartbeat. 'Well, as I don't want that to happen, I suppose I'd better say yes.'

It was a moment when the release of tension seemed to flood through the room, and where seconds before they had all been tense and apprehensive, now it had completely disappeared as Alec put his mother's ring on Grace's finger, and they saw the lovely cluster of rubies in their diamond setting. Alec kissed the ring on Grace's finger, and it was a token to seal their love.

'So where in goodness is that hot drink?' Owen said, clearing his throat. 'I'm parched after all that yakking. And I hope you don't think you're going to whisk my girl off straightaway, Macleod.'

'We haven't had time to think about setting a date, but I was thinking maybe at the turn of the year, if Grace approves. Hogmanay will suit us just fine.'

It was clear that Grace was so deliriously happy that she

was going to approve of anything her new fiancé had to say, and Jassy felt a sharp twist of envy. Both of them had always assumed that she would be the one who would marry first and that Grace might not even marry at all, and now everything had changed. But she was happy for her sister. Grace would make a wonderful doctor's wife.

She had slipped out into the kitchen alone while the other three were offering tentative plans for the future. She was waiting for the kettle to boil when she became aware that she was no longer alone. Her heart thumped as she turned to face her father, remembering her part in all this.

'I'm sorry to learn the way you feel about me, Jassy. I don't deny that it was a shock to hear you speak to me in that way, although they always say that a few home truths never did anyone any harm.'

It was a shock to hear him speak that way too, showing a touch of unaccustomed humility, however disjointed – and however short-lived it was destined to be.

'You know I didn't mean half of it,' she said, choked.

'Of course you did, so don't back down now. It was probably deserved, anyway. People often say things in anger that are more truthful than at any other time, no matter how hurtful they may be.'

She didn't quite know what to make of this newly humble reply. It wasn't his style, and it wouldn't last. It made her want to rush at him and hug him, but she wasn't sure how it would be received. But he hadn't finished yet.

'Anyway, it's cleared the air, and your sister's happy, so we should be too. And at least while we're away, I shall know that Grace is being looked after, since her beau will keep an eye on her.'

'Are you still coming to the cottage with me then?' She hadn't known whether to hope for this or not.

'I gave my word, didn't I?'

There was no holding back her emotions now, and seconds later she was in his arms, her eyes smarting after all that had gone on during this strangest of days. After a few moments, Owen extricated himself.

'All right, that's enough keening for one day. There's something I have to do, so I'll leave you three young 'uns to discuss matters of the heart between yourselves. I'll have that tea later.'

He left her, and she rejoined the other two slowly, wondering what he could possibly have to do that was so urgent now. Grace was flexing her fingers and admiring her engagement ring, her eyes for no one but Alec. Three was definitely a crowd here now, and they should be alone, thought Jassy. She needed some fresh air, and she left the flat, breathing deeply, as if she had come a very long way.

Without noticing where she was walking, she realized she was nearing the churchyard where her mother was buried. A familiar figure was standing very still near her mother's grave, and her eyes began to smart again. Then, as she saw his lips moving, Jassy drew in her breath in a kind of horror.

He was talking to his wife. He always came here on the day she had died – Jassy's birthday – but she had no idea he might come here at other times, presumably to find some solace in being near the place where she was buried.

She didn't want to be observed in these most private of moments, and she started to move away, but her father must have heard some movement, and he turned towards her. She had no option but to join him, feeling like an intruder between two people who had known and loved one another before she was even born. Yet she had every right to be here, for she was part of them.

'I often come to see her,' Owen said in a tired voice. 'I find peace here, and I talk to her. You may find it a strange thing to do, Jasmine, even an unhealthy thing, but she still helps me to see things properly, the way she always did.'

Jassy swallowed her earlier feelings of horror. 'I don't think it's so strange. I think it's a lovely thing to do. Perhaps you could apologize to her for me, for shouting at you the way I did.'

She wasn't sure how sensible that sounded, but this whole day was beginning to feel very surreal. And if her father thought for one second that she was mocking him, they might lose the fragile rapport they now had. To offset any such feelings, she slipped her hand in his, and felt his fingers close around hers.

'She'd have been proud of both my girls, and she'd have understood without my telling her again,' Owen said.

Jassy started to feel uneasy once more. It was nearly twenty-one years since Celia Wyatt had died in childbirth and it was surely too long a time to imagine that her aura was still surrounding her family. It was sweet . . . but it was also morbid, and it was living in the past. A time must surely come when it was wiser to let go, which was the one thing Owen seemed incapable of doing.

'I think it's time to go home, Dad,' she said gently.

'You go. I'll stay a while longer. I'll be back in time for supper.'

Whatever else happened, war or flood or earthquake, he wouldn't miss his supper, Jassy thought, trying to smile, but she was still uncomfortable by the time she reached the flat. Grace and Alec were talking animatedly, and she knew she couldn't spoil their happiness by revealing what she had just witnessed. She had the feeling that the fewer people who knew about it, the better Owen would like it.

She supposed he was lucky in a way, though, if that was the right word for it. He still believed he had some kind of connection with his wife, however ethereal and unfulfilled it might seem to other people. While Jassy, the daughter who had caused his beloved Celia to die, felt nothing for the woman who had given her life. How could she, when all she knew about her were a few old photographs, and what Grace had told her? She couldn't be blamed for her mother's death, any more than she could be blamed for her lack of feelings towards her, but the knowledge still filled her with guilt, the way it had always done.

Fourteen

Nothing could curb Jassy's exuberance for long. It was catching, and during the next week she sensed that Owen was actually starting to look forward to having two weeks away as well. He so rarely took time off from his shop, and she couldn't help remembering something her old boss and mentor, Giles Devenish, had always said. All work and no play didn't just make Jack a dull boy. It narrowed his horizons, and stupefied his brain.

Not that anyone could say that Owen's brain had stupefied. In many ways he was as sharp as he had ever been, but there must surely come a time in anyone's life when it was wiser to slow down and let someone else take over. Someone like Grace, for instance, who seemed more than eager to be in sole control of the shop while he was away. Or maybe she was just making the most of it, because when she became a doctor's wife she would surely have enough on her hands without working in a haberdashery shop. Doctors' wives were reputed to have busy lives, and she knew Grace would make an excellent one.

'Have I got something on the end of my nose or something?' her sister asked Jassy over supper that evening. 'You've been staring at me for the last five minutes.'

Jassy laughed. 'I was just wondering which part of being a doctor's wife was going to suit you best – graciously dispensing advice to Alec's patients, or soothing the angry ones who telephone in the middle of the night who are wanting his best bedside manner.'

'Well, I hope that won't happen too often,' Grace said, a small flush creeping up the sides of her face at the image Jassy was unwittingly painting.

The prospect of sharing a marital bed with Alec frequently

gave her delicious attacks of the collywobbles. She had known him for so long, and their friendship had almost imperceptibly grown into love, and yet it was as if it had always been there. She also thought about children . . . and she didn't deny that that scared her too, remembering that her own mother had died in childbirth, but not for anything would she allow such morbid thoughts to deny herself the fulfilment of having a baby – Alec's baby. Her heart swelled at the thought.

'She's got that soppy look in her eyes again now,' Owen said with a grunt. 'But you've got to remember, Grace, that when you marry a doctor, you marry his patients as well.'

'What do you mean?'

'I mean that they all think they own a little bit of him and that they *can* call on him at any time, day or night, and he has to come running.'

'Well, I'm sure you certainly believe that, although I wouldn't say Alec's the type of man to be at anyone's beck and call, unless he thought it was medically necessary,' Grace answered quickly, before the images of herself and Alec in intimate circumstances betrayed her even more. 'I wonder if you'll still be arguing with him when he's your son-in-law?'

Owen grinned. 'Good God, of course I will, girl. A good old argument helps to keep my ticker going, and he knows that, if you don't.'

'Just as long as it doesn't get out of hand,' Jassy put in.

As they both looked at her, it seemed as if they had almost forgotten she was there. They had something even more in common now. They had Alec. She swallowed the silly jealousy that had sprung up from nowhere, and reminded herself how glad she was that Grace had found happiness at last.

And so had she, in a different way. She had her cottage, and she had new friends in Horton. Her spirits lifted again, because her dad was going to share all that with her, for two weeks, anyway. For the first time ever, he would be all hers. Any other problems that might arise could be dealt with, and she was going to do all she could to make his stay a happy one, especially after the episode in the churchyard when she had discovered just how vulnerable he could be.

Owen got up from the supper table, his eyes quizzical as he looked at her.

'I swear the two of you have got wedding-itis tonight. You're the one with the soppy look in your eyes now, Jasmine, and there's just so much a man can stand for one night. I'm going to bed.'

But the twinkle in his eyes as he left the room took the sting out of his words, and Grace smiled happily.

'He's pleased about me and Alec really – and he's pleased to be going to the cottage with you too, Jassy. I know it will do him good to be in different surroundings and different company.'

'And you'll hardly miss us at all, will you?' Jassy said with a laugh.

'Would you, in my position?'

By the time Sunday came, Jassy had done a huge amount of grocery shopping, ready to stock up the cottage larder. There was a local butcher and baker in Horton, and milk was delivered daily when ordered. Everything they needed could be bought locally, but the basics like tea and sugar and cleaning materials needed to be there when they arrived. Even planning what they would need gave Jassy a lift. She had always likened it to playing house, but this time it was real.

They arrived in the early afternoon to find a large envelope on the doormat inside the front door. When Jassy opened it, she flushed with pleasure.

'Well, isn't that thoughtful?' she exclaimed. 'It's a card from Mrs Lester, wishing us a happy stay in Blackthorn Cottage. William's signed it as well, and so has Ted,' she added, pleased and surprised to see his scrawled signature.

'That woman has a very kind heart,' Owen said. 'Didn't I say so from the day I met her?'

'Yes, you did, Dad,' Jassy said solemnly, putting the card on the mantelpiece above the fireplace, thinking that whether or not he had said it didn't matter.

Grace had gone to the kitchen with the groceries which allowed his daughters to resist glancing at one another. One hint that they thought he might be finding Kate Lester attractive in a more personal way could spell doom to any hopes they might have of their father ever finding love again. It was something he had to discover for himself, and Jassy very much hoped that he would. He'd had too many years to mourn.

They settled into the cottage, putting things away in bedrooms, and filling the larder and cupboards until Grace decided it was time for her to return home. It would be odd for her too, Jassy thought, returning to an empty shop and flat, but not as odd as it would have been before she and Alec had become engaged. She gave her sister a big hug before she left.

'If Alec can tear himself away next Sunday, we'll probably come down to see how you're getting on,' Grace said. 'He mentioned something about it.'

'I suppose you mean he'll want to see if I'm behaving myself,' Owen said.

'Of course I do, though he hardly chases up all his patients like this.' Grace laughed mischievously. 'Well, only the one whose daughter he's going to marry! We've got to be sure you're going to be around to give me away, haven't we?'

They watched her drive away and there was a small silence between the two who were left behind.

'She'll do all right,' Owen said at last. 'She's got a good head on her shoulders and she won't stand for any nonsense from that old goat Macleod.'

Jassy hid a smile. He had his own way of dealing with things, and it would be a long time before he let go of his banter with Alec, if ever.

'Do you feel like a walk down to the village after supper?' she said.

'There's time enough for that. I'd rather settle down and get the feel of this place,' Owen replied. 'It's a fine evening, so I think I shall sit outside in the garden for a while.'

'All right. I'll join you when I've cleared up inside.' She wasn't sure if that was what he wanted, or if he would prefer to be alone, but she was determined to show that what she wanted was to share these two weeks with him.

They had been sitting outside quite companionably for more than an hour when they were disturbed by the sound of a car in the lane. By then Owen had told her how to prune the roses and that she'd have to keep the weeds down to stop them encroaching on the garden again. For a city man, he had the air of having a fair knowledge of country ways, and if it wasn't authentic, he wasn't letting on.

The car came to a halt outside the cottage, and Jassy's heart leapt as she saw William and his aunt getting out of it and coming towards them.

'We thought we'd call on you on our way back to the village,' Kate Lester said with a smile. 'We've been to the farm to see how Ted's getting on.'

Guiltily, Jassy realized she had completely forgotten Ted's accident.

'How is he?' she said hastily.

William gave a short laugh. 'Living the high life with Mrs Cooper waiting on him hand and foot.'

'William, that's not fair. It was a nasty gash, but he's back at work now. It was an unfortunate accident, but he's not the sort to let it get him down for long.'

Not like the way he was spooked at Blackthorn Cottage all those years ago then, thought Jassy.

'Anyway, you put the sparkle back in his eyes,' Kate went on approvingly. 'You did a generous thing, William, offering to let him take your place in the best dressed horse and cart event on Midsummer Day.'

William shrugged. 'He's hankered after it for so long, it just seemed like the right time. And he can handle Raven better than I can handle him myself now.'

Not being part of this little exchange, Owen cleared his throat. 'Where are your manners, Jasmine? Aren't you going to ask these good folk in for a drink of something?'

'Of course. Please come in, both of you. The sun's going down, and I think we've been outside for long enough.'

It was all too cosy, she thought a little while later, making the cocoa that they requested, and seeing the other three making themselves comfortable in the tiny sitting-room. Pleasantly cosy though ... and when they had gone she explained to her father all about the village fair on Midsummer Day that was always held at Cooper's Farm, and about William's part in it that he had now handed over to his cousin Ted. It was nice gesture, and he was a nice man to have thought of it.

It was hard to sleep that first night. Staying in Mrs Lester's flat hadn't been so different from sleeping at home, with the proximity of the village wrapping itself around them. Here, away from the village and more isolated, Jassy was aware of every creak and rustle in the cottage and in the trees outside. Just before four o'clock in the morning, she was sharply awoken by a cacophony of bird song. She groaned. One, louder than all the rest, seemed to be practically inside her bedroom, and, still half asleep, she tottered to the window and pulled back the curtains to see a large blackbird sitting on the branch of the tree nearest to the cottage.

'Good morning to you too,' she muttered. 'Don't you know what time it is?'

Her heart gave a sudden jump. It was hardly daylight and there was a fine mist spangling the trees and bushes, giving it a beautiful, ethereal appearance that heralded a lovely day. But Jassy was in no mood to appreciate it as she heard stealthy movements somewhere below. Her instant alarm gave way to anger. If there was an intruder in the cottage, and trouble brewing, it would be sufficient to make her father turn tail and go back to Bristol. It wouldn't be out of fear, but out of certainty that this had been a crazy idea after all.

Her heart jumped again as she saw the latch on her bedroom door being lifted, and then it slowly opened.

'Dad!' she spluttered. 'What are you doing? It's barely daylight!'

'Best time of the day,' he said, reminding her that he had always been an early riser – although never this early! 'I couldn't sleep with all that racket going on, so I thought I'd go down and make us a cup of tea. Get something on before you freeze and I'll bring it in.'

She hastily put on her dressing-gown over her nightie, and saw that he had put a tray with two cups of tea on the small table on the landing outside. There was a plate of biscuits too, and she felt a lump come to her throat, realizing what a gesture this was for him to make. He hadn't really wanted to come here at all. She and Grace and Alec had schemed to get him here under the pretext of looking after him, and now he was looking after her. It was a sweet and generous moment, and if she didn't know he wouldn't thank her for it, she'd have thrown her arms around his neck and hugged him. But he'd picked up the tray again and it wouldn't have been a good idea, anyway.

'This is a first!' she said instead.

'And it'll probably be the last, so don't get used to it, girl,' he said gruffly. 'I guessed you'd be awake as well, so I thought we might as well share this ghastly start to the day.'

She laughed. 'It's not so bad, is it? When would you ever hear anything like such heavenly bird song in the city? Or see a scene like this? It's like fairyland in the early morning, Dad. Take a look out of my window and see for yourself.'

He had put the tray down on her bedside table now and he walked across to the window, silently taking in the panorama in front of him, the fairylike fronds of the trees and bushes, the undergrowth that seemed to float on a sea of foam, the fresh, cool scent of early morning. She willed him to be thrilled with what he saw, knowing no artist could have captured it more beautifully than nature herself.

'It's a picture all right,' he conceded. 'Everything looks pretty at this time of year, but it'll be a bit different when the leaves are bare, and it's covered in snow.'

'I know that. It'll be a winter wonderland then.'

He gave a short laugh and turned around to drink his tea.

'You're an optimist, girl, I'll give you that.'

'Is that such a bad thing to be? I'd rather look on the bright side than wallow in doom and gloom all the time.'

She realized she could be on dangerous ground now, and she changed the subject quickly as she saw her father's frown.

'So are we going to walk to the village later today? You promised we would last night. You enjoyed chatting to the old men on the village green when you were here before, and from what I've seen they're in the same spot every day.'

She had curled up on her bed now to drink her tea and dunk her biscuits, and he was sitting on the end of it.

'Is that how you see me, then? Being put out to grass and

169

having nothing else to do but sit and chat to a group of ancient old codgers?'

'That's not what I meant at all, and you know it,' she began crossly, and then she saw that he had stopped frowning. 'What I see,' she went on carefully, 'is that you're taking a couple of weeks out from your busy life and are sensibly using the time to relax and enjoy yourself.'

He squeezed her hand. 'That's what I'd better do then. That old duffer Macleod would be proud of his nurse, even if she's not as tactful as she thinks she is. But don't think you're getting me out walking just yet. I'm going back to bed to read for an hour or so and you can call me later when you've made some breakfast.'

'Yes, Captain!' Jassy said with a grin, but her eyes were salty as he went out of the room, because it was going to be all right. They would get along just fine. She was sure of it, but to be on the safe side, she crossed her fingers as usual as she snuggled down under the bedcovers for a while longer too.

The smell of frying bacon brought Owen downstairs before Jassy needed to call him. It was still only seven o'clock in the morning, and the sun had burned off the early morning mist and was now shining brilliantly in a cerulean blue sky in these early May days.

'You didn't need to get up yet,' she told him.

'It's what I'm used to,' he reminded her. 'Just because a man's not doing a job of work, it doesn't mean he can become a sloth.'

'That's something you'll never be,' Jassy told him dryly. 'If you stayed here long enough, I'm sure you'd have a hand in plenty of village activities.'

He didn't say anything for a few minutes, and then he spoke more sharply.

'I know what you're trying to do, Jasmine, and it's not going to work. I'm here because I choose to be, but it's only temporary. Much longer than two weeks and I'd probably go mad, so don't try putting any nonsense into my head about making it a permanent arrangement.'

She slapped down a plate of bacon and eggs in front of him, her patience ebbing away at his stubbornness.

'I don't know why you'd think I'd want to make a permanent arrangement of us living here together, either,' she snapped. 'I know you'll be counting the days until you can get back to your blessed shop, so don't let's fool ourselves.'

She poured him a cup of tea with shaking hands. As he himself had said, 'honour thy father (and mother)' seemed a long way from her range of thoughts right now, and she waited for his response to her outburst. He took a few minutes before he spoke again.

'The trouble with us, Jassy, my love,' he said, the endearment taking her by surprise and making her eyes prickle, 'is that we're too much alike. Too headstrong and ready to take offence when there's no need. I see the echo of myself in you far too often for comfort.'

'Is that such a bad thing?' she mumbled, momentarily off guard.

'Not if it gets things out in the open, I daresay, and providing it makes no difference in the long run to the bonds between a father and daughter. At least it's a lot livelier than living with a cabbagey sort of woman. But it's far too early to be having this kind of conversation, so I'm going to get on with my breakfast before it gets cold.'

He could still surprise her, thought Jassy. Maybe he had always been like this, weighing things up in his head, even though it had always seemed to her that he bellowed before he stopped to think, and his replies frequently erupted in bouts of temper. Perhaps it had needed her time away from him while she was working for Giles Devenish, to finally appreciate more about him than she had ever done before. She was under no illusions, though. They weren't going to live here in perfect harmony for the next two weeks, but at least they both realized it.

'I'm going to the shops later to get some bread and a newspaper and something for our supper,' she announced. 'Are you coming for the exercise?'

'Is this one of Doctor Macleod's requirements?'

'No. It's one of mine. And it's not a requirement. It's a request to have your company.'

'Then I'd better say yes, hadn't I?'

God, he could be so contrary, Jassy fumed. Why couldn't

he simply say yes and be done with it, without always querying her motives? But the day was turning out far too lovely to be arguing, and halfway through the morning they set out on a gentle stroll to the village. People recognized her now, and a few of them recognized her father too, and they passed the time of day with many of them. Owen told her coolly he might as well sit on one of the benches on the green for a yarn, while Jassy did the necessary shopping. His eyes dared her to say I told you so, and she didn't risk it.

She couldn't avoid seeing William in his office, efficient as ever, as he studied some papers on his desk. It would be churlish to pass by, she thought, and so she went inside, not missing his wide smile when he saw her. He got up at once, ever the gentleman.

'This is a pleasant surprise, Jassy. How did your first night go?'

'As expected. Strange, and surprisingly noisy, but far more so this morning when we were so rudely awakened by the dawn chorus,' she told him.

He laughed. 'You'll get used to it. It's called part of country life. And how did your father like it?'

'He survived,' Jassy said cautiously not really knowing how to answer that.

They both turned as Owen entered the office and greeted William.

'I called in at the post office to buy a stamp, expecting to see your aunt, but there was a strange woman behind the counter.'

'She doesn't work on Mondays. She'll probably be at the village hall with the rest of the Friendship Ladies, organizing who's going to do what for the tea party on Wednesday to celebrate the Coronation. They'll all be baking and planning like mad between now and then.'

'You make it sound like a military operation,' Owen said.

'You have no idea,' William said grimly. 'Anyway, Jassy, will I be seeing you at the Monday Club this evening?'

It was odd that he'd chosen that particular phrase, reminding her instantly of the way they had sung the song together. *I'll be seeing you . . .*

'I don't know.' And then she had to explain about Monday Club to her father.

'Well, of course you must go if you want to, girl. I'll not have you staying in on my account. I don't need coddling.'

'I know you don't, but it's only our second night here, Dad.'

'Well, I shan't stay indoors every night, either. You go to your Monday Club, Jasmine, and I'll drop in at the Rose and Crown. My new pals say they have a darts match most nights.'

'That's settled then,' William said, giving her no time to reply, or to ponder on how quickly the ancient old codgers on the village green had become her father's new pals.

'I hadn't actually made up my mind about going to the Monday Club,' Jassy said, as they started back.

'Well, what's stopping you? If it was on my account, then you needn't concern yourself. I told you, I don't need nurse-maiding. If you want me to find my feet in this place, then let me get on with it in my own way and don't fuss.'

She hid a smile as his voice became stronger. When did anyone ever tell him what to do, other than Alec when his health was involved?

He took one of the bags of shopping from her and strode on purposefully. As they neared the village hall, a crowd of ladies spilled out into the sunshine, chattering like magpies. Kate Lester was one of them, and her face brightened as she saw the other two.

'It's good to see you out and about, Owen, and you too, Jasmine, dear.'

'How is the organization for the Coronation tea party going? William told us you were busy planning it today.'

Kate laughed. 'Not well enough! All the shops will be closed on Wednesday, and we all have our tasks to do, jellies to make on Tuesday evening, and fairy cakes to make for the little ones. After the ceremony on Wednesday morning the men will be decorating the green with Union Jacks and bunting, and then setting out the chairs and trestle tables ready for the tea.'

'I can help with that,' Owen said.

Kate looked flustered. 'Oh, but are you sure you should? I didn't mean to imply that I was looking for your assistance as well.'

'Of course I can help. I'm not dead yet, woman.'

Jassy groaned. It was all very well for her father to talk to his daughters in that familiar way, but she wasn't sure how Kate Lester would take it. Then she realized the other woman was laughing.

'I can see that. Well, then, I won't say no. And how about you, Jassy? Do you want to help? I wouldn't have asked, but since your father is keen to be involved, perhaps you would be too.'

'Tell me how many jellies you want, and put me down for that.'

'Wonderful. Call in at the village hall tomorrow, where a skeleton team of ladies will be working, and collect as many dishes as you require.'

They parted company and Owen spoke thoughtfully, a touch of admiration in his voice.

'There goes a very efficient woman, Jasmine. She got her way without any fuss and bother, and I like that.'

'You like *her*, don't you, Dad?'

'Who could help liking her?' he said evasively. 'Now, let's get this shopping home and have a sit down and a cuppa. I'm parched.'

In a small village like Horton, it was hard to avoid people unless you became a total recluse. It was clear that Owen had no intention of becoming such a thing, if only to prove to his daughter that he was far from ready to stagnate, as he put it. On Monday evening, while Jassy went to the Monday Club and joined in the poignant Noel Coward songs as before, Owen was establishing himself at the Rose and Crown as a reasonable darts player and buyer of jugs of cider. Not too many, just enough to make him feel more mellow than he had in years. He liked the old codgers. He liked the way they yarned in their thick Somerset accents, even if some of it was unintelligible to him. He liked the camaraderie that was quickly being extended to him, and he was starting to admit that it hadn't been such a bad thing to come down here for a couple of weeks with Jassy after all.

That was all it was for, just a couple of weeks, and the man who couldn't spare that amount of time out of his busy working life was a fool to himself. By the time he left the pub that evening, intending to collect his daughter after the Monday Club, Owen was convincing himself that it was all his idea.

The village hall was all in darkness when he got there, and for a moment he was disorientated. In his mind, he was sure he'd asked her to wait for him so that he could escort her home through the dark lanes. Instead of that, he had to walk back alone, and not being as familiar with the area as Jassy, he was more and more flustered by the time he saw the lights of the cottage ahead of him.

He flung open the door angrily, hardly noticing the startled looks of the two people inside.

'Why the devil didn't you wait for me as we arranged? I could have gone wandering off anywhere before I found this place again,' he snapped, as petulant as a schoolboy, seconds before he registered that his daughter and William Hedges were sitting close together on the sofa. They were poring over some book or other, and looking very cosy indeed.

Fifteen

'Dad, I'm sorry! I don't remember making any arrangement, and William offered to walk me home so that we could discuss some of the songs for next week.'

'Is that what they're calling it now?' Owen said, in no mood to be pacified, even though he knew that this was a perfectly reasonable explanation. After a lifetime of finding it hard to back down, it was even more so with these two looking at him so indignantly.

William got to his feet. 'I'm sorry, Mr Wyatt. If I had had any idea you expected Jassy to wait for you, this would never have happened.'

'Well, considering all the alterations that have been made to this place,' he went on angrily, changing to a different tack, 'it might be a good idea to have a light installed at the end of the lane so that it shines down here. People could break their necks in the dark.'

'That's a very good idea, Dad,' Jassy said quickly, before he went into full flow again. 'What do you think, William?'

Owen didn't give William a chance to reply. 'Damn it, girl, I'm not asking for a consensus of opinions. I'm saying it should be done, and I shall make it my business to see about it tomorrow. Now, goodnight to you both. I'm tired and I'm going to bed. I shall leave my door open until I hear you come upstairs, Jasmine.'

The implication was so clear and so ludicrous that Jassy had a job not to laugh. Did he think William Hedges was about to ravish her the minute her father's back was turned? And if he did, would she react like a Victorian maiden and scream rape . . . ? In an instant, she knew that she would not . . . Even as the jumbled thoughts raced around her head, she heard William's smothered laughter.

176

'Well, that's telling me, isn't it, Miss Wyatt! I've definitely turned into a black sheep now, haven't I?'

'I'm sorry about all that,' she muttered. 'He treats me like a child, and it's really embarrassing at times.'

Without warning William pulled her gently into his arms.

'And we both know you're not a child, don't we? Nobody could put over the words to a song the way you did tonight, without being capable of the emotional feelings of a woman.'

She was both startled and annoyed. *Was that all he saw in her, then? Having the capability of putting emotion into a song?* She gave an awkward laugh.

'Well, I'm glad you find me a suitable singing partner,' was all she could manage to say.

'I think we both know I think of you as more than just a singing partner.'

'Do we?'

She heard her father cough loudly, and it was enough to make her pull away from William, and break this suddenly charged moment. 'Oh, of course. How could I ever forget that I'm a business client, and if I decide to sell or let Blackthorn Cottage, it will be to your advantage, won't it?'

He gave her a little shake. 'Sometimes, Jasmine, I think you're the most short-sighted woman in the universe. But thank you for reminding me that we have unfinished business arrangements between us. Now I'd better let you get upstairs to your beauty sleep before your father comes after me with a shotgun. Sleep well.'

He gave her a mocking wave, and seconds later she was alone, and fuming. It wasn't only her father treating her like a child now, but William obviously couldn't see it that way. She tried not to analyze just why she was so annoyed, because she knew very well. When he had pulled her into his arms, she had been anticipating that he was about to kiss her, and she had been more than ready to respond, like the gullible idiot that she was.

She made more noise than was necessary going upstairs to bed, and called out loudly to say goodnight to her father.

'You can close my door now, Jasmine,' he replied, and it was all she could do not to slam it.

*　　*　　*

During the following day she was very aware that both she and her father were at pains to be pleasant to one another. It was easier on the nerves, but it wasn't entirely natural, either. To her own surprise, Jassy realized she almost preferred the old blustery Owen to this newly affable one. But she also realized Kate Lester had more than a hand in keeping him placid.

He came home from the village in time for supper that afternoon to say they had happened to meet, and they had discussed his idea of writing something about the church from an outsider's viewpoint.

'Kate thinks it's a good idea,' he enthused. 'It will give me something to do to look through the old archives, and she's sure the vicar will agree to include the article in the parish magazine.'

Oh well, if *Kate* thought it was a good idea . . .

'Kate also gave me the name of a man who could see about installing a light at the end of the lane as I suggested. I telephoned him from the post office, and he's agreed to come round on Friday.'

'You seem to have been very busy. You and Kate.'

Owen frowned. 'What's that supposed to mean? I thought you wanted me to feel at home in this God-forsaken place – begging your pardon, vicar,' he added with a touch of humour.

'I did. I do. And I'm glad you're finding things to do. I'm sorry, Dad. I just feel a bit out of sorts today.'

He nodded. 'It happens to all of us, my dear. Women in particular, of course.'

Well, that was rich, coming from him, but Jassy knew better than to make any comment as she heard him whistling as he washed his hands before supper. Far better to have him in a good mood than to antagonize him unnecessarily.

'By the way,' he added, 'I'm glad that man will probably come on Friday to see about putting up the light at the end of the lane, as I suggested. If a thing needs doing, there's no point in delaying it.'

She had to admire him for that, Jassy thought, even if, as she suspected, he'd probably had to badger a local handyman to see to it so quickly. In any case, everyone would be in good spirits on Wednesday. It was Coronation Day, and her father would be glued to the wireless in the morning to hear all the pomp and ceremony in London. Then there were their own festivities to attend in the afternoon. She wished Grace could be here to join them. But Grace would be sharing the celebrations with Alec, and they wouldn't be here until Sunday.

That evening she was going to make the jellies for the party, and it had been arranged that William would drive to the cottage to collect them early tomorrow afternoon. Owen decided to leave her to it, and went off to the village again. One or two of his old codgers went to what they called the Sunset Club on Tuesday evenings, and he was vaguely thinking about joining them. It seemed to Jassy that for a small village they had their fair share of clubs, but it certainly drew people together in a way that never happened in a busy city. Or maybe it did, if you had the time to look for it. Down here, community spirit was definitely alive and well, she thought, as she boiled water and put the first packet of jelly crystals into a measuring jug.

The cottage was filled with an enticing aroma by the time she had finished, and ten bowls of jelly filled every spare surface in the kitchen and sitting-room. She was relaxing with a book when she heard her father return. She couldn't quite read the expression on his face.

'Well, that was certainly an evening and a half,' he greeted her.

'What do you mean?' Jassy said cautiously.

He chuckled. 'I looked in at the Sunset Club, and you never saw such a collection of old fogies with two left feet trying to do the veleta to the vicar's encouragement. He wouldn't win any medals for his footwork, either.'

'You mean there was *dancing*?' Jassy echoed.

She knew it was a club for the older people in the village. Anyone over fifty was eligible, and the old boys propping up the benches on the village green were well over that age! But Jassy had expected it to be something more sedate than dancing. And she had never known her father dance before – if indeed, he had joined in. She hardly dared to ask.

'Only one or two, in between the card games and the

179

amateur poetry readings.' He snorted at that, never having had much time for poetry. 'It was pleasant enough, though, and they're a cheerful crowd, I'll say that for them. I might go again next week. I'll see how I feel.'

His casual voice said far more than the actual words. He had definitely enjoyed himself. If it hadn't seemed to be tempting fate, Jassy could almost think that her father had suddenly realized there was a life beyond grieving and work.

'Did many of them get up and dance, Dad?' she asked delicately.

He laughed. 'You're about as subtle as a bull in a china shop, girl. If you want to ask me if I did the veleta, why don't you just ask me?'

'Well, did you?'

'I did. Me and Kate did a twirl or two around the floor, and I even remembered the steps. I daresay it's something you never forget, however long it is since you've done it.'

Like falling in love again, Jassy thought, however impossible it would have once seemed. And Kate had gone to the Sunset Club too. Of course. She wondered if her father had known Kate was going to be there. But before she got carried away with speculating, she said she'd make him his bedtime cocoa, since he looked just about all in now.

'Nonsense. I've found more energy tonight than in all the blasted medicines that goat Macleod gives me.'

'You can't go on calling him that,' she called out as she put the kettle on. 'He's going to be your son-in-law, remember.'

But her heart felt lighter than it had done in ages, and she had a good feeling about the future. Grace had found love, and there were tentative signs that her father might even do the same. That just left her – and providing Freddie Patterson hadn't soured her for ever as far as men were concerned, she was optimistic enough to believe that it could happen someday. Or had it happened already?

The party on the green was scheduled for three o'clock in the afternoon, which meant that before then, most people in Horton, and everywhere else, were listening to their wireless sets to hear all that was going on in London on that important day. It was like hearing about something that was happening in another world, hearing the reverent voice of the announcer relate what was happening in Westminster Abbey; the soaring, triumphant music; the glowing descriptions of the robes and coronets of the aristocracy, and the moments when the royal couple were crowned, followed by King George's liegemen paying homage. They were ancient words that only emphasized the solemnity of this event.

It was medieval and splendid, and Jassy wondered how the two little princesses must feel. They would be sitting with their grandmother, the formidable Queen Mary, now the Queen Mother, as they watched all the pageantry, and then the moment when their parents became crowned before the nation as King and Queen. In particular, she wondered how the young Princess Elizabeth felt, knowing that one day this role would be hers. It must give everyone listening – and watching – a feeling of fierce patriotism and loyalty towards a destiny that had existed for generations, and was part of the fabric of all their lives.

'Well,' Owen said, letting out his breath when the main part of the event was over, and they had had a quick snack, 'now perhaps we can get down to enjoying ourselves in a more modest way this afternoon. It's grand to have all that pomp and ceremony, but I wouldn't have their job for all the tea in China.'

Jassy laughed. 'You wouldn't want to live in a palace then, Dad, and have servants waiting on you all the time?'

'I would not! Would you exchange Blackthorn Cottage for it all?'

She looked around at the little cottage that had become indelibly stamped with her own personality now, and knew that she would not. Before she could answer they heard the sound of a car horn tooting, and the next minute William had knocked on the door.

'Jelly service, Ma'am,' he said cheerfully. 'Are you all ready for this afternoon's fray with the kids?'

'Just about,' she said with a grin. 'It was lovely, though. Did you hear it?'

'Some of it, although it's been a bit hectic in the village today.'

181

'I'm sure that's an understatement,' Jassy said. 'Look, you'll need somebody to keep an eye on these jellies in the car. I'll come back with you and help to set everything up.'

'Then I'll come too,' Owen said. 'I'm sure you can do with as many helping hands as possible.'

A while later, with excited children as well as adults milling about, Jassy thought there was more danger of them all getting in each other's way. The trestle-tables had been set up, and single bedsheets did double duty as tablecloths. Cups and plates and cutlery appeared as if by magic, and the food was covered efficiently to stop sandwiches and cakes from drying up. This might be a unique occasion, but it was obvious that Horton was a village that took its community closeness very seriously, and everyone was working together to make this day very special. Every child would get a Coronation mug and flag to take home, and the vicar would say a few words to bless the proceedings, and to send every good wish to their new King and Queen.

Jassy saw a familiar figure waving to her, and she recognized Daphne Smith, the young schoolteacher she had met previously.

'It's all going well, isn't it, Jasmine? Are you impressed with our industry?' she said with a laugh, as several of her infants screeched and raced around her.

'I certainly am,' Jassy said. 'I just hope the weather holds up. It didn't look too good this morning, but it's brightening up now, thank goodness.'

Daphne said airily that she didn't think the heavens would dare open on such an important day as this, and then said what was on her mind.

'Have you thought any more about what I said, about the job of school secretary? We really do need someone like you, and before you say you still don't know if you're staying in Horton, would you consider taking it on temporarily?'

'I'm not sure that would be any use to you,' Jassy said.

'I assure you it would. If we had someone efficient until the end of this term, at least we could restore some sort of order to Miss Oldfield's system, if that's what you can call it. We've all been so busy helping the children with their fancy dress costumes for today, everything else has been rather neglected.'

'My current plans are really only to stay here for two weeks to help my father have a little rest and relaxation.'

They both looked across to where Owen was laughing heartily with some of his new friends, while helping to drape bunting around the oak tree in the middle of the green.

'I'd say he was pretty well recovered,' Daphne said with a smile. 'Please think about it, Jasmine. I've spoken to my head teacher about it, and we both think you would be ideal.'

'I'll think about it, and I can't say any more than that,' Jassy said, wondering why she didn't say no right away. But Daphne could be very persuasive, as her infant charges would have discovered.

She thought about it all during that long and exciting day, and didn't miss the way her father seemed to throw himself into organizing and helping, as if he'd been born to it. She didn't miss the fact that Kate Lester seemed to be by his side very often too, and she wasn't the only one who noticed it.

Ted Hedges had come back to the village for the celebrations, along with the Coopers and his workmates. He winked at Jassy as she was pouring out endless cups of lemonade for the children. They had finished their fancy dress parade to the applause of doting parents and grandparents, and finally got through the mountains of sandwiches, cakes and jellies and blancmanges.

'I see the old folks are getting along all right,' Ted said, nodding to where Owen and Kate were chatting together. 'Not going to hear the sound of wedding bells there, are we?'

It might be what Jassy was half hoping for, but hearing him say it in that mocking way made her quickly defensive of her father.

'Don't be absurd. Your mother is a very sociable woman, and she's merely being pleasant to a stranger.'

'Doesn't seem to me like he's being much of a stranger, sweetheart. I'd say he's getting his feet under the table.'

She stared at him. 'Does that bother you, Ted?'

'I don't know. What do you make of it?'

She didn't like this conversation, and nor did she want to discuss her father's feelings or intentions with Ted Lester.

'I think it's none of my business,' she said pointedly.

He grinned. 'In other words, I should keep my nose out of it, but if they got hitched it would definitely become our business, because then we'd be related.'

Jassy wasn't sure she wanted him for a stepbrother, nor William either. But William wouldn't be a stepbrother, since he wasn't Kate's true nephew. Even if her father and Kate Lester ever did become more than friendly, William wouldn't be related to her. From that first day when she had expected to see a starchy, middle-aged businessman, she knew she was growing more and more drawn to him. The thoughts whirled around in her mind, and she wished Ted hadn't spoiled this lovely day by making her think about things she didn't want to consider. But he wasn't spoiling it. The children were running about excitedly now, the helpers were starting to clear away the chaos of the tea-tables, and groups, old and young, were still crowding about discussing the events of the Coronation they had all listened to that morning, and their own celebration of it in Horton.

Owen and Kate came walking towards them, looking very happy in each other's company, Jassy thought. But if Ted made any silly, snide comments about it now, she knew her father would withdraw like a clam.

'Don't you dare say anything to spoil things,' she told him fiercely.

'I wouldn't bother,' he said. 'In fact, I'm not stopping any longer. Me and my mates have got better things to do than to stick around here all afternoon.'

He waved to his mother and went off to join the group of young men he had arrived with. Kate frowned.

'Now where's that boy going? I was going to invite you and your father to join William and me for supper tonight, and I'd hoped Ted would join us too.'

'He's off with his mates,' Jassy said lightly. 'This is probably all getting a little tame for him, Mrs Lester. But thank you for the invitation – if Dad agrees.'

It was hard to think that he wouldn't agree to spending more time with Kate. Jassy had never seen him looking so content with life, and it was such a rare event that she felt quite emotional. If her father's future really did lie with Kate

Lester, then something good had definitely come out of her inheriting Blackthorn Cottage. It was a twist of fate that no one could ever have foreseen. But that was the way of fate. Sometimes good, sometimes bad.

There was plenty of work to do on the green before supper-time, and people still seemed reluctant to move away, so it was a long while later before the four of them had a late supper. Knowing they wouldn't be too hungry after all the nibbles on the green, Kate had made a cheese and potato pie which only needed to be heated through to be eaten with pickles and hunks of bread and butter. It was such a harmonious evening that Jassy decided to broach the subject of the school secretary job. Better to let her father know about it before Kate or William let it slip.

'I've been offered a job, Dad,' she said, keeping her voice amused. 'Working at the infant school as a school secretary, just temporarily until the end of July.'

'You said no, I presume.'

'I said I'd think about it. It sounds interesting.'

'I see.' He was no longer looking quite so affable, and the atmosphere had gone several degrees cooler. 'You intend staying here that long then?'

Before she stopped to think, she made a huge decision and acted on it.

'I will if you'll stay too. Why not, Dad? You seem to be getting on so well with everybody, and I'm sure Grace is loving the chance to be so independent.'

His face went so dark that for a moment she thought he was about to blow up, and she immediately regretted her impulsiveness. It had probably been wrong to talk about personal decisions in Kate and William's company too. It wasn't fair to make them party to whatever mood her father was about to display. But she had reckoned without the blossoming friendship between Owen and Kate. Disbelievingly, she saw Kate put her hand over her father's and give it a little squeeze.

'Now, Owen, before you go off half-cocked, why don't you think about this sensibly?' Kate said calmly. 'It's obvious you're really enjoying the country life. It suits you, and it suits Jasmine too. Your other daughter will be getting married soon, and having a new life of her own. She'll be off your hands, and there's no reason why you couldn't make a complete break if you wanted to. You could even retire to Horton and become a country gentleman. I can just see you in tweeds and a pork pie hat, and you'd be organizing events at the Sunset Club before you knew it!'

By the time she finished, Jassy and William could hardly contain their mirth at Owen's expression. He wasn't used to anyone organizing his life in this gentle and not-so-subtle manner. He was used to Grace's teasing and keeping him sweet, and to Jassy's feisty behaviour that irritated him more often than not. But Kate was quite different. Kate was just as independent and capable as himself, but there was a softness about her that he liked. Their pasts were different, and yet it was similar in so many ways, both widowed, but learning to cope with life, both at an age when companionship was important. He cleared his throat.

'Is this what you really want, Jassy? Do you really think we could stand each other for several more months, instead of two weeks?'

'We haven't done so badly so far, have we?'

No, but it had been less than a week, the weather had been fair, and they had both been able to get out of doors. It would be different if they were housebound together while the rain pelted down and the wind screeched and moaned through the trees in the woods. Although, if she was working at the infant school, they wouldn't be incarcerated together all the time . . .

'So shall I tell Daphne Smith I'll take the job?' she challenged him, ignoring everything else, and forcing him to make the decision.

'If it's what you want.'

There was a sudden explosion from William, and the others looked at him in surprise.

'It's not my place to say so, but since we've all become embroiled in each other's business, I have to say that you two are the most stubborn people I've ever come across. I thought Jassy was bad enough, wondering what to do about the cottage, when it's obvious they were made for each other, but when you both get started, it's worse than listening to

186

two schoolkids wrangling over who's having the last toffee. It's clear that you both want the same thing, so why the dickens can't you come out and say so!'

Jassy felt her mouth drop open in fury, while Kate glowered at her nephew for such rudeness to their guests. Then, to everyone's surprise, Owen began a slow handclap, and Jassy saw the same reaction that he usually gave to Grace's teasing.

'Owen, I'm so sorry,' Kate began, 'and William, you will apologize at once.'

Owen waved his hand at her. 'Nobody needs to apologize, Kate. He only said what needed to be said, and it probably takes an outsider to see what a stubborn pair we truly are. So what do we decide, Jassy? Do we stay for a few more months, as it seems we both want to do?'

'You're still asking me to decide,' she said weakly, hardly able to credit how this was all going.

'Then I'll answer for both of us. We stay, and if we end up fighting, so be it.'

'We shall also have to see what Grace has to say about it on Sunday,' Jassy pointed out, still bedazzled by it all.

'Or you could telephone her before then, and get her approval,' Kate said. 'Why don't you do it now, before you change your mind again?'

He was actually laughing at her cheek as they went down to the post office below to make the call to Grace, leaving the other two alone. Everything was taking such a bizarre turn, Jassy thought. It wasn't what she had expected to happen, but she couldn't deny a bubbling excitement as she realized that it was William who had taken a hand in it all. Kate had begun it, but it was William who had put the final seal on it. It was William who wanted her to stay in Horton. She looked at him directly now.

'It seems as if I'll have to put any plans for the cottage on hold for the time being then. No more business coming your way, William.'

'I think there's business enough for me, sorting you out,' he said with a small smile, 'and I hope you don't think I overdid it just now.'

'I think it was wonderful,' she said with a catch in her

throat. She put out her hand to touch his, and before she knew what he was about to do, he had raised her hand to his lips in a sweet, old-fashioned gesture.

'And so are you, my lady,' he said.

Sixteen

On Friday it was all settled. A local handyman had arrived to instal a light at the end of the lane, according to Owen's instructions, and Jassy had been to the infant school and met the head teacher, Mrs Willmott. She was to start on Monday, and by the time she left for home, she had acquired an ancient bicycle that one of the cleaners had left behind, and she rode it precariously back to the cottage.

'I'm out of practise,' she called out to Owen, as she wobbled to a halt at the cottage gate. 'But at least it will get me to the school on time.'

He straightened his back from weeding around the rose bushes. 'As a matter of fact I was thinking about getting a small car too. It would give us the chance to look around the countryside, and I don't like to be always dependent on Grace, so we could also go back home whenever we like.'

Jassy didn't respond to his last statement. A car would give him the perfect excuse to take Kate Lester farther afield too, though she wouldn't say as much. But Owen never wasted time when he had a plan in mind, and when Kate and William arrived for supper on Saturday night, Owen brought up the subject.

'There's a reputable garage on the Taunton road,' William told him. 'If you like, I can spare a couple of hours next week to drive you over there.'

'That would be grand. If you could make it on Monday perhaps you'd care to come too, Kate, since it's your day off.'

There was no missing the fact that Kate went pink at the invitation. It was almost as if the fates were conspiring to get them together, thought Jassy. Or else it was themselves who weren't missing an opportunity. She thought so again as the older couple went for a stroll through the woods after supper, while she and William stayed behind to clear away the supper things.

'What do you think?' she asked him abruptly. 'Are those two becoming more than friends? They've hardly known one another more than five minutes!'

The thought had crossed her mind that it could even be her father who was more enamoured of Kate Lester than she was of him, and she couldn't bear it if he was to be rejected and retreat into his almost reclusive ways again.

'How long does it take for two people to be attracted to one another?' William countered. 'I'm told there's a strong case for believing in love at first sight, and I daresay when you get to their age, you don't want to waste any time.'

'You wouldn't object then?'

'I would never object to my aunt finding happiness with a man she clearly admires at the very least. Would you?'

'No, but I think Ted might have other ideas.'

She told him quickly of the odd little conversation they had had on Coronation Day, and William shrugged.

'Ted's still an immature boy. He sees love the way it's portrayed on the silver screen, only for young and glamorous people living out fairy stories. In any case, he's unlikely to come back to Horton to live now he's firmly settled at Cooper's Farm, so I can't see what difference it would make to him.'

Jassy was relieved to hear him say so. They agreed that they were merely speculating on something that may never happen. It was a lovely dream to think of two nice people finding happiness in what the romantic novels called their twilight years, but in practical terms it would probably never happen. The most Jassy could hope for was that meeting Kate had at last pulled her father out of his long-term grieving for his wife. When they returned to the cottage, their faces were glowing from the soft evening breeze, and Jassy refused to think anything more of it.

The arrival of Grace and Alec next day temporarily put anything more out of her head. Grace was proudly wearing her glittering engagement ring now, and oozed a confidence that had never been evident before. They approved of all the alterations to the cottage and wanted to know everything about the village.

'I can't believe how different Dad looks,' Grace confided to her sister later, when the men had gone outside to admire the roses. 'Alec will be really pleased at how relaxed he is, and I don't know how you persuaded him to stay longer.'

'Oh, I don't think it's solely on my account,' Jassy told her. 'He's become quite friendly with Mrs Lester, including going to the Sunset Club and dancing with her, and he's invited her along when he and William go to see about buying a small car tomorrow,' she finished triumphantly.

It was worth saying it all in a rush to see the astonishment on Grace's face.

'Good Lord, there must be something in the water down here,' she said with a grin. 'Is he really keen?'

For the first time, Jassy wondered how Grace would really feel about it. Grace was her father's pet, and Jassy had always known that. But now she had Alec, and she surely couldn't begrudge her father his happiness.

'I think he might be,' she said cautiously.

But thankfully Grace was viewing the world through rose-coloured glasses now, and thought it was hilarious. She couldn't wait to tell Alec.

'For heaven's sake don't tease him or anything,' Jassy warned. 'One hint from us that we're tickled pink about it, and he'll back off.'

Grace promised, but neither she nor Alec could hide the arch glances they kept giving one another whenever Kate Lester's name was mentioned during the afternoon and early evening.

'What's wrong with you two?' Owen said at last. 'Is it too impossible for two people to like each other's company without you looking so daft about it? It's not as if we were eloping – and if we were, we'd be darned sure not to let you two jackasses know about it!'

He stumped out to the garden where he took refuge these days whenever he wanted to think. Alec followed him out.

'Don't take on so, man. You're looking so well now, and if this woman has got anything to do with it, then good for her.'

'She doesn't,' Owen raged. 'Don't you people ever listen?'

'Of course she doesn't. I merely said *if* she had anything to do with it. Don't you ever listen, either, you dumbbell?'

Watching them through the kitchen window as they continued arguing with many gesticulations, their arms occasionally flailing about like windmills, the Wyatt sisters sighed.

'Just look at them,' Jassy said. 'It didn't take long for them to start their usual nonsense, did it? Dad probably misses that, though I suspect he always has plenty to say with his new pals on the green and at the pub.'

And then they saw Alec clap the older man on the back, and wondered just what had been going on between them after all.

Monday started out dull and cool, and ended in pelting rain that chilled the bones, even in May. Pedalling home from her first satisfactory day at the infant school, Jassy wished she'd had the sense to wear or take some wellington boots and a decent mackintosh. While she was living in the country, she might as well look the part, especially when the weather was unpredictable. She kept her head well down against the rain until she reached home, and then almost ran into the unfamiliar car standing in the lane outside.

Owen was watching for her to come home, and opened the front door before she reached it. 'What do you think? She's a little beauty, isn't she?'

Jassy was in no mood to admire a car. 'I'm soaked,' she snapped. 'Let me get out of these wet things and then I'll be able to think more sensibly.'

'Well, there's no need to snap my head off,' her father said.

No, that was usually his style, thought Jassy. She slid out of her sodden jacket and grabbed a towel from the kitchen, rubbing her wet hair before she cocooned it in the towel. But she recognized the hurt note in Owen's voice, and knew he'd been dying to show off his new toy. She gave a sigh and put on a brighter face as she rejoined him.

'All right then, show me this magical machine!'

'I wouldn't call it that, but it'll get us around,' he grunted, but his enthusiasm wouldn't be dampened for long, and five minutes later they were both sitting inside the small black car while he explained the finer points of it.

'It's no good trying to make a mechanic out of me, Dad,' she said with a laugh. 'As long as it goes, that's all that matters. And as long as you're happy.'

He looked at her. 'I am,' he said simply. 'I'm happier than I've been in a very long time. And I've got you to thank for that, Jasmine.'

She was taken aback. She hadn't expected such a reply, and she was fairly sure she wasn't the one to lift his spirits.

'Why? For being so obstinate and persuading you to come to Blackthorn Cottage?' she said lightly.

'Mostly that,' he said. He gave her arm a squeeze. 'Let's go indoors and have a cup of tea. You'll want to thaw out before you go to the Monday Club tonight.'

'I'm not sure that I'll bother in this weather.'

'Of course you will. I want to get in some driving practise, so I'll take you there and collect you afterwards. I'm due for a game of darts at the pub tonight, and a little drop of rain isn't stopping me.'

He was being so positive and so energized that Jassy didn't have the heart to say she'd almost decided not to go. She wouldn't have told him the reason, anyway, that it was because she found it too uncomfortable to look into William Hedges's eyes and sing a romantic song with him. She wasn't an actress, and she found it hard to pretend an emotion she didn't feel . . . or to hide one that she did.

So that evening saw her arriving at the Monday Club, to find that the others were already there. She sensed at once that there was excitement in the air, and she soon learned why. It had been arranged that the Monday Club would give a small concert at the Midsummer Day Fair, and Esme Dunn strolled across to Jassy as soon as she saw her.

'What a pity you won't be here by then, Jasmine, so it looks as though I'll be singing the duet with William instead,' she said sweetly.

'The village gossip evidently hasn't reached you yet, then. I've taken a job at the infant's school until the end of July at least. I'm not going anywhere just yet.'

William overheard them, not missing the flash of annoyance on Esme's face.

'Sorry, Esme, but I'll still have my singing partner by then, and you'll get plenty of applause in any case. You do a terrific job of *Mad about the boy*.'

The irony of the song wasn't lost on Jassy, even if it was on William. Esme obviously saw him as her own property, whether or not there was any foundation for thinking that way. Somehow Jassy didn't think there was. Esme wasn't the type of girl William would find attractive . . . but it was no business of hers, anyway.

'When you've all finished gossiping, can we get started, everybody?' Jim, the organizer, said impatiently. 'And let's put some heart into the songs tonight.'

The *frisson* of tension disappeared as they listened to the arrangements for the small concert. They would only have a spot of about twenty minutes, and they would be expected to put on a good show, with a few traditional numbers, and their Noel Coward repertoire.

'So we get to sing again,' William breathed in Jassy's ear as Jim struck up the first few chords of their song. 'Let's do as Jim says, and pretend we're in love – if it's not too difficult for you!'

She gritted her teeth at his mocking tone, knowing it wasn't going to be too difficult. She wasn't in love with him, but for the purposes of the show she would darned well do her best to convince everybody listening that she was!

They finished to spontaneous applause, and one of the older ladies wiped her eyes, gushing that it had been beautiful . . . just beautiful. And just as before, it was easy, after all, Jassy discovered, to feel the words of the song, and pretend that they applied to a lover. It was also vital to remember that it was strictly a performance. It wasn't real.

The days merged into weeks, and the roses in the front garden of Blackthorn Cottage were in full blossom by mid June, filling the air with their heady, overpowering scent. Jasmine had slipped easily into the role of infant school secretary by now, and loved it. Owen had become the new darts champion at the Rose and Crown, and was everybody's good ol'

pal as he bought the old codgers a round of drinks to celebrate, and he had drafted out his first article for the parish
magazine, with the help of Kate Lester and the vicar. The
Monday Club had perfected their concert plans for Midsummer Day and Ted Lester told his mother keenly that he
had every hope of winning the best dressed horse and cart
at this year's fair.

The Sunday before Midsummer Day Owen and Jassy went
back to Bristol to collect some more clothes and belongings.
Grace was to make dinner for all of them at the flat, including
Alec. It was a cheerful and light-hearted occasion, with Owen
regaling them with anecdotes about his old codgers, and yet
Jassy had the feeling all along that something wasn't quite
right. By the time they were amicably replete after the meal,
it was then that Grace dropped her bombshell.

She and Alec were sitting together on the sofa, and Jassy
saw how her hand stole into his, as if for moral support.

'Dad, Jassy, we've got something to tell you,' she began.
She glanced at Alec, who nodded encouragingly.

'Well come on, whatever it is, it can't be anything too
bad,' Owen said, but a frown was beginning on his face as
he looked from one to the other of them. His thoughts were
clearly etched. If that bastard Macleod had done anything to
hurt his girl or bring a scandal to his family, he'd throttle
him . . .

'It rather depends on how you view it. Certainly, Grace
and I are excited about the prospect,' Alec said carefully.

When she seemed reluctant to go on, he spoke in a firm
voice. 'Grace knows I've had a hankering to go back to
Scotland for some time. My father has a practice near
Aberdeen and he's always wanted me to go in with him as
a partner. He and my mother are both getting on a bit now,
and he's made the offer again. It's a wonderful part of the
country, and in a nutshell, I'd be a damn fool to refuse it.'

'I see,' Owen said without expression, 'And what does
Grace say about this? I presume she has some opinion on
it.'

The hand holding tightened. 'Grace agrees. You'll recall
what the Bible says – whither thou goest, I will go,' Alec
said finally.

'Don't quote the Bible at me, man,' Owen roared, instantly back to his old form. 'You're suggesting taking my girl to some northern God-knows-where and expecting her to be happy about it? I want to hear that from her own lips.'

Grace snapped back. 'Dad, of course I'm happy about it. This is a wonderful opportunity for Alec and for me too. We'll be part of a family business.'

'You're already part of a family business.'

The silence was as sharp as a knife cut.

'But that's just it,' Grace said slowly and deliberately. 'You won't want to be in business for ever, and already you look a different man since you've taken time to relax. I don't want to spend my life behind a shop counter, either, which is what will happen if I don't go with Alec. I have to think of my own life now.'

'I see,' Owen said.

'Grace, I think it's wonderful for you both,' Jassy said swiftly, even though she knew her father must feel as if his family was being torn apart. First Celia, now Grace . . . but he still had her, if only he would see it that way.

Grace flashed her a smile. 'Alec's father wants him to take over much of the practice by the end of October, so we want to bring our wedding forward. Alec's parents won't be able to travel all this way, so we're thinking of having a small wedding here in early October, and then we'll have a blessing in Alec's kirk in Scotland for his family to attend.'

'You seem to have it all planned, miss!' Owen said.

'Yes, we do, and don't think we haven't given it considerable thought before we both agreed on it,' Alec said. 'But we want your blessing as well, Owen. This is a great chance for us to start a new life, but we want you and Jassy to be happy for us too. I know my darling Grace will never rest easy unless she has that.'

They all looked at Owen, and he saw the anxious look in his precious girl's eyes. He saw the protective way Alec Macleod had put his arm around her, and despite his own feelings, he didn't have it in him to refuse, even though he knew a part of him would go with her.

'Then you have my blessing, and I wish you all the luck

in the world,' he said gruffly at last, and was rewarded by hugs and kisses and tears.

Owen was quiet for most of the journey back to Horton that evening, and Jassy wisely didn't interrupt his thoughts. By then, the four of them had talked themselves out until they were hoarse, but Owen was satisfied in his mind that Grace was going to have a good husband and a secure and happy future, even if it was so far away. But not as far as death, he reminded himself in one poignant, sober moment. And he wouldn't dim her joy by his own sadness at losing her.

Although it was truly strange how fate had a habit of deciding things that a few months ago, he would never have considered. There were more things in heaven and earth, etcetera, etcetera, he thought, with a glimmer of wry humour.

They got nearer and nearer to Horton, and eventually the outskirts of the village came into view, and he finally spoke.

'I don't know what to think about the future now, but it's only right that Grace and Alec should do what's best for them,' he said abruptly. 'But I have to think about the shop as well. Grace has worked with me for so long that I don't care too much for the thought of breaking in someone new, and I imagine it's out of the question expecting you to come back and work with me, isn't it?'

She knew she had to answer this very carefully, and she delicately avoided any mention of Kate Lester.

'I just don't think it would be a good idea, Dad, and the longer I stay in Horton, the more I think I want to stay, at least for a while. I love working at the school and the cottage belongs to me, so I've got every option of staying as long as I like, but what I'd like more than anything, is for you to stay there too. Grace was right. You do look so much better now, and you've found some new interests of your own there, haven't you?'

She prayed he wouldn't think there was anything too personal in what she said. He was still capable of losing his temper over the slightest thing, as he had shown back at the flat. Grace and Alec's news had been a shock to him, but he finally seemed to have come to terms with it.

'You'll be able to do whatever you think fit after your

twenty-first birthday,' he said. 'At least Grace will still be here then, and we must be back in Bristol for it, of course. I won't decide on anything until then.'

'Well, really, you don't have to make any decisions until October when they leave,' she reminded him, knowing better than to try to rush him.

Her birthday would be the anniversary of the day his beloved wife had died too, but his replies were as much as Jassy could hope for, and she said no more as they drove through the twilit village and out to where the welcome light surrounding the cottage came into view. It looked so tranquil, as if nothing bad had ever happened here in the past, and as if something good was surely going to happen for it in the future. It may be no more than a fanciful thought, but one that Jassy was determined to keep uppermost in her mind.

It was almost as if Owen had decided to put all thoughts of the future out of his mind for the time being. He threw himself into village activities until even Jassy was bound to call a halt.

'You don't have to do everything at once, Dad,' she protested. 'You go to the pub several nights a week, you drive Mrs Lester into Taunton now and then, as well as up to Cooper's Farm to see Ted, and you've even joined the Sunset Club. Slow down, can't you?'

'I thought this was what you wanted, for me to integrate into village life.'

'I wanted you to relax, not kill yourself,' she muttered.

'I am relaxing. Keeping busy is what I'm used to, and that relaxes me. You do things your way and I'll do them my way, and then we won't get on one another's nerves.'

There was no arguing with him and she gave up trying. His article about the church eventually appeared in the parish news, and the vicar told him it was well received, and if he wanted to do more on village life from a city man's view, it would be more than welcome. Jassy was enjoying her job at the school immensely, but in a way Owen seemed almost more integrated than Jassy herself. Of course it was what she wanted, but it was somehow unnerving. And it was

198

thoughts of the coming performance on Midsummer Day that were unnerving her most of all.

It was almost upon them now, and there was much activity up at Cooper's Farm to get things ready, with preparations for the usual tombola stalls, the best fruit and vegetable tables, the home-made cake and jams competition, and the best dressed horse and cart, as well as the games for the children.

Most recently, Owen had taken it on himself to make ye olde village stocks, as mentioned in the archives from times gone by. From the rear of the cottage, the sounds of sawing and hammering, interspersed with mild cussing when a nail missed its mark, was one that Jassy became well used to before the object was proudly displayed.

'Isn't he clever?' Kate Lester exclaimed, when she and Owen were preparing to take it to the farm. 'This is going to be such a novelty, and next year we'll have to think of something else for him to make.'

'I shan't be here next year, remember?' he said.

Kate flushed. 'Oh, Lord, yes. You've become such a part of the place now, I forgot this was only a temporary arrangement.'

Jassy didn't dare look at either of them. They seemed to be fencing around one another so often now, and their relationship seemed so delicately balanced that she didn't want to say the wrong word. The one thing that was undeniable, however, was that they truly enjoyed one another's company. It was obvious to everyone, including William. After the Monday Club's final rehearsal before the big day, he asked her a blunt question.

'So when is your father going to make an honest woman of my aunt?'

Jassy hid her surprise at the question and laughed.

'What a quaint, old-fashioned phrase. Can't two people become good friends without marriage coming into it?'

'You tell me. Can they?'

'Have I told you my sister and her fiancé are bringing their wedding forward and moving to Scotland in October?'

'No, you haven't, but Aunt Kate said something about it. And what does that have to do with what I just asked you?'

She didn't know why he was putting her on the spot like this, or why she had fudged answering the question directly. She answered crossly.

'It has quite a lot to do with it, since my father may want me to go back to Bristol to help him run the shop when Grace leaves.'

'I see,' William said. 'Somehow I can't see that happening.'

'Why not?' For one blinding moment, she wanted him to say that he wanted her to stay here, with him . . . she willed him to say the words . . .

'I can't see you ever being satisfied with being stuck behind a shop counter, selling ribbons and cottons to old ladies, that's why. You're doing a far better job at the school, using your brain.'

'Well, I'll do it until the end of July, as promised, but after that, I can't say what I'm going to do. We'll definitely be going back to Bristol for the first part of August, anyway.'

He knew it would be her twenty-first birthday on the first of the month, but she wasn't going to draw attention to it. And she no longer wanted to talk about it. There would be enough upheavals in the forthcoming months, what with Grace and Alec's wedding, lovely though that occasion would be, and then their departure to Scotland. She drew in her breath, knowing just what a wrench it would be, and not only to her father. Grace had always been a huge part of her life, a substitute mother in Jassy's early years, and a big sister she could always rely on ever since.

'I'm sorry, Jassy. I didn't mean to upset you.'

She heard William's voice as if through a fog, and looked at him through blurry eyes.

'You didn't. I was just having a bad moment, that's all.'

'And somehow I seem to have made it worse.' He put his arms around her and held her close, and she had no inclination to move away. They were outside the hall, waiting for Owen to come by and drive her back to the cottage, and Esme emerged from the Club to witness what looked like a very cosy embrace.

'I see the lyrics of your song are having their desired effect,' she said distantly. 'You'd better hold on to him while you can, Jasmine. There'll be somebody else for him to

200

cuddle up to once you're out of the picture. It was my turn last year. Who knows who'll be next!'

She left them to it, her blonde head high in the air, and Jassy felt acutely embarrassed and annoyed. Esme was jealous, of course, but it was undoubtedly true. When – if – she went back to Bristol, this relationship would be finished for ever. She need never see William again once she put the cottage in his estate agent's hands. But for now, with Grace planning to move away, she was fast coming to the conviction that she must abide by whatever her father wanted to do. She owed him her loyalty – and in many ways, she was just as confused about her future plans as she had been on the first day she arrived here.

'Take no notice,' William said harshly, bringing her back to the present. 'Esme's always got some bee or other in her bonnet, and just because she and I sang several duets last year, she thinks she has territorial rights on me.'

'But it doesn't apply, does it?' Jassy said, moving away from him as she saw her father's car approach. 'It's only a song after all.'

That night, with moonlight lighting up the soft darkness of her bedroom, she faced her feelings squarely. The words of their song were emotive, but in her heart she knew she was starting to believe they were real. That he was real. That he was her sweetheart, her destiny, and that the sentiments of the words were real.

She smothered a small sob. This wasn't meant to happen. She had been so wrapped up in the thrill of seeing her father and Kate Lester edging so sweetly towards a happy ever after ending, and then the excitement of Grace's engagement, that she had ignored her own feelings. But they had grown just as imperceptibly and inevitably as night following day. She could no longer ignore the fact that she was falling in love with William Hedges.

Seventeen

By the end of July, Jassy reflected that time had never gone so fast. Working at the school had given her a new incentive for living in Horton. She loved the work and she loved the village. She had become quite friendly with Daphne Smith, and they had spent several evenings at the cinema in Taunton. She also knew that, no matter how much Owen was throwing himself into every activity he could, she was going to abide by whatever he wanted to do. When Grace and Alec left for Scotland, it was going to be a huge upheaval in his life. If easing that blow for him meant she had to go back to Bristol and work with him in the shop, for a while at least, she had virtually resigned herself to it. It needn't be for a lifetime, she told herself, and it might be easier on her nerves than seeing William Hedges as often as she did.

She could either leave the cottage empty for a while, or let it for the rest of the long summer season as she had once intended. In any case William would need to know her plans, and she mentioned it to him after one of their evenings at the Monday Club. She was startled to hear the anger in his voice.

'So you've decided to be a martyr, have you? It doesn't become you, Jassy, and I thought better of you.'

'What do you mean by that?'

'I mean I thought you had more guts, to put it crudely. You've got a life of your own, and just because your sister sacrificed most of hers to your father, it doesn't follow that you have to do the same.'

She felt her mouth drop open in fury. He was tactless and hateful to say such things to her. He had no right . . .

'That's a rotten thing to say. Of course Grace didn't sacrifice her life! She loved looking after Dad, and she was like a mother to me – the one I didn't have,' she finished, her voice choking.

The break in her voice did nothing to make him compromise. 'Exactly. And now she's got a new life of her own, and she's not wasting it by considering what her father wants any more, which is only right and proper. You should do the same.'

'Well, I can't, and I think it's callous of you to suggest it.'

'Really. So if your knight in shining armour came along on a white charger, or more likely on a motor bike, you'd tell him you'd rather stay with daddy than get married and have a family of your own, would you? Did it never occur to you that Owen might very well want grandchildren in his old age?'

'I know he would, because he once said so,' Jassy snapped, even more angered at his reference to a motor bike and the day Freddie Patterson found her at Blackthorn Cottage. 'But you're twisting my words. I didn't say I was going to go back to Bristol for ever, just that if Dad needs me, I think it's my duty to go with him, at least for a while. It's called loyalty, in case you've never heard of it. And he's not in his old age, either.'

'No, he's not, and remembering that little talk we had once before, he might even consider marrying again one day, and where will that leave you?'

Her temper flared. 'You're like all men, aren't you? You think a woman's happiness is solely dependent on finding a man to marry. Well, I'm not sitting around waiting for a knight on a white charger or anything else, and some of us can manage perfectly well without all those trappings, thank you very much.'

'Oh well, that's telling me, isn't it? I'll be sure not to make any rash proposals of marriage then! Not that I was thinking of making one!'

How on earth this conversation had descended into something far too personal, Jassy wasn't quite sure. But the sound of a motor car slowing down beside them made her turn sharply away from the insufferable man. Seconds later she had yanked open the car door and was sitting beside her father, her face stony, her arms folded tightly around herself.

'Do I take it that this evening hasn't gone too well?' Owen said mildly as he drove off with a wave to William.

'You could say that. That man's impossible sometimes. I was right in what I first thought of him.'

'I seem to remember you expected him to be some pompous old goat.' Owen was clearly in a better mood than his daughter, and his words were laced with a barely disguised chuckle.

'Well, a third of that was right. He's pompous, and irritating, and a know-it-all, so that's my new assessment of him. I could add plenty more as well.'

Owen laughed outright now. 'Sometimes, Jassy, methinks the lady protests a little too much.'

'I haven't even started yet,' Jassy muttered as the cottage came into view.

'Well, you'd better prepare to be pleasant to him on Saturday evening.'

It would be the last day of July, and the next day they were going back home. Owing to the circumstances of her birth there had never been any wild celebrations for Jassy's birthday, but this was a special one when she came of age, and Grace and Alec were planning a special supper for them all. Before then, they all knew that Owen would be spending an hour or two alone at the churchyard as usual.

They left the car and walked into the cottage, each with their own thoughts, and Jassy's were centred now on what Owen had just said.

'Why should I be pleasant to him on Saturday evening especially?' she said suspiciously.

'Kate's invited us to a small party in honour of your birthday,' Owen told her. 'She's asking William and Ted too, and she wondered if you'd like to invite that nice school-teacher friend of yours. It's a very nice gesture, Jassy, and I won't have any nonsense between you and William ruining it for Kate,' he added warningly.

She knew it was a lovely gesture, and presumably her father had had plenty of time to discuss it with Kate. His evenings weren't all spent at the pub with the old codgers now, she had discovered. But this was definitely a thoughtful thing for Kate to do, and she could hardly refuse.

'It's very sweet of Mrs Lester, and I'll ask Daphne tomorrow,' she muttered, thinking that at least there would be sufficient numbers for her not to have too much conversation with William.

What she hadn't expected was that Kate would be making quite such an occasion of it. Supper consisted of cold meats and salad and tiny new potatoes, and then the most enormous apple pie with Somerset cream from Cooper's Farm that Jassy had ever seen. But if that was not enough, it was followed by a birthday cake with twenty-one candles on it. The fact that Kate had gone to so much trouble made Jassy's eyes prickle.

'Oh, this is so lovely of you, Mrs Lester,' she said with a catch in her throat.

'Well, I know it's not your proper birthday until tomorrow, but we couldn't let you go off to Bristol without marking it in some way, and to let you know how highly we think of you, my dear. You've become a real part of the village now. Light the candles, William.'

'We all think highly of Jassy,' Daphne said with a smile. 'We've found a treasure for the school in her, and I only hope she'll stay with us – but I know better than to press her on that. She'll decide in her own good time.'

'Meanwhile,' Ted put in, 'the birthday girl has to blow out every candle and make a wish.'

Jassy stood up with a shaky laugh. All this was so much more than she had expected, and because it wasn't the actual day, when her father always had mixed feelings, he looked tremendously happy to be here too. But that wouldn't be solely on account of his daughter, of course . . .

She blew out all the candles with one enormous blow, making a wish and closing her eyes as she did so. She opened them again to find herself looking directly through the drift of smoke into William's eyes on the other side of the table, and his gaze was so enigmatic that she felt her heart thump. Just as though he could read the wish she had just made . . .

'So what did you wish for?' Ted said.

'Oh, you mustn't ask her that,' Daphne told him. 'If she says it out loud, it won't come true.'

It probably wouldn't anyway, Jassy thought, but she put on a bright smile and told everyone that Daphne was exactly right and that birthday wishes were private.

'It's a lot of rot anyway,' Ted said, becoming bored now.

'You're too cynical for your own good, cuz,' William said. 'There's no reason why wishes can't come true if you want them badly enough.'

Daphne looked at him admiringly. 'Why William, I didn't know you could be such an old romantic.'

He grinned back. 'Not so much of the *old* if you don't mind!'

Kate stood up. 'Well, now I'm going to cut this cake and you can all make your own wish when you eat your slice. I'm sure we've all got something to wish for.'

For a moment Jassy wondered if William's wish could possibly be the same as hers, or if they had just grown too far apart to ever make it happen. They wouldn't have the companionship of the Monday Club now, since the previous one had been the last until September, so there would be no more romantic singing duets to mend any cracks in their relationship.

But she deliberately wouldn't dwell on that, and instead, as the plates of cake were handed around, she wondered even more just what Kate Lester might be wishing for . . .

After the meal came the unexpected gifts. Kate gave her a silk scarf, and Daphne gave her a book she had wanted. Ted had made her an ornament out of boughs, and William handed her a large packet. Inside was a beautifully bound copy of Noel Coward's music and lyrics. The little written message on the front merely said: 'I'll be seeing you – William'. It was sweet and emotive, and it was all she could do not to fling her arms around him and thank him properly, but the thought of doing so in front of all these people made her merely thank him for his thoughtfulness, while wondering if it meant anything, or nothing at all.

August the first fell on a Sunday that year, and it was an appropriate day for Owen to be visiting the churchyard where his wife was buried. He and Jassy left Horton by mid-morning and were back in familiar surroundings in time to have hugs and kisses and presents, and then a quick snack with Grace before Owen left them to what he called their female gossip. He had been fairly silent on the drive back, and Jassy knew he was trying to make an effort not to let the memories of the past overshadow her special day. And it *was* her special day, and once the sisters were alone in the flat, the details of last night spilled over.

'There's definitely something going on there,' Grace said sagely. She didn't need to pinpoint the fact that she meant her father and Kate.

'Do you think so?'

'Don't you? He looks so different now, Jassy – even today.'

'I know. And I can't help wondering just what sort of a one-sided conversation he's having with our mother today. Does he think it's time, after all these years, for him to tell her he's found a new lady in his life, and to ask for her blessing?'

She felt foolish just saying such things, but after witnessing her father at the churchyard on that other occasion, she was convinced that if he really felt the way she thought he did about Kate Lester, he would also feel the need to do this.

Grace gave her hug. 'You're getting far too intense over all this, darling, and I won't have you looking gloomy on your birthday. I've got something very special to ask you, although you must have guessed it already. I want you to be my bridesmaid when Alec and I get married.'

Jassy's face lit up. 'Oh, of course I will!

'Then we'll have to get our heads together and decide what we're going to wear. We need to give the dressmaker plenty of time, so I'll see her next week and ask her for some pattern books, and the next time you come home we can go through them. What do you say?'

The anticipation was the best thing to put a smile on their faces, and when Owen came back he found them deep in conversation about fabrics and styles. They hardly noticed how quiet he was, because it was no different from the way he always came home on this particular day, but he couldn't help but be drawn into his daughters' excitement about the prospect of a wedding in the family. When Alec joined them, they were all more relaxed at the special birthday supper.

'Jassy, we decided on your favourite chocolate sponge in place of a rich birthday cake this year,' Grace told her. 'We also thought it might be a bit much to remind you that you're not a child any more by putting twenty-one candles on it, so we've decorated it in a different way.'

Alec brought in the cake, lavishly decorated with edible flowers and sweetmeats, and Jassy knew how thoughtful her sister had been in not drawing attention to what was also the end of an era for Owen.

'It's beautiful, and I love it,' she said. 'It's almost too good to eat, isn't it, Dad? But I'm sure we shall!'

'It's a work of art,' he agreed, 'and don't think I don't know why you've done this, Grace. You're a sweet girl, but there was no need to protect my feelings. In any case, we had a birthday cake with candles on it at Kate's last night.'

'Oh!' Grace said in surprise.

'Excuse me, all of you. Get on with cutting the cake, Grace, and I'll be back in a moment.'

He left the table and went to his bedroom, leaving them momentarily subdued and looking at one another.

'Don't cut it until he comes back,' Jassy said sharply. 'This is as much for him as for me, isn't it? I hope he's all right.'

He returned with a small box in his hands.

'This is for you, Jassy.'

'I've already had my presents.'

'Not all of them. I made a promise to your mother that I would keep this for you until your twenty-first birthday. It's only costume jewellery and not of any great value, except sentimentally, but she always loved it, and she insisted on wearing it on our wedding day as her "something old". It's the brooch she was wearing on the day we met. We were dancing, and the brooch scratched my cheek, and she told me teasingly that I'd probably have to marry her now. Three months later we were married and shared the happiest ten years of our lives. She was twenty-one when we met, and she wanted you to have this on your special birthday, Jassy.'

It was hard to say who was most affected by the simple way he spoke, and neither of his girls had ever heard this story before. Owen had always been a private man, and such memories had been locked up in his heart for far too long.

But such pent up emotions couldn't be held in check for ever, and Jassy gave a little cry and flung her arms around her father's neck, tears running down her cheeks.

'It's the most beautiful gift I've ever had, and I'll treasure it for ever,' she whispered.

Alec cleared his throat. 'So now can we cut the cake? I didn't spend all day wearing my pinny and baking it for it to sit there like an ornament.'

It was the final release of tension, and everybody laughed at the thought of the very masculine Alec baking a cake. The day ended in a way Jassy would never have expected, with Owen finally talking about his beloved wife and the years they had spent together. She didn't know how or why it had happened, and twenty-one years seemed far too long a time for it to emerge, but it was his way, and she had to acknowledge that.

Before the day ended and Jassy and Owen drove back to Horton, the sisters spent a little time together in Grace's bedroom, mulling over all that had happened.

'You don't begrudge me this gift, do you, Grace?' Jassy said tentatively, fingering the pretty turquoise and gilt brooch she now wore on her dress.

'Of course I don't. I had my years with Mum that you didn't, and this was such a lovely thought. She was a wonderful person, Jassy, and you're just like her.'

'Well, that's the best birthday present I've had,' she said, choked.

The drive back to Horton that evening was done in companionable silence, as each sensed that the other was disinclined to talk. Jassy reflected that in many ways she had dreaded this birthday, and yet it had passed more peaceably, and certainly more unusually, than she could ever have imagined. And surely now was the time for her father to move on. The long period of grieving must now be over, and there was a future for him and Kate, if he would only grasp it with both hands. But it had to be in his time, and on his terms – unless Kate Lester proved to be a more formidable lady than she appeared on the surface!

But since the subject of weddings had been on everybody's

mind the previous day, on Monday evening Jassy mentioned the plans she and Grace had already made.

'I'll need to go home from time to time, Dad. Grace is arranging for us to see the dressmaker in a couple of weeks' time, but before then we want to look through her pattern books and decide on the styles.'

'That's fine. I have a suggestion of my own, anyway. Grace will obviously be busy making plans for her wedding, and it's only fair that I should be back at the shop so that she can have some time to herself. You don't have to work at the school for the holidays, so why don't we go back home for a part of every week? We can still be here for the weekends, or whenever you like. In any case it's time I got back in the swing of working in the shop and seeing to the books. I can't leave it all to Grace now.'

Jassy felt an enormous shock at his words. If he was starting to think about working again, it sounded like the beginning of the end of his time in Horton, and it wasn't what she wanted at all.

'I thought you really liked it here, Dad,' she stammered.

'I do, but I've still got a business to run, and it won't happen by itself. This was only meant to be a temporary arrangement, Jassy.'

She knew that, even if she had been hoping for something different, and she felt depressed at hearing him say it.

'You wouldn't ever consider moving down here permanently, then?' she asked tentatively. 'When Grace and Alec move to Scotland, I mean.'

'Are *you* considering it?' he countered. 'It seems to me we've had this conversation many times before, and never resolved it.'

Jassy realized he wasn't giving her a straight answer, either.

'We're obviously as undecided as each other, so let's sleep on it, Dad.'

All the same, she couldn't help feeling anxious that after so much rapport between her father and Kate Lester, he was going to throw away a second chance at happiness. It wasn't a daughter's place to ask bluntly about it, especially not with an unpredictable man like Owen Wyatt, who would probably revert to his old black moods in an instant if he thought

210

he was being manipulated. She couldn't make any such hints to Kate, either, but there was surely nothing wrong in mentioning that they would be spending a few days back in Bristol from time to time.

She went shopping in the village the following morning, calling in at the post office as she did so, ostensibly to tell Kate about the birthday in Bristol, and to show off the little brooch that she had vowed to wear always.

'And how was your father?' Kate said casually. 'Was everything well with him?'

'I think so. He seemed a lot calmer on the drive back here, anyway, although I think he's quietly dreading the day that Grace leaves home.'

'That's something all parents have to face, Jassy. Children have to make their own way in the world. They grow up, get married, have their own homes – and if the parents are very lucky, they eventually have grandchildren to worry about,' she finished with a smile.

'I suppose you'd like that too,' Jassy said daringly.

Kate shrugged. 'It will be a long while before Ted provides me with any, but I can always hope that William will find the right girl and get married. His children wouldn't be my natural grandchildren, but they'd be near enough.' She began to laugh. 'But just listen to us, getting quite gloomy on this lovely morning. Tell your father I hope I'll see him at the Sunset Club tonight.'

'Oh, I'm sure he'll be there,' Jassy said hastily, and left her to attend to the next customer.

She hesitated before going back to the cottage. It was so obvious that those two were made for one another, and she was afraid that once Owen resumed his shop duties he might find it all too attractive to leave.

It seemed hard to believe that a few months ago none of them had met, and now their lives seemed to have become imperceptibly intertwined. Today was a day very like the one when she first arrived, she reflected. The green was peaceful, and the old men were sitting on the benches beneath the oak tree, cogitating on putting the world to rights. Birds were singing, and it was going to be a heavenly summer's day. Across Horton Green she could see the estate agent office, and on an impulse, she walked over and went inside.

'We have to do something,' she said flatly.

William looked startled. 'Do we? What about?'

She sat down on the client's chair. He looked more businesslike and formidable on the other side of his desk, but she wasn't going to let that stop her. Not that she knew exactly how to begin, nor what his reaction would be. While she was still trying to find the right words, he came around to the front of the desk and sat on it. He leaned forward, taking her hands in his.

'Why don't you tell me exactly what it is you think we should do, Jassy?' he said.

She looked down at their linked hands. 'I don't know,' she mumbled.

He let her go, leaving her feeling a fool for bursting in like that. Then she realized he had put the 'closed' sign on the door, and was coming back to her.

'Come through to the back and I'll make you a cup of tea. You look as if you could do with one.'

'Do I seem so feeble?'

'More or less,' he said with a grin, and she followed him meekly.

There was hardly room for two in the tiny back area, but her words finally tumbled out in a rush as she explained about her father's sudden wish to go back and work in his shop.

'I doubt that it's so sudden,' William said. 'He might have been thinking about it ever since Grace decided to get married. Even if he chooses to give it up, he could hardly leave it to her to settle everything up, could he? It seems a perfectly sensible thing to do, and you're probably reading the wrong signs into it.'

'Am I?' she said. 'So you think I'm wrong to have been imagining a happy ever after for my dad and your aunt? I thought you agreed with me about that.'

'Maybe I do, but you can't run other people's lives for them, darling. As for doing something about it, my advice is to leave well alone. If it's meant to happen, it will happen, and I'm sure your father wouldn't thank you for interfering.'

'Probably not,' she said, annoyed that he could be so logical about it all, when she had rushed in without thinking things through.

She took her mug of tea, and scalded her tongue by drinking it too fast.

'In any case,' William went on, 'you know the old saying about absence making the heart grow fonder, don't you? A few days apart now and then might make them both see what's right under their noses. What do you think?'

Jassy felt her cheeks flame. They were standing so close, and it seemed that she was the only one who could see what was right under their noses too. She put down the mug of tea, not bothering to finish it, and feeling acutely embarrassed now.

'I know you're right, and it's obviously best to leave it to fate. Thanks for the advice, anyway.'

He pulled her into his arms and planted a less than gentle kiss on her lips.

'It's nice to know you care so much,' he said lightly.

She stalked out of his office, thinking that he would never know *how* much. And thinking too, that a few days away from time to time, might do them all good. It might help her to realize that there was never going to be a future for her and William Hedges – and secretly, to wonder if that kiss meant otherwise.

Owen enjoyed his Tuesday Sunset Club evenings, so it was arranged that they would return to Bristol on Wednesdays and go back to the cottage on Sunday mornings. That would give Owen the remainder of each week to be in charge of the shop, and allow Grace to have as much time off as she wanted to with Jassy. And once the new arrangements took place, the excitement between the sisters over the approaching wedding grew apace. They pored over pattern books and had several consultations with Mrs Forbes, the local dressmaker. They finally decided on a long, ivory satin gown for Grace, and a powder blue one for Jassy. Jassy had discussed something privately with Owen, now was the time to tell Grace.

'Dad and I both want you to wear Mother's brooch on your wedding day, either as your, "something borrowed", or as your "something old", the same as she did. Will you do that?'

'I think it's a lovely idea, darling, thank you,' Grace said.

There were still weeks to go until the date for the wedding, but sorting out a lifetime of memories in the flat meant laughter and tears for both Grace and Jassy. Alec was arranging to wind up his practice in Bristol, and there were so many of his patients and Owen's customers who wanted to come to the church to wish them well that it could all have got out of hand. It was decided for all their sanity, that although all were welcome at the church, there would only be a very small reception back at the flat afterwards.

'We'd like to invite Mrs Lester and William,' Grace told her father at the beginning of September. 'We've got to know them both so well, and it would be a nice gesture, don't you think?'

It was agreed, and the invitations were duly written and would be delivered by hand when Owen and Jassy returned to Horton on the following Sunday morning. Apart from when he was working in the shop, sometimes on his own, and sometimes with Grace, Owen had been busy on his own account all that week, and Jassy had seen little of him. Rather than stir up any kind of mood on his part, she refrained from asking any questions about where he had been. It was only when they got back to the cottage and both gave a sigh of relief and kicked off their shoes, that he spoke to her seriously.

'You may wonder what I've been up to all this week, Jassy.'

'I know you've been extra busy, and Alec may well have something to say about it,' she said, determinedly light.

He snorted. 'Never mind Alec. I feel as right as rain now.'

She desperately hoped this didn't mean he was taking up the reins of the shop again full time, and expecting her to join him. She really didn't want that . . . and nor did she know how she could refuse, other than to persuade him to hire an assistant, and Owen had always prided himself on his solely family business.

'So what have you been up to?' she repeated his words.

'I've been discussing matters with my solicitor and my accountant, and I've got a proposition to make to you, Jassy.'

Here it comes, she thought, groaning inwardly. She forced herself to keep her expression bland and not to give away how her heart was sinking.

'What would you think about selling Blackthorn Cottage to me?' he said.

She gasped with shock, but before she could say anything, he went on talking.

'You're absolutely right in saying we both love Horton, although I never thought I'd hear myself say it. Nor did I think about retiring, until Alec nagged me into taking things easy. And yes, I'm willing to concede that he did me a favour,' he added. 'So we could go on living in the cottage as we are, and probably getting on one another's nerves for ever. But I've no wish to be beholden to a daughter for my home, my dear, and so what I'm proposing is that I sell the shop and the flat and buy the cottage from you. Naturally, we shall still live there together for as long as you wish, or until things change.'

Amid all the amazing things he was saying to her, it was that last phrase that caught her attention the most.

'Until things change?' she said huskily. 'What things, Dad?'

To her astonishment, his face reddened slightly. He gave a small shrug.

'Oh, I don't know. You'll probably think about getting married someday, and when that happens, I might want to find a new tenant, rather than live there alone. All sorts of things.'

'Such as a new tenant who once had a dream of living in Blackthorn Cottage herself, you mean?' she said daringly. 'Or maybe you weren't thinking of a certain person just as a tenant.'

She held her breath. He could so easily rant and rave at her now, the way he used to do, but he looked more rueful than anything else.

'I know what you're thinking – that I'm an old fool. Such dreams aren't for people of my age, are they?'

She put her arms around him, holding him tightly.

'I don't think you're an old fool at all, and dreams are for people of any age, Dad. I'd love to see you happy

215

again – really happy, I mean, and I'd be thrilled to sell the cottage to you. It makes me realize why I was so reluctant to sell it, because I never wanted to let it go completely, and now I won't have to, will I?'

He released her slightly. 'Well, don't think I'm going to make any hasty proposals of a romantic nature, because these things grow slowly, and they might not be welcome.'

Jassy laughed. 'Oh, I think we both know a certain proposal would be well received! And so does everybody else, you old daftie.'

She was teasing him in the way Grace did, and it felt so good to know that he was taking it in good part. Jassy found herself mentally crossing her fingers, and hoping desperately that if and when her father did get around to proposing to Kate Lester, she wouldn't say no!

'We'll also say nothing about what we're planning for the cottage for the time being,' Owen went on. 'I want to let Grace know, of course, but at the moment it's all in my head.'

'You won't even let William know?' Jassy said.

'Not yet. William can handle everything here when the time comes, but I'll contact a Bristol firm to handle the sale of the shop and flat. Once that has gone through, it will only be a formality for William to deal with our personal business.'

It might be all in his head, but he had obviously gone through everything very thoroughly, Jassy thought. The next time they were in Bristol they told Grace and Alec, and Owen saw a local estate agent to start the ball rolling for a mid October sale, if possible. Grace was clearly thrilled, knowing she need have no more worries about her dad once she and Alec moved away. It was such a simple and exciting idea to sell the cottage to her father, keeping it in the family, so to speak, that by now Jassy wondered how she was going to keep the news to herself.

She decided to avoid William as much as possible. He was going to be involved later, but the last thing she wanted to do was to blab out her dad's plans before he was ready. It wasn't that easy to avoid people in a small village like Horton, though, and he turned up at the cottage on Tuesday evening when Owen was at the Sunset Club.

'Why are you avoiding me?' he demanded.

'I'm not!'

'Don't give me that! I've seen you in the village a dozen times and you never look my way, or pop in for a chat – or more likely, an argument.'

She had to smile at that. 'Do I take it that you've missed me then?'

'Of course I've darned well missed you,' he said, almost angrily.

'You know we've been back home for a few days every week. Dad still has a business to run, and he can't leave it all to Grace in these weeks before her wedding. There are a lot of other things to sort out as well, for both of us, if you must know.'

'What things? Does it have something to do with that fellow who came here before?'

Jassy couldn't think where his thoughts were going for a moment, and then she flushed, realizing he meant Freddie Patterson. She would dearly love to spill out all her father's exciting news, but she daren't, not until he was ready. There was only one way to stop his persistent questions.

'It may have,' she said defiantly. 'Freddie has been a friend of mine for a long time, and we once knew one another very well,' she added meaningfully.

William didn't speak for a moment and then his voice was harsh.

'I was hoping you'd forgotten him. I was going to ask you to come to the dance with me on Saturday night, but I suppose you'll still be in Bristol, seeing your old friend, I daresay.'

'I might not be,' she said quickly. 'Dad might want to come back earlier.'

'Well don't do me any favours. If you're back in time and you turn up at the dance, I'll be seeing you there.'

He turned and walked swiftly out of the cottage, leaving Jassy's heart thudding, wondering if there was meant to be any significance in his last words, or if it was completely unintentional. He needn't have asked her to the dance, and she needn't have been so stupid as to let him think there was still something between herself and Freddie Patterson.

217

But she had, and now she was going to be utterly frustrated until Saturday night, because she was quite determined that she would return to Horton by then. If Owen didn't want to drive her, she would get the bus . . .

When he came home that night, she found he was more than amenable to coming back from Bristol on Saturday morning, and she discovered he wasn't the only one finding it difficult to keep a secret. Kate was now in the know about him selling up in Bristol and buying the cottage from his daughter. And from the light in his eyes and the jaunty way he walked, Jassy had a shrewd suspicion that that wasn't the only thing they had talked about.

They were leaving for Bristol early the next morning, and it was a busy week for Owen, organizing things with the local estate agent, and being assured that the sale of a thriving small business with living accommodation would go through smoothly. Jassy could hardly wait for Saturday to come, and on the way back in the car, she said frankly that she didn't know how much longer she could stop herself from saying something to William, especially if she went to the dance that evening.

'Of course you're going. You like William, don't you? More than you ever thought you would, I'd say.'

'Well, that wouldn't be hard would it? I didn't expect to like him at all!'

'And maybe it's more than liking.' At her gasp, he went on gently. 'I'm not blind, my dear, and he's a good man. You could do a lot worse.'

'I'm not thinking of *marrying* him, Dad!'

'Aren't you? Then you're not the daughter I thought you were.' He went on calmly. 'You also have my permission to divulge our plans to him tonight. It might be interesting to see where that conversation leads.'

She started to laugh at his cheek, but her hopes were high at this virtual blessing on something she had hardly dared to dream about. It was true, though. Dreams weren't only for children, and sometimes they did come true.

She was more nervous than usual as she got ready for the dance that evening, and a bit uncomfortable at entering the

218

village hall alone. She wore a cream-coloured dress, and her mother's brooch. She thought of it as her talisman now. It had brought love and happiness to her parents, and maybe it would do the same for her. She had got to the hall a little late, not wanting to be too conspicuous, and her nervousness increased when she couldn't see William at first. All her doubts came rushing back, wondering if she had ruined everything by her stupid comments about Freddie. And then, almost to her disbelief, the small band began playing the tune she and William knew so well, and she felt a lump in her throat.

'I believe this is our dance,' she heard a familiar voice say behind her.

She twirled around. 'I can't do the foxtrot,' she stammered, for want of something to say.

'Neither can I, so we'll just stumble around together,' William said, drawing her into his arms. 'I requested this song, so stop being so stubborn, Miss Wyatt, and just feel the music. More than that, feel the words.'

She didn't need to feel them, she knew them so well.

She felt a weak sob begin in her throat as they swayed and floated to the music, and when it ended, William's lips were close to her cheek.

'I think you and I have unfinished business. There's a harvest moon tonight so why don't we go outside and take a look at it?'

The dancing seemed immaterial then. Outside, there was the most beautiful moon of the year, and it was a night meant for lovers, for soulmates, and she so much wanted to be his . . . in the fragrant autumn darkness, his arms were around her, and before she knew what was happening, he was kissing her, not just a friendly kiss, but as if it meant something far more.

'Now tell me, Miss Wyatt, just how much this other man means to you,' he demanded, his mouth just a fraction away from hers as the kiss ended. 'I'm not in the habit of muscling in on another man's girl, but you came to the dance tonight, so you'd better tell me the truth before it drives me wild.'

'He means nothing at all,' Jassy said, her heart

hammering now. 'Whatever there was between us was over long ago.'

'Then I want to know if you're definitely staying in Horton, because my aunt has been giving out some very strange hints in the last few days.'

Jassy felt a laugh bubbling up, savouring the secret for a moment longer, because it was going to be so sweet to be able to tell him everything now. Well, nearly everything. At least she could tell him about her father wanting to buy the cottage and that they would both be living in it, until circumstances changed.

'What circumstances would those be?' William asked.

She gave him a little shake. 'You know very well! You were the one who asked when my father was going to make an honest woman of your aunt! I can't imagine it would be soon, but I hope it will happen someday. I know how much your aunt always dreamed of living in Blackthorn Cottage too, so if it all happened as we surmise I suppose I'd have to move out,' she finished, not wanting to think that far ahead.

William's arms tightened around her until their silhouettes became one.

'You would, and you could always marry me and share my place, which is by far the most sensible suggestion. Not that I'm finding it at all easy to think sensibly when you're dazzling me with all that moonlight in your eyes. What do you think?'

Jassy sensed that this was as important to him as it was to her. But still she held off, wanting to hear the words he hadn't yet said.

'Why would I want to marry you?' she countered, a waver in her voice.

'Because I love you, you impossible woman. Is that reason enough for you?'

'I think I could be persuaded,' she said unsteadily.